Praise for

THE GLOBAL WAR
ON MORRIS

"[I]t's an unexpected delight to find *The Global War on Morris*, a political satire by Rep. Steve Israel (D-N.Y.), so spirited and funny . . . writing in the full-tilt style of Carl Hiaasen, Israel . . . skewer[s] his way through one gaffe after another in the fight against domestic terrorism. Imagine *It's a Mad, Mad, Mad, Mad World* with a soupcon of al-Qaeda."

—Ron Charles, *The Washington Post*

"Rep. Steve Israel reveals his inner Jon Stewart in his debut novel. . . . The book amounts to a critique of what Israel deems the overreaching of the Bush-Cheney efforts."

—*New York Daily News*

"If Joseph Heller had served in Congress instead of the Second World War, he might have written *The Global War on Morris* instead of *Catch-22*. Congressman Steve Israel's tale of how the war on terror sweeps up an unassuming salesman from Long Island is both darkly hilarious and hilariously dark. Somehow Israel has combined his access to top-secret national security briefings with a finely tuned sense of the absurd as he skewers Washington bureaucrats, Machiavellian politicians, and a certain Darth Vader–like Vice President. On every page he displays a wicked wit and an irony that never descends into bitterness."

—Paul Begala

"I was laughing out loud."

—Dana Bash, CNN

"If there's a writer currently serving in the U.S. House of Representatives funnier than Steve Israel, I have not been made aware of their work. *The Global War on Morris* is a great, smart, and funny read."

—Paul Reiser

"I haven't laughed so hard since I read my last novel. Steve Israel is as funny, witty, and satirical on paper as he is in person. He's also a master of political insight and an accurate observer of Washington absurdities. *The Global War on Morris* is a bipartisan skewer that will annoy both sides of the aisle. At a time when America could use a good laugh, Congressman Israel comes to the rescue. Fast and furious, fair and balanced. A great read!"

—Nelson DeMille

"This very funny political satire, set in 2004, reads like it could have sprung from the keyboard of Christopher Buckley. . . . As political satires go, it's really good; as debut novels go, it's even better."

—*Booklist*

"Brandishing biting wit and a Washington insider's perspective, U.S. Congressman Steve Israel (New York) takes aim at the United States' global war on terror—revealing true casualties—in his hilariously shrewd first novel. . . . Israel's wicked sense of humor highlights the absurdity of his subject matter. . . . Readers will doubtlessly find analogs to Israel's exaggerated characters among their coworkers, neighbors, maybe even family."

—*Shelf Awareness*

"The novel is funny, fast-paced and cinematic."

—*The Jewish Week*

"*The Global War on Morris* is a laugh-out-loud funny book. I don't mean a chuckle here or there. This yarn by Congressman Steve

Israel is downright hilarious. The NSA types in Washington, we discover, have picked up this unlikely pair with its state-of-the-art surveillance operation: Morris is a medical supplies salesman—a real nebbish guy—who can't wait to get home to Long Island each night and catch the old black-and-white movies on Turner Classics. Hassan is a "sleeper cell" terrorist down in Miami waiting for his call-up, and with it that dreamy reward of seventy-two virgins. Guess which of these two the U.S. government has marked as the country's number-one security threat? But the greatest surprise in *The Global War on Morris* is how a U.S. congressman can be such a world-class satirist. Steve Israel is right up there with Tom Wolfe and Christopher Buckley, and, believe me, that's as great as it gets. This first book of Steve Israel's is a race between laughter and absurdity with you as the referee."

—Chris Matthews

"Israel's tongue muscles still must be hurting. After all, he had his tongue firmly planted deeply in his cheek for virtually every sentence through this 289-page romp. This is pure satire, biting sarcasm filled with laugh-out-loud digs at Cheney and his crew, overstuffed federal bureaucracies, headline-grabbing politicians, the excesses of the war on terrorism and even America-spoiled sleeper-cell terrorists."

—*Buffalo News*

"This debut novel from Congressman Israel is hilarious. . . . A political satire that isn't just witty but also ripped from the headlines."

—*The Kentucky Democrat*

"Hilarity and broad satire of the bureaucracy ensue. . . . Why read this when one can see Washington insiders acting like buffoons in farcical situation on CNN? This is funnier than Wolf Blitzer, that's why."

—*Library Journal*

THE GLOBAL WAR
ON MORRIS

STEVE ISRAEL

SIMON & SCHUSTER PAPERBACKS

NEW YORK   LONDON   TORONTO   SYDNEY   NEW DELHI

To former vice president Dick Cheney.

And to my dad, who didn't particularly care for him.

———————

Simon & Schuster Paperbacks
An Imprint of Simon & Schuster, Inc.
1230 Avenue of the Americas
New York, NY 10020

This book is a work of fiction. Any references to historical events, real people, or real places are used fictitiously. Other names, characters, places, and events are products of the author's imagination, and any resemblance to actual events or places or persons, living or dead, is entirely coincidental.

First Simon & Schuster trade paperback edition November 2015

SIMON & SCHUSTER PAPERBACKS and colophon are registered trademarks of Simon & Schuster, Inc.

For information about special discounts for bulk purchases, please contact Simon & Schuster Special Sales at 1-866-506-1949 or business@simonandschuster.com.

The Simon & Schuster Speakers Bureau can bring authors to your live event. For more information or to book an event contact the Simon & Schuster Speakers Bureau at 1-866-248-3049 or visit our website at www.simonspeakers.com.

Interior design by Ruth Lee-Mui

Manufactured in the United States of America

10 9 8 7 6 5 4 3 2 1

Library of Congress Cataloging-in-Publication Data is available.

ISBN 978-1-4767-7223-3
ISBN 978-1-4767-7224-0 (pbk)
ISBN 978-1-4767-7225-7 (ebook)

Author's Note: While this book is entirely made up, many news and sports events did take place on the dates indicated. All of the public statements by President Bush and Vice President Cheney are true. Which may be harder to believe than the story itself.

CONTENTS

PART ONE

PART ONE

TSURIS AHEAD

SUNDAY, AUGUST 1, 2004

tsu·ris *(/tsŏŏris/) n.—1. Trouble or woe; aggravation.*

Tsuris ahead.

That's what Morris Feldstein, a man who spent his entire life avoiding anxiety, danger, or tsuris, thought as he sat in his dining room. He was chewing on Kung Pao chicken from the Great Neck Mandarin Gourmet Takeout. His wife, Rona, had just asked him a question.

"Morris. Do you plan on watching the Mets game tonight?"

He mumbled: "I was planning to. Unless you want to watch something else. Benson is pitching. The Mets just got him. They're playing the Braves."

And now, as Rona considered his response, Morris detected the possibility of tsuris. He resumed chewing, avoiding any eye contact with Rona, and hoping that the only sound in the Feldstein dining room would be the Kung Pao shifting between his cheeks. He hoped

Rona would accept his answer with a silent affirmation, rather than the clucking of her tongue against her teeth, the drumming of her fiery-red fingernails against the table, or that sigh. God had implanted what Morris called Rona's "guilt pipes" deep within her.

The sounds of tsuris, like the wail of a tornado warning, the stirring of a police siren, or a wave drawing back on itself before breaking in white foam.

The dining room was lit by a crystal chandelier purchased at Fortunoff department store when the Feldsteins moved to 19 Soundview Avenue many years before. Faded photographs smiled from the walls, distant memories of what Morris used to call "Feldstein family fun!" Back when the Feldstein family was fun. The pastel suits and flowing gowns and voluminous hair at Jeffrey's bar mitzvah and Caryn's bat mitzvah. The trip to Disney World when Rona summoned a weary smile for the camera even though "you could *plotz* from this heat." The weekend upstate at Lake George when Rona refused to go into the lake because "I don't swim where living creatures swim and God only knows what diseases you can catch in there."

Morris ate, watching the steam rising above the white cartons from the Chinese restaurant.

The next moments would define the rest of Morris's evening. Silence would mean Rona had accepted his response, and that he was free to finish dinner, sit in his RoyaLounger 8000, and watch the Mets. Anything other than silence meant certain tsuris.

"Okay," whispered Rona. "That's fine. I guess."

Fine, I guess, in Rona-speak meant that things were anything but fine.

"Well, did you—" Morris stammered.

"Did I—" Rona replied.

"I mean, do you want to watch something else?"

"Me? No. Why would you ask that?"

"I mean, if you want to watch something else—"

"Look," Rona said, her voice beginning to quiver. "So I'll miss

Wolf Blitzer tonight. A CNN special on the War on Terror. I'll watch him another time. No biggie. It's just the War on Terror."

Morris lifted his head and locked his eyes on his wife. She pushed her food around her plate while resting her chin on one hand. Her red hair was cropped, thanks to her weekly appointments at Spa Daniella, which Rona liked to call "my sanctuary." Even at fifty-seven, she had retained the qualities of youth that attracted Morris to her so many years before: the glimmering green eyes over a high ridge of cheeks, the protruding lips, a slender frame that time and two pregnancies seemed to ignore.

That was the amazing thing about Rona, he thought. Everything about her resisted time itself. She used passion and guilt like gravity—the heavy force that kept everything together, including their marriage. Three months after their wedding, in 1980, Rona asked Morris to attend a rally to protest the Soviet invasion of a place called Afghanistan. Morris didn't even know where Afghanistan was. Or why the Russians invaded it. But Rona's concern for people they had never met and a place they never knew attracted Morris to her.

It was at that protest that Morris realized what he now remembered thirty-four years later. Someone had to do those unpleasant things that Morris hated about life: asking strangers for directions, arguing with sales clerks, protesting invasions of foreign countries. That was Rona! Morris Feldstein's wife.

For thirty-four years.

"If you want to watch CNN, we'll watch CNN," Morris said.

"No, no, no. God forbid you should miss the Mets tonight, Morris. And, by the way, you're not eating your spareribs. What's the matter with them?"

"The spareribs are fine, Rona. We'll watch Wolf Blitzer. It's settled."

"Are you saying you want to watch CNN, Morris? Or are you placating me?"

"Yes, I want to watch CNN." *I do not want to watch Wolf Blitzer talking. I want to watch Kris Benson pitching.*

"I just think it's important that we stay informed. With all that's going on in the world. Everywhere you turn is *mishagas!*"

"I agree." *Why get involved? What difference does it make?*

"Then, if you want to watch CNN, it's fine by me. We'll watch. Now tell me: What's wrong with your spareribs? You haven't even touched them. What's wrong, Morris?"

It had been the biggest dilemma of Morris's day. A day that, until that moment, had gone just as smoothly as the day before, and the day before that, for fifty-seven consecutive years. If every day was a winding road, Morris was pretty much doing a tick under the speed limit in the right-hand lane of the longest, straightest, levelest stretch of unbroken pavement ever. Every weekday at eight-fifteen, he kissed Rona good-bye. And it was always the same kind of kiss, more habit than affection. His central nervous system sent a signal to his lips, his lips pursed, and his body lurched forward, there was an instant peck, followed by a mumbled exchange of "love you"-"love you too."

It wasn't loveless. Just automatic.

Then he worked his territory as a pharmaceutical sales representative for Celfex Pharmaceutical Laboratories Inc., doctor's office to doctor's office. From one exit of the Long Island Expressway to the other. Stocking samples, pecking out orders on his BlackBerry. Stocking more samples and pecking out more orders. Plying the North Shore communities of Long Island, dispensing blue and yellow and pink boxes in the enclaves of Long Island Sound.

At about five thirty every night, Rona would hear the soft thud of the car door in the driveway, then Morris's plodding footsteps against the brick walk, as if he were shuffling toward the electric chair. The two exchanged polite small talk over whatever Rona had ordered in for dinner that night. (Mondays usually meant the pastrami platter from The Noshery.) Morris would then descend into his so-called office; a partially finished basement adorned in 1970s' brown mahogany paneling and faded orange shag carpeting. There, he worked at a wooden and wobbly junior desk, doing the day's paperwork and tapping at his computer, in a room he shared with piles of clothing in various stages of laundering and a sadly drooping Ping-Pong table last used when their youngest child, Caryn, was in junior high school. Later, he would return upstairs, sink into his RoyaLounger 8000, and raise his arms with the scepter that the king of every suburban castle wielded: his television clicker. If it wasn't a Mets game, it was Turner Classic Movies. Morris felt safe in the comfort and the distance of black and white. At about eleven each night Rona tapped him on the shoulder and reprimanded him: "Morris, you fell asleep!" Which was the last thing he would hear from her until the next morning.

Morris Feldstein's entire life was tucked in the safe confines of anonymity. If Morris clung to any life philosophy, it was "Don't make waves." Whenever Rona wanted to return a purchase to Saks or Nieman Marcus, Morris would cringe and ask, "Why make waves?" then wait in the car while she made the return. When he and Rona flew somewhere on vacation, Morris wouldn't recline in his seat. That would make a wave for the person behind him.

One night, when Caryn was in high school, she proclaimed at the dinner table that she was going to be a documentary filmmaker "to expose injustice and inhumanity." Morris chewed his veal Parmesan from Mario's Takeout Gourmet and deliberated. He wanted to watch movies to escape the world. Caryn wanted to make movies to change the world. But Morris knew the only way to change the world was by pressing the TV remote: channel up or channel down. He didn't raise his objections with Caryn. That, too, would be making waves.

Morris Feldstein was so averse to making waves that he demurred when the leaders of the Temple Beth Torah synagogue of Great Neck asked him to become president of the Men's Club. When they suggested instead that he accept the vice presidency, he declined again. After two weeks of prodding, Morris agreed to the position of second vice president, and then only for two reasons. First, because the second vice presidency of Temple Beth Torah of Great Neck seemed like a pretty good place not to be noticed. And second, he didn't want to make waves with the synagogue leaders who continued their appeals.

Morris sat in the RoyaLounger 8000, viewing CNN with detached interest. It was 2004 but it could have been any year since the War on Terror was proclaimed. The same rolling crescendo of music, the unmistakable voice of James Earl Jones heralding to CNN viewers who may have forgotten that "Thisssss . . . is CNN." Then Wolf Blitzer broke the day's news: the Attorney General of the United States announcing the discovery of a terrorist plot that revealed "critical intelligence in the War on Terror." And after that pronouncement, Blitzer reported that "Administration sources have told CNN that the Department of Homeland Security may—may—raise the threat alert tomorrow for unnamed financial institutions in Washington and New York. Those sources cite intelligence reports suggesting a possible—possible—al-Qaeda attack. CNN is watching this story closely. And will report on it as it unfolds. Right here. On CNN." There was also increased fighting by a radical cleric in Iraq whose name Morris couldn't pronounce. And President Bush was expected to urge Congress to create two new intelligence agencies with acronyms Morris would never remember, because, evidently, the current alphabet soup of federal agencies wasn't up to the task of protecting the homeland. And with that rosy recap of the day, Wolf Blitzer promised to "be right back" after some commercials about depression medications.

Not a word about the Mets. Or their new pitcher, Kris Benson, who had just arrived in a dubious trade, thought Morris.

Then it got worse. During the commercial, Rona asked: "Now, isn't this better than a baseball game?"

Morris couldn't understand why anyone would frighten themselves by watching the news, when the worst thing that happened in a Mets game was the relief pitching. "Yes, Rona."

"I wish you would pay more attention to what's happening in the world, Morris."

This was the difference between Morris and Rona. Rona wanted to change the world. Morris wanted the world to leave him alone. She read news magazines and subscribed to the *New York Times* and watched Wolf Blitzer. He was like the Public Access channel on cable television: there but rarely observed. In 2000 she had planted herself in front of the television for four straight nights watching them count ballots and peer at chads in Florida before the Supreme Court anointed George Bush the new President. And then clapped when their daughter, Caryn, announced that she was going to protest in front of the Supreme Court and bring her camera. She sent modest donations to the Nature Conservancy and occasionally attended meetings of Hadassah, and her eyes filled with tears whenever she watched the news about the genocide in Darfur. She believed she could make the world better, when, Morris knew, she could not. All watching the news did was to prove how unalterably miserable the world was. Why bother watching what you couldn't change?

ORANGE ALERT

MONDAY, AUGUST 2, 2004

As soon as the gate to West Executive Drive began swinging open, Jon Pruitt felt the usual pain in his stomach and sighed. He was about to meet with Vice President Cheney, who would feel similar pain in his chest. That was the bond between these two men: it hurt them to see each other.

Pruitt peered at the scenery from the backseat of his car. The avenue was a sealed-off stretch of pavement between the West Wing of the White House and the majestic Eisenhower Executive Office Building. Now it doubled as a secure passageway and narrow parking lot. There was little movement outside. No scurrying White House aides. No bustling reporters and correspondents. It was a typical August Monday in Washington. The heat and humidity had invaded, driving Congress into its summer retreat and withering the White House press corps to a skeletal crew. West Executive Drive was like the main street of a parched western ghost town. All it lacked was the tumbleweed.

"Side entrance," Pruitt instructed his driver. He thought, *Freakin' Cheney. Ordering me to use the side entrance.* Sigh.

The West Wing side entrance. Not the front, where the marine guard stood frozen at attention, where the press could see who was coming and going, where one entered to the impressed gaze of the whole watching world. No, Pruitt's access was through the side door, like the servants' entrance. Which is why Cheney instructed his visitors to use it. You slipped in the side entrance that led to the back steps that climbed to the dim corridor that brought you to the Vice President's office. The exalted senior officials privileged enough to get an office in the West Wing ordinarily wanted proximity to the President or at least a decent view of the grounds. But when Vice President Cheney saw that office near the back steps by the side door that no one noticed, he said, "I'll take it!"

The car stopped near the door. As Pruitt emerged, the heat smothered him.

"Thirty minutes," he told his driver. And then thought, *If I'm not back by then, check Guantánamo.* Sigh.

He pushed through the door and gulped the air-conditioned oxygen. A receptionist gave him the "isn't this heat brutal" smile that everyone wore this time of year.

"I have an appointment with the Vice President," Pruitt said. At the start of his career in government, the thought that he would one day say the words "I have an appointment with the Vice President" was unfathomable. Now, when he uttered them, it was like saying, "I have an appointment with the assistant principal" after being caught instigating a food fight in the high school cafeteria.

"Yes, Mr. Pruitt. Go right up."

He smiled, and began climbing the stairs to the West Wing's second floor. There was a time when Pruitt's compact and muscular body—sculpted from his days as an athlete at Saint David's School in Manhattan—would have bounded up those steps. But in the year since becoming Special Legal Advisor to the Secretary of Homeland Security, his steps had become tentative, as if feeling his way in the dark. His smile had been reduced to a slight pucker, as if everything left a bad taste in his mouth.

And he sighed. Constantly. Sighing almost the way most people breathed.

The stomach pain flared with each step. *Why did I take this job? It was so much easier when I did legal affairs at the CIA. Sure, there were a few failed coups. And that shitstorm when those Predators misfired into that school in Somalia. But on the whole, every day was a holiday compared to the crap I get here.*

He reached the top step and looked down a darkened corridor toward the Vice President's office.

In an anteroom, a few staffers sat at desks, straight and proper. One, without even looking at Pruitt, said, "The Vice President is waiting inside."

And there he was, at the far end of the room. Leaning on his desk, his arms spread and his wrists locked. Vice President Richard Cheney. In person. Which, Pruitt thought, was more frightening than the way all the caricatures portrayed him. The editorial cartoons didn't do Cheney justice. They didn't capture that permanent sneer, the upturned lip that made it look like he was always on the verge of spitting from the side of his face; the uniform blue suit and red tie (which Pruitt was convinced Cheney wore to bed at night); the way he seemed to duck his chin beneath his collar, like a turtle retreating in its shell; the thinning white hair above the skeptical eyes. He was all the more frightening in person.

Out of the corner of his eye, Pruitt detected Karl Rove lurking in the back of the room. In this administration, the most indispensable talent was good peripheral vision.

The office was smaller than the Oval Office, and more functional. Cheney's guests sat close to the door. The less they saw of the office, the better. Plush couches faced each other, and a large blue Victorian chair was reserved for the Vice President. Cheney's favorite photograph, from the 2000 election, was prominently displayed on a mahogany table. There was President Bush, wrapping his arms around his running mate. That was the afternoon that Cheney, as head of the campaign's vice presidential search committee, announced that the search was over. And he had found himself.

Cheney looked up from the stacks of papers on his desk then nudged his eyeglasses up the bridge of his nose. "What do you have for me this morning?"

"Nothing new. Nothing since last night. The last time you asked . . . sir."

Cheney's sneer seemed to dip, then clicked back to its usual place. "What about that report I sent you?"

"The Florida threat?"

"That one."

"We checked it out. Turns out it's a bunch of Quakers planning a war protest."

"So?"

"Quakers. Elderly . . . Quakers. You know, the Quaker meeting house. Nonviolence. 'Kumbaya.' That sort of thing. They're planning a peaceful protest against the war in Iraq."

"Protesting Quakers. Isn't that a contradiction in terms? Doesn't that seem suspicious to you? Put more people on them."

"Sir, it's a group of religious pacifists at a Friends meeting house planning a peaceful protest. We can't spy on religious—"

Cheney gave him the death glare, and Pruitt felt his perspiration freeze-dry along with the inside of his mouth. Still, while Pruitt's stomach was now grinding, he knew that the Vice President's pacemaker had to be shifting gears as well.

"Are you the Department of Homeland Security or the ACLU? Because if you don't have the stomach to do the job, we may have to look for people who will."

Pruitt knew what the Vice President was doing. Psychological warfare in the biggest Washington war of all: bureaucratic turf. If you can't do it, I'll find an agency that can. And further marginalize your existence. And cut your budgets.

"Yes, sir," he muttered, sighing.

"Now, item two. The Democratic Party had their convention up in Boston. Christ, if naïveté were a disease, then that convention was a telethon." Cheney seemed to snicker. "Kerry came out of it with a bounce"—he waved a stack of polling data in the air—"and now it's our turn. Our convention is in New York on the thirtieth. I think DHS should upgrade the terror alert."

"But we have no credible—"

"There's intel out there about a possible al-Qaeda attack against the World Bank, the IMF, and the New York Stock Exchange!" The Vice President waved another document from his desk. "If ever there was a time to raise the alert, it's now. Today."

"Mr. Vice President, there are no credible warnings of an imminent attack. Just media speculation. From unnamed sources. In this Administration. On Fox News."

"Does DHS want to wait for the mushroom cloud over the New York Stock Exchange? Let me remind you of something," Cheney said. This time his lip seemed headed straight for his right eye. "You're supposed to be my guy at DHS. The only reason I agreed to Ridge's appointment as Secretary was because I'd have a guy there to keep an eye on things. To protect the President's agenda. But lately I think you're going a little soft on us. Like Rice. And Powell. Are you going soft?"

Pruitt asked, "Is President Bush asking DHS to raise the alert?"

Cheney rolled his eyes. "I will remind you that the reason we have the color alerts at DHS is to insulate the President from the criticism that he is politicizing threat. Or scaring the American people."

"Well, I—"

"And besides, the President has a different announcement. We're asking Congress to create a National Intelligence Director. And a National Counterterrorism Center."

"And where does that leave us over at DHS?"

Cheney's sneer seemed to elevate to a quasi-smile. And his eyes sparkled. "That remains to be seen. If DHS won't do the job . . ."

"I'll speak with Secretary Ridge. I'll let him know how strongly you feel about raising the threat level."

"That would be advisable."

Rove chimed in: "Don't raise it too high. Has to be credible. Can't look political. What color makes sense?"

I'll see if I have something in a nice orange, Pruitt thought, and left the office.

THE TOWEL ATTENDANT

MONDAY, AUGUST 2, 2004

Flesh. Hassan tried so hard not to notice, but it was impossible. Flesh encircled him at the main pool of the Paradise Hotel and Residences at Boca. Fleshy breasts taunted him from low bikini tops, and fleshy thighs sloped from bikini bottoms. There were stomachs, taut and flat, but also undulating bellies, soft and bloated from the breakfast buffet. There was deep brown flesh, and bronze flesh, and pallid white flesh, and flesh turned red from the hot sun. Creases in the flesh ran in all directions, plunging into and swooping out of swimsuits, leading Hassan's eyes to forbidden places. There were also the fleshy remains of the seniors who migrated to Florida from all points north. The nanas and poppies and grannies and grampses who flocked there to roast in the sun. They became so brown and shriveled that they looked like walking beef jerky with New York accents.

And how these people positioned themselves! Sprawled on chaise lounges with their knees high in the air and their legs spread wide. They splayed their arms across each other's bodies, or sometimes wedged themselves into a single chaise lounge, interlocking their perspiring bodies in a helix position, flesh on flesh.

It wasn't easy being a celibate terrorist and pool towel attendant at the Paradise.

This is the test of my worthiness, Hassan thought. *They promised me seventy-two virgins in Paradise. Then they send me to the Paradise Hotel and Residences and tempt me with flesh, and try to break me with the constant calypso music over the loudspeaker, turning my mind into steel drums.*

Hassan was feeling the strain. How could he concentrate on leading his sleeper cell with these pounding headaches? Not to mention that stabbing pain in his groin. Maybe a hernia, he had read on *WebMD*. But the Paradise Hotel didn't offer health insurance to part-timers, and the budget guys at the Abu al-Zarqawi Army of Jihad Martyrs of Militancy Brigade declined his request for more money for medical expenses. They did, in their infinite mercy, make one suggestion: "How about a forged Medicaid card? That we can do." So Hassan filled out the paperwork and emailed it to Tora Bora. Every week for the past six weeks a functionary had promised him, "Hand to God, it will only take one more week, Hassan." Meanwhile, the groin pain was getting worse.

"This is my test. I will not fail," Hassan coached himself every day. From early morning, when he dispensed fresh towels poolside, to the evening, when he limped from chair to chair, swiping off clumps of towels saturated with sweat and chlorine and sand and suntan oils and God knows what else. And in the hours in between, he stood guard in the towel hut, battling the infidels all day about . . . towels. What was it with these people and their insatiable demand for towels? He would dispense the maximum two towels per guest, and then fight with each guest about the two-towel maximum. He would point to the massive sign with the huge red words: TOWEL LIMIT: 2 TOWELS PER

GUEST. THANK YOU, and still they would demand three towels or four or even more. *No wonder they won't give us back our land,* he thought. *Look how they fight for an extra towel!*

Of course, it didn't matter to Hassan that the Americans who visited the Paradise never took any land from his people. To him, they were all Zionists. The Italian Americans, the Irish Americans, the African-Americans, the Hispanic Americans. If they were American, he was sworn to destroy them. He had even said so, in the video that awaited his final act. He took an oath to destroy them, to annihilate them, to consume them in a wrathful, unmerciful, apocalyptic fireball.

But until then, he had to keep them dry.

His reward was nearing. Within months, God willing, his task would be complete. The sleeper cell would be activated. Azad, Achmed, Pervez, and he would be roused from their long hibernation. Azad would be freed from his job at Bozzotti Bros. Landscaping; Achmed liberated from the humiliation of cleaning planes of the mess left by first-class infidels; and Pervez would serve his last Happy Meal as a McDonald's counterman. They would attack. Then Allah be praised, Paradise wouldn't be the name of the hotel where he worked, but the afterlife he had been promised. Paradise, where he would meet the seventy-two virgins. In the flesh.

He closed his eyes, imagining the virgins, imagining away the pain in his head and groin.

NICK

Scooter Libby would do almost anything for his boss, the Vice President. Anything. He would fabricate and obfuscate. He would offer half-truths and untruths. He'd even go to jail, for God's sake (though he knew the prospects of such a thing was unlikely as Cheney would always have his back). But sitting in the rear seat of a White House pool car with Karl Rove for a long drive on the foliage-lined Baltimore–Washington Parkway, winding through the Maryland suburbs, was really testing the limits of his patience. The air conditioner fought against the heat outside, and Rove had just asked, for what seemed like the tenth time, "Where are we going?"

"I told you, Karl. An undisclosed location."

"I know that. But where?"

"If I told you where, it would be a disclosed location."

"I'm Senior Advisor to the President," said Rove. "You can tell me."

"I'm Chief of Staff to the Vice President. I can't."

"I've told you before, Scooter, Senior Advisor to the President outranks Chief of Staff to the Vice President. Technically."

"Maybe in the Office of Management and Budget flowcharts. But not in the Vice President's mind."

That was the big debate in the Administration. In the labyrinthine staffing structure that Cheney built, who outranked whom?

"You might as well tell me now. I'll know when we get there."

"Then why keep asking?"

Rove grumbled then mustered a smile, a malicious, settling-of-the-score smile. Libby wondered whether Rove was planning his demise behind that smile, right there next to him, right there in the backseat of the White House pool car. The roadkill of individuals who had gotten in Rove's way littered America's political landscape. Congressmen, senators, governors. Enemies real and imagined. Past, present, and future. Direct threats and potential threats. Libby shifted his body toward the backseat window, staring as the car passed communities named Landover and Greenbelt and Laurel.

Rove realized their destination: the National Security Agency. In Fort Meade.

(He could tell by the road sign that read: NATIONAL SECURITY AGENCY. FORT MEADE. For terrorists and traitors who felt awkward pulling off and asking for directions to the place where America's most vital secrets were hidden, the road signs were helpful.)

After producing their IDs at several checkpoints, they pulled into a remote underground garage tucked into the massive black-glass complex. The tires squealed as they turned from one level to the next, descending deeper and deeper into the concrete bowels. Libby thought of the parking garage scene in *All The President's Men*, when Deep Throat leaked Nixon Administration abuses to the *Washington Post*. Deep Throat. Nixon. Watergate. Those were the days. When a two-bit break-in could turn into a constitutional crisis. Iran–Contra.

Abscam. Child's play. Christ, if only the *Post* knew about this! They could all go to jail!

In a far corner of the lowest level, the car came to a stop, only a few feet from an elevator.

"Follow me," Libby ordered.

They approached the doors, and Libby pressed a button. "Fingerprint scan," he said. The doors parted. Once inside, the elevator rattled through a short descent. The doors hissed open, and Rove found himself face-to-face with a group of uniformed NSA Police nodding politely at Libby.

"Welcome to COG," Libby said.

"What?"

"Welcome to COG."

They were in one of the underground, undisclosed, undercover outposts of a Cheney-inspired project called COG (Continuity of Government).

Here is where the Vice President would be whisked to ensure the survival of the government if the White House fell under attack.

On the other hand, his boss, the President, would stay at home. At the White House. Under attack.

It was a small suite with all the essentials of a standard bunker: sleeping quarters, food rations, and emergency communications equipment. Knowing he might need to spend weeks or months riding out the survival of the United States, Cheney added a few personal comforts: the entire works of Rush Limbaugh (propped on a small coffee table), his favorite hunting rifle, and a list of major Republican National Committee donors who would be prioritized in any search and rescue operations as the nation emerged from its apocalypse.

Libby led Rove through a narrow corridor that led to another locked door posted with a sign that read: RESTRICTED. COG LVL 1.

"This is what the Vice President wanted you to see," Libby said, fishing through his pocket for a plastic card, which he waved in front of the door to the sound of a soft buzzing.

They entered a massive room, brilliantly lit and frigidly air-conditioned. Rove saw endless rows of giant cubes, encased in glass and metal. Glittering black walls of computers whirred and blinked red and green lights. Technicians dressed in black uniforms strolled casually down narrow aisles, stopping occasionally to inspect a cube, as if price checking at the supermarket. Rove thought he wasn't in the top-secret, undisclosed location of the Vice President in 2004, but on the mother ship of some alien fleet.

"What is this?" Rove asked.

"The Vice President's reorganization of the intelligence community. His name is NICK. Stands for the Network Centric Total Information Collection, Integration, Synthesis, Assessment, Dissemination, and Deployment System."

Right there, deep in the bowels of the NSA, where no one would notice, NICK noticed everyone's business. So clandestine that even President Bush could not be briefed on it. You couldn't find NICK in any federal budget (unless you had the fortitude and the magnifying glass to find a three-point italicized typeface entry within the "Supporting Projections Tabs" of the Department of Agriculture, Office of the Deputy Secretary for Public Nutrition, Office of the Assistant Deputy Secretary for National School Lunch Programs, Division of Compliance, Assistance to State and Local Governments, Education, and Outreach, Misc.). The leadership of Congress was vaguely informed about NICK—just enough of a dose so they would feel as if they were in the know without knowing anything at all. The last thing the country needed was one of those pesky federal judges deciding that the constitutional right to privacy was more important than the nation's need for security.

NICK was one of the most potent defenses in America's anti-terrorist arsenal. Programmed to follow tens of millions of lives in real-time, assessing patterns of behavior, and predicting threats against the nation. NICK was the ultimate voyeur, with an insatiable curiosity and a ravenous appetite for data. He would hunt it, sniff it, taste it, chew it, swirl it around his hard drive, and digest it. And if it left a bad taste, creating the slightest irritation, indigestion, or queasiness, NICK would spit it right out in an alert to dozens of law enforcement agencies.

NICK performed investigative triage in a country on threat overload. Everyone was either suspicious or a suspect, a patriot or a Democrat. America was a population of tipsters, snitches, and informants. The limitless American vision that had built a continent, forged a democracy, defeated the Nazis, peered through the blackness of space, and landed a man on the moon was now reduced to peaking through window shades and checking over shoulders for Muslims in our midst.

Enter Professor Roger Dierker from the Rensselaer Polytechnic Institute and his theory of "graduated threat probability patterns." Dierker, a consultant to the NSA, programmed NICK to dig through the infinite streams of information coursing through cyberspace and then pan it, sift it, sluice it. Separating nuggets of information from worthless muck. NICK channeled information through an elaborate series of constantly updated filters. He could process billions of reports, accounts, files, and records, and recognize any one of eighteen hundred (and growing) separate "terrorist behavioral indicators." He knew the hundreds of word patterns most likely to be used in a terrorist e-mail or phone call, as well as the hundreds of code words to mask those communications. He knew the nearly two thousand favorite terrorist training camps, neighborhoods, and vacation spots, as well as the terrorists' "fifty preferred hedge funds." NICK even knew the top twenty songs most likely to be downloaded to the My Favorites category of a terrorist's iPod.

NICK was a high-tech police profiler. He didn't pull people off the highway based on how they looked; he pulled them from the information superhighway based on what they did. It didn't matter whether data was fed directly to him, or just happened to be passing by on its way to a Google Search. NICK saw it all. Police reports filed, arrests made, and tip lines called; passports presented, countries visited and miles traveled; Internet sites viewed and music downloaded; DVDs rented, books bought and books borrowed. Reservations for planes, trains, cars, hotels, motels; certain magazine subscriptions ordered, certain organizations joined, certain petitions signed, certain donations sent; applications for drivers' licenses, pilots' licenses, or licenses in any one of one hundred and sixty-five "occupations of elevated threat"; purchases of guns, uniforms, fertilizer, or any of over two thousand substances that didn't mix well; credit reports with balances that spiked or slumped, as well as charges made, charges paid, cards applied for, and cards declined, cards reported lost, stolen, damaged; bank accounts opened, bank accounts closed, transfers in and transfers out; suspicious deposits or unusual withdrawals; birth certificates, death certificates, changes of address, visas, and passports; tax forms, immigration forms. Any form of information that could be useful to NICK.

Scanning, checking, comparing, contrasting, and cross-referencing in a ceaseless search for patterns. Reaching across innumerable bytes of information and making them all add up.

If someone blew a stop sign and received a ticket, NICK knew it. If they had a foreign birth certificate and blew a stop sign near an apartment on the federal terror watch list, NICK noted it. If they also used certain word patterns in their e-mails, NICK wouldn't like the taste of that. He would try to wash it down with phone records, bank statements, travel information, and plenty more. He would gorge on private details. And after sucking it all in, if NICK learned of some unusual fluctuations in a savings account and some wire transfers from certain places, he would exhale a well-nourished, satisfied breath, and transmit a threat-pattern advisory. It could be a Level 5, meaning NICK wanted to keep his eternal eyes on you and your records. Or it could be a Level 1, which meant that you were about to hear a knock on your door. A few people in suits and sunglasses would ask you some questions. You've been nailed by NICK.

Rove blew a long whistle from his lips and asked: "What's to stop this from spying on innocent Americans? Accidentally, I mean?"

Libby exhaled impatiently. "We take privacy rights very seriously, Karl. We have checks and balances. Safeguards. This government does not spy on the American people."

MORNINGS WITH MORRIS

WEDNESDAY, AUGUST 4, 2004

Just as on every morning for the past thirty-four years, Rona's alarm clock that Wednesday was the sound of Morris awakening at precisely seven fifteen she heard him stirring beside her in bed. He lifted himself with a resigned sigh, and shuffled toward the bathroom. Rona knew that Morris would pee at seven eighteen, gargle his mouthwash and brush his teeth by seven twenty, and shave, shower, and dress by exactly seven forty. Then the slightest breeze of Calvin Klein aftershave would pass over Rona as he left the bedroom. By seven forty-five AM he would be sitting in the kitchen sipping his coffee, chewing on a toasted bagel with two slices of Swiss, and turning the pages of the newspaper that he retrieved from the curb. That scent of coffee and a toasted bagel was Rona's signal. At eight fifteen she would join Morris in the kitchen for a good-bye kiss. At eight thirty he would close the door with a soft thud and go to work. That was Morris's morning. Every morning. As precise and predictable as an atomic clock.

Rona pulled the blankets to her cheeks, blinked at Morris as he dragged his feet to the bathroom, and thought, *God forbid the man should sleep late one day. Or go really crazy and have his bagel before getting dressed. God forbid he changes his routine.*

There was a time when Rona tried to change Morris's routine. To coax him from his seat in front of Turner Classic Movies by changing the scenery of their marriage. Once, she enrolled them in the adult lecture series at Long Island University. The course was American History. Morris never made it any further than the Pilgrims. She tried to accommodate his love of old movies by joining the Cinema Arts Centre in Huntington. But Morris said he didn't like movies with subtitles or post-film discussion groups.

So she gave up on trying to change Morris and kept trying to change the world. Which seemed easier. She joined the Great Neck Democratic Committee and the Hadassah Social Action Committee and the North Shore Breast Cancer Action League. She volunteered for local political campaigns. She conducted on-line debates. Not on computers, but on lines at supermarkets and bakeries and the women's apparel department at Bloomingdale's. She reconciled to her and Morris's uneasy truce. Morris survived by not making waves. Rona survived by acting like one of those wave machines at the science fair.

Which is how their marriage survived.

Plus, she thought, *With all the* mishagas *in the world—this one divorcing that one, almost half of Great Neck having affairs with the other half—I should count my blessings.*

She knew one thing about Morris: A man who won't take chances by attending adult education wasn't a high risk for adultery.

Of that much she was certain.

THE TYPE-A G-MAN

THURSDAY, AUGUST 5, 2004

It was in parking lot section L-5 that Agent Fairbanks's infamous temper erupted for the first time that morning.

He stomped on the brake pedal. His car screeched to a stop. He grabbed the steering wheel as if he were strangling it, and emitted a "Jeeeeeeeezuuuz H" so long and loud that it rattled his car windows, carried clear across the parking lot.

In the Department of Homeland Security Employee Assistance Program, Fairbanks would angrily insist that all mistakes didn't make him angry—only mistakes caused by laziness made him angry. And right there, sitting for the entire world to see in Section L, Row 5, Space 8 of 285 Melville Corporate Center, Quadrangle 1, was a lazy mistake. A lazy mistake that could result in an elevated threat to the United States of America.

Fairbanks poked hard at his cell phone.

"May I help you," Marie's voice answered, in a bureaucratic tone that sounded as if she meant to say, "Only a few months to my retirement, must I help you?"

"It's me. Get me Agent Russell."

A few seconds passed, and Russell's voice trembled into the phone.

"Agent Russell. I'm curious. Do you by any chance recall where you parked your vehicle today?" Fairbanks felt his throat constrict around his words, chafing his voice.

"Uuuuhhhh—"

"Because I do. I know where you parked today. And yesterday. In space L-five-eight."

"Yes, sir."

"Now, Agent Russell. Tell me. Why does parking your vehicle in this particular location violate my DHS Subagency Parking Directive NYM-PD-three?"

"Sir," Russell quivered. "NYM-PD-three states that employees using the parking lot should avoid parking in the same parking space every day. Sir, I was going—"

"And why should we avoid parking in the same location, Agent Russell?"

"Sir, because if a terrorist cell is conducting surveillance, we self-identify our vehicles to them."

"And why don't we want to self-identify our vehicles to them?"

"Sir, to avoid anything that may compromise homeland security or cause potentially life-threatening actions against our persons or property."

"Which is why our vehicles are what, Agent Russell?"

"Unmarked vehicles, sir."

"And when you park in the same location, on two consecutive mornings, in a building publicly known as the site of a DHS office, what have you done?"

"Sir, I have marked the unmarked vehicle."

"Yes, you have. Now, get your ass down here and move this vehicle, or I will have it and you both transferred to North Korea!"

"Yes, sir. On my way, sir."

To say that Agent Tom Fairbanks's temper got the best of him was to describe his entire career in federal law enforcement. Thirty years of personnel files were splattered with similar evaluations: "A ticking time bomb"; "A grenade with the pin pulled halfway out"; "We gave him a gun?," and "STRONGLY recommend anger management therapy" (with three red lines scrawled angrily under the word "STRONGLY").

Agent Fairbanks could not contain his temper, and so his temper contained him—in the Melville, Long Island, regional field office of the Department of Homeland Security's Subagency of Intelligence and Analysis. The field office was Washington's latest strategic doctrine in the global War on Terror: the best offense is a good flowchart. No looming attack, no catastrophic hurricane, no national emergency, was so grave that it couldn't be handled with a good reshuffling of the bureaucracy.

Agent Fairbanks had been shuffled and reshuffled. He was frayed and brittle and now discarded to the bottom of the deck: in Melville, Long Island. Of course, were it not for his reputation for uncontrolled rage, he might be starting his day in more challenging locales: FBI offices in Manhattan or perhaps even in Delhi or Mumbai. But his FBI days were behind him. The FBI had been a stop in his federal law enforcement career. A brief stop.

Fairbanks entered his corner office. A small window, shielded by dented and stained aluminum blinds, offered surveillance of the immense parking lot four floors below. He separated two slats and saw Agent Russell racing back to the office, darting through the endless lanes of cars, like a rat navigating a maze.

The office was spartan. A lonely leather chair sat caddy corner to his desk, and dark gray file cabinets were pushed up against a far wall. The walls were decorated as an afterthought. A Census Bureau map of Long Island dominated the wall opposite the window, resembling a trophy fish. Above his desk were two framed citations in cheap black frames: the Huntington Township Rotary Club "Law Enforcement Man of the Year Award" from 2003, and a Proclamation from the Town of Oyster Bay ("Whereas Agent Thomas Fairbanks has made a vital contribution to the safety of the residents of Oyster Bay . . . Whereas Agent Thomas Fairbanks represents the qualities of leadership, dedication, and sacrifice that emblify"—was that a word, Fairbanks wondered when he received it—"public service; Now, therefore, be it resolved that the citizens of Oyster Bay do hereby thank Thomas Fairbanks for his service to our Town and to the United States . . .").

The only evidence that Fairbanks had a life outside the department was the gold, tri-fold picture frame on his desk, displaying his three children. There was TJ (now president of his junior high school class); Trisha (who had just organized the Sweethollow Middle School Christian Conservative Kids' Club); and Timothy (who, last summer, led his T-ball league in stolen bases, despite a league rule against stealing bases). "They are their father's children," people remarked when they gazed at the photographs, in the same tone they used after clucking their tongues and nodding their heads when they passed a traffic accident on the highway. The boys' shining blond crew cuts gave them a halo effect; and their bright blue eyes sparkled with a pride and confidence that some mistook for a disturbing, possibly psychotic, arrogance. Trisha's long blond hair fell to her shoulders. She parted it just like her favorite television star, Ann Coulter. And each child boasted what the family called "the Fairbanks smile": thin lips pressed together, angular jaws clamped forward, cheeks clenched. As if their faces had to be bolted on tight to contain the volcanic anger within. The Fairbanks children looked angry just like Daddy.

He removed the only item from his in-box. It was a copy of the DHS NEW YORK REPORT, the department's monthly newsletter.

Fairbanks despised it. Every glossy issue taunted him with graphic re-
minders of his current predicament. There was a photo of McCarthy,
the female director of the Buffalo office, announcing the break-up of
an attempted border infiltration from Canada. There was Schiff, at a
press conference with the Governor, announcing a bust in Binghamton. Binghamton, for Christ's sake! Serrano in the Bronx, and Bishop
in Syracuse. But no room for Fairbanks. As if his office wasn't even a
part of the department. As if they weren't on the map. As if nothing
ever happened on Long Island.

Marie's lethargic knocking rescued him from his anger. "You told
me to remind you. So I am," she whined.

Fairbanks stared at her. "Remind me about what?"

Annoyance spread across her face. "Your conference call. It starts
in fifteen minutes."

As if the employee newsletter isn't bad enough.

It was the weekly ITACCC—Interagency Threat Assessment
and Coordination Conference Call. It would be like all the others.
He would sit at his desk, holding the phone with one hand as if to
choke it, while beating a pen against his desk with the other hand.
Each of his colleagues would report on the latest threats in Buffalo
and Brooklyn and Onondaga and Oneonta and Saugerties and Syracuse. Threats here, threats there, threats everywhere. There would
be all the hoopla about what happened in Albany. Two leaders
of a mosque had been arrested for participating in a terrorist conspiracy. In Albany! Sting operations and investigations and threats
everywhere except Long Island. Cut off from the United States by
some damned glacier eons ago, cut off now from the color-coded
warnings, advisories, and alerts that rolled in from Washington
every morning. And at the end of the conference call, the senior
agent would ask, almost like a set-up joke in a nightclub comedy
act, "How 'bout you, Long Island? You got anything out on Long
Island? A break-in at the mall? Not enough low-fat skim milk at the
Starbucks? Bada-bing!"

Still, there was some hope. Maybe something came up over the weekend.

Fairbanks had two ways of finding out.

"Send in Agent Russell. When's he's back from his little stroll through the parking lot," he ordered Marie.

Russell appeared minutes later, panting and disheveled, his blond hair blown in all directions across his head, his tie flipped over his shoulder. He hugged a thicket of unruly files against his chest.

"You're late," Fairbanks snapped. "I have my conference call in ten minutes. And you're late."

"I was moving my—I'm sorry sir."

"What do you have for me? Anything?"

Russell repositioned the files against his chest and struggled to pull one out. "Actually, sir, I think this time we do have something."

Fairbanks's eyes widened. "Really?"

Russell rarely saw his boss pleased. And right now, he seemed on the brink of pleasure. "Yes, sir. We received a call from the county police. One of their undercover guys picked up some intel at a mosque in Bay Shore Friday night. Next week, the Long Island Council of Islamic Clerics will be hosting a meeting with a special visitor. So special, that he is on the watch list's offfff . . ." his voice trailed as he pulled another paper from the stack against his chest ". . . the NSC, the DIA, the JSC, the BFIA, Interpol, Mossad, the Saudis, the Paks, . . . and us."

Jesus, Mary, and Joseph! "Who is it?"

"We have some surveillance photos," continued Russell. "Taken in Karachi, Amman, Kuwait City, Madrid, and Detroit. And now he's on his way here. To our neck of the woods, sir." He tried to balance himself as he hugged the files with one arm and pulled out a dozen black-and-white photographs with the other. He spread the images across Fairbanks's desk, like a card dealer in Vegas. Fairbanks leaned forward, his eyes squinting.

"What's his name? Give me his name!"

"Sir, he goes by the alias of Akrim al-Dulaimi."

"What else do you have, Russell? Anything? Jesus H!" He gathered the photographs on his desk and was going to fling them at Russell. But Russell's arms were holding the other files against his body, and all that would do is create a mess. So he tossed them in the garbage behind him.

"But, sir. Our sources believe that Dulaimi is a credible threat. And he's having a meeting right here—"

"I know what our sources think!" Fairbanks barked. He rubbed his throbbing temples. An anger-management coach taught him this technique. Visualize the pressure dropping, lower and lower. Down, down, down. Visualize it subsiding. But he couldn't. *He's one of ours*, he wanted to shout. The county's undercover unit is hot on the trail of an FBI undercover asset. Let the meeting happen. There'll be twenty cops and ten real people and not a terrorist among them!

But Fairbanks couldn't say these things to Agent Russell. Or anyone else. He couldn't even tell the county police that they were wasting resources trying to bring an undercover operative to justice. At some point, they would either drop him or arrest him. As with so many others. Fairbanks knew that everyone jumped on judges for appearing so lenient with certain suspected terrorists. Half the time they get a friendly phone call from Washington at the last minute. "Hey, Your Honor . . . errr, you know that the defendant you're about to put away for plotting the destruction of the United States of America? Errr, he's actually in the Federal Employees Health Benefits Program . . . that's right . . . yes, he's very convincing . . . no, we couldn't say anything earlier because it would compromise national security assets . . . thanks for understanding . . . just a heads-up . . . keep it quiet . . . bye now."

"Strike one," Fairbanks muttered to himself. "Is there anything else?"

Russell wrestled with another file as sweat gathered across his forehead. "Sir, some messages from Colonel McCord. In Great Neck."

McCord! Another Frankenstein creation of the DHS community-relations imbeciles in Washington. They had printed up hundreds of thousands of laminated cards embossed with the agency seal and "Honorary Agent." DHS local offices dispensed the cards to foster goodwill and encourage cooperation as the agency's eyes and ears. Which would have been okay if the eyes and ears had included brains. McCord, for example. A retired paramilitary guy who treated that little card like a license to drive an urban tactical assault vehicle to defend the village pond.

"Sir, the Colonel reports on illegal aliens at Great Neck Diner . . . one, uhhh, 'Middle East–looking' gas station attendant at the Exxon, who he believes has infiltrated the gas station to blow it up. Also, a report of—and I quote here, sir—a 'foreign-tongued' family that moved into his neighborhood. The caller believes that they are—quoting again—'hostile to US interests.'"

"What language do they speak?"

"French, sir."

Hmmmmm, thought Fairbanks. "Anything else?"

"Yes, sir. Colonel McCord reported seventeen instances of speeding on Soundview Avenue and one possible violation of the Village of Great Neck zoning code. Illegal deck expansion."

Jesus H! Strike two. Fairbanks looked at his watch. The conference call would begin in five minutes.

"Let's keep an eye out, Agent Russell. On everything. Especially that French family. Dismissed."

He was down to his final strike. He locked the door behind Agent Russell and made sure the aluminum blinds were shut tight. Then he returned to his desk, logged on to his computer. He typed in his primary password and his secondary password. And then scanned the home page. There, at the bottom right of the screen, was the icon he sought, that tiny computer monitor floating above the name NICK. He clicked and the screen flashed:

YOU ARE ENTERING A RESTRICTED SITE. AUTHORIZED PERSONNEL ONLY. VIOLATORS WILL BE PROSECUTED TO THE FULL EXTENT OF THE LAW. PRESS ENTER FOR NICK. PRESS EXIT FOR HOME PAGE.

Fairbanks poked at the Enter key.

The screen flashed again then went dark. Several seconds later white letters scrolled against the black background.

ENTER NICK AUTHORIZATION CODE

He tapped at the keyboard.

ENTER NICK PASSWORD

He complied.

RE-ENTER NICK PASSWORD

He did.

WHAT IS THE NAME OF YOUR DOG?

He typed: HOOVER, J. EDGAR

The monitor blinked. A dark blue background with the department logo and the screen heading appeared:

NETWORK CENTRIC TOTAL INFORMATION COLLECTION, INTEGRATION, SYNTHESIS, ASSESSMENT, DISSEMINATION, & DEPLOYMENT.

Then there was an entire paragraph of helpful legal informa-tion—the dozens of federal statutes that one was currently violating if they had no business on the site, followed by a list of potential conse-quences, up to and including the death penalty.

"TYPE FIELD CODE" NICK asked Fairbanks.

6-3-1.

"C'mon, baby," Fairbanks pleaded as he heard his computer gurgle. "Give me something. Anything. For once!"

And then this:

NICK HAS FOUND 0 THREAT PATTERN[S] IN YOUR JURISDICTION. PLEASE TRY AGAIN LATER. :(

Strike three.

THE RECEPTIONIST

MONDAY, AUGUST 9, 2004

Even as he crept through heavy rush-hour traffic, Morris Feldstein said to himself with a slight smile, "This will be a good day." He tapped his steering wheel with his thumbs to punctuate the sentiment.

Morris didn't normally forecast whether or not his days would be good or bad. As they rarely fluctuated, he could tell you only two things with certitude. One was the score of the prior day's Knicks, Giants, Islanders, Mets, or Yankees games. The other was that the day ahead would not be good, it would not be bad. It would just . . . be. Early in his marriage to Rona, he'd return home from a day of pitching pharmaceuticals to doctors, and she would ask, "So? How was your day?" Morris would stare at her expressionless, and respond with a languid "No runs, no hits, no errors." After four years of no runs, no hits, no errors, she stopped asking.

Today, however, was different.

Today will be a good day, he thought.

True, the Mets had lost to Saint Louis the day before. But Morris chalked that up to a pitching meltdown by Al Leiter in the third and fourth innings. Plus, it was Monday, which meant Rona was bringing in kosher deli for dinner. The morning offered slight relief from the recent heat. And he was on his way to a Celfex sales call at the office of Dr. Kirleski, where his favorite receptionist, Victoria D'Amico, worked.

Victoria D'Amico always greeted Morris with an excited smile and a cheery, "Hello, Morris Feldstein!"

And he was on his way to see her. With something special.

This morning Morris had a gift for Victoria, tucked between three pens in his shirt pocket. He tapped his thumbs on the wheel again, to the overheated blaring on the car radio of *The Angry Andy Morning Rant*. Angry Andy was spewing about the Mets game in Saint Louis, with a chorus of grumbling ascent from Tony from Astoria, Woo from Flushing, and Pete from Seaford (who announced that he was a "longtime listener, first-time caller" to Andy's incessant ringing of his "welcome bell"). Meanwhile, Morris inched through an intersection of gas stations on every corner and continued past a monotonous canyon of big-box retailers, the Costcos and Walmarts and Home Depots. The endless, rusted chain of America's corroding chain stores: the same Blockbuster Videos and CVS drugstores, the same family restaurants with cheerful names and scrubbed brick facades and circus-themed canopies. The same fast-food franchises on Long Island, the land of franchise opportunity.

"Almost there!" he chirped, and it was as close as he'd ever come to singing (except during his High Holy Day visits to Temple Beth Torah, when he felt compelled to mumble a monotone and ambivalent drone). Finally, Morris eased his car into an intersection and waited to approach the Roslyn Plaza Medical Arts Building, listening to the rhythmic ticking of his turn signal.

He had arrived.

Morris slipped his car into a spot and turned off the ignition. He gathered his Celfex sales forms and promotional literature from the backseat. One glance at his paperwork told him that Dr. Kirleski needed resupplies of Celf-Assure (impotence), CalaFLO (incontinence), and CelaREM (insomnia). He walked across the parking lot, checking his shirt pocket for Victoria's gift.

Inside, Morris found Victoria sitting behind the glass partition, her head bowed toward some paperwork, her blond hair cascading forward. When she heard the door open, and saw that it was Morris, her lips curled into a smile and dimples implanted themselves in her cheeks and Morris thought, *She looks like a young Doris Day. Doris Day in* Pillow Talk. *With Rock Hudson. I think she was nominated for Best Actress. Nineteen fifty-eight or fifty-nine.*

"Hello Morris Feldstein!" For some reason, Victoria seemed to enjoy saying his full name.

"Hullo, Victoria." His hands felt awkward and heavy at his sides.

"What happened to our poor Mets this weekend?"

That was an invitation to Morris. "Well, if you really think about it, they won three in Milwaukee. And in Saint Louie, on Friday, Glavine was scoreless most of the game. Just had a bad ninth. Then on Saturday it was a two-to-one game. That was close. And yesterday, you take those two bad innings out of the game and we would have won. So it wasn't so bad."

"Let's go Mets!" Victoria squealed. "So you wanna see the doc?"

"Yes. Actually, no. Not yet. I mean, I have something for you. From Celfex. The home office. I thought you would enjoy it. Hold on." Morris felt his tongue stumble against the inside of his cheeks as he fumbled through his pocket. He produced the gift: two tickets to the Celfex Diamond View Suite at Shea Stadium. "These are for you. Mets versus Astros. Tomorrow night."

The tickets were "customer-relations incentives," dispensed by the home office in Plattsburgh like bars of gold. There was no quid pro quo involved in Celfex dispensing gifts to the doctors who dispensed Celfex products. That would be wrong, according to chapter four of the Celfex ethics manual. This gift was simply a matter of good customer relations. Celfex encouraged Morris to entertain doctors at the luxury suite. But Morris was uncomfortable with the entire concept of luxury-anything at a baseball game. Shea Stadium should not require jackets and ties; the sipping of white wine and eating of hors d'oeuvres he couldn't pronounce; the making of small talk for nine innings. Especially when normal Mets fans in the cheap seats outside hurled curses and swilled beer and accumulated small piles of discarded peanut shells under the seats in front of them. So he didn't mind giving away the tickets, and enjoying the game from the comfort of his RoyaLounger 8000. That made him happy, as well as his supervisors, the doctors, and now, perhaps, Victoria.

Behind the glass partition Victoria's eyes widened. She sprang out of her seat and disappeared, which confused Morris. Then the door to the lobby burst open, and she charged him with outstretched arms, blaring, "You are the best! Gimme a hug, Morris Feldstein!"

Morris refused to do many things in public. Hugging was near the top of the list. Morris didn't do hugs with strangers. They were too complicated. They involved excessive motion and calibration. Too many things could go wrong. Limbs moving in all directions. Uncertain where his arms were supposed to go, or whose head went where, or what body parts could come into contact with the other person's body parts. And when two bodies are that close, there's no room for error.

So when Victoria rushed toward him, it was as if he was watching a highway collision in slow motion. Morris braced for impact, his face screwing into a tortured grimace, his arms reflexively rising to protect his chest, his fingers locked around the Mets tickets as if he was clutching a football that he might fumble. Victoria wrapped her arms around Morris and pulled him against her. So powerfully that it forced an anxious *oooohhhh* from his mouth; so close to her that he felt her chest against his and smelled a fresh lemon scent in her hair. Morris's arms felt like steel beams as he extended them around her. And he robotically patted her on the back, as if consoling her at a funeral.

She drew back and stared at the tickets. Then her lips sank and her eyes grew sad.

"Oh," she whispered.

"Oh?"

"Well, it's just that—I guess I never told you. I'm divorced, Morris Feldstein." Her eyelids twitched and she looked at the floor.

"I didn't know, Victoria. I'm sorry."

"Oh, don't be sorry," Victoria chuckled, but Morris detected the slightest trace of bitterness. "It's better this way. I mean, it took me eighteen years to figure out that Jerry—that's my ex—was no good. But now I've-started-my-new-life-and-I-just-hope-he's-happy-with-that-slut-he-met-at-the-pizza-place-because-the-two-of-them-deserve-each-other."

Morris blinked.

"It's just that, to be honest, Morris Feldstein, I haven't been to a Mets game since the divorce. Jerry and I used to go all the time. Of course, we sat in the nosebleed section because he was such a cheap bastard. Anyway, I don't know who I could go with. At the last minute like this." She scrunched the corners of her mouth and her nose twitched. "Unless . . . I mean, are you going to go?"

Going to a Mets game with Victoria had never occurred to Morris. Even when Victoria and two Mets tickets were staring him in the face. "No. They're for you," he said.

Victoria looked at him strangely, as if he just didn't get it, which he didn't. And she shrugged with a giggle. "You know what, I bet Doctor K would go. I'll ask him."

Only later, after Morris arrived home to the smell of fresh kosher deli and a quick greeting from Rona, only when he was ensconced in his RoyaLounger 8000 watching the highlights of the prior weekend of Mets games, did he wonder if Victoria was suggesting that they go to the game together. And even though that realization was about eight hours too late, it made Morris feel something new and strange.

Maybe he wasn't such a schlub after all. No Rock Hudson, mind you. But not so bad after all.

8

THE MATCHMAKER

"Uccchh. I hate this day," Victoria D'Amico thought the next morning as she pulled her car into the parking lot of the Roslyn Medical Arts Building. And the reason for this departure from her usual good cheer was in the passenger seat, right next to her.

Morris's Mets tickets. Unused from the night before.

She stared at the dull yellow brick walls of her office building. The morning was gray. The first drops of a light rain pinged at her windshield. The radio blared Billy Joel's "Uptown Girl"—one of Victoria's favorites and, she was known to say, her "theme song." She would raise her palms outward, gyrate her shoulders, contort her face, and sing. Now, all she could do was echo the words half-heartedly.

Some uptown girl she was. Even with two tickets to a luxury skybox at Shea Stadium to see the Mets play the Astros, she had spent the night alone, without a date, without a friend, cross-legged on her couch, wrapped in a pink terry-cloth robe, dipping into a bag of microwave popcorn and watching the one movie that she always reserved for such nights: *Sleepless in Seattle.*

Tom Hanks and Jerry D'Amico. Contrast and compare.

Hanks: suave, sensitive, inquisitive.

Jerry: "I don't watch chick flicks."

No one was able to go with her to the game. No boyfriends to speak of ("I'm not ready for the dating scene so soon after Jerry ruined my life."). Not Dr. Kirleski ("I'm sorry, Victoria. Mrs. Kirleski is dragging me to one of her charity medical dinners."). Even Morris Feldstein turned her down. *I mean, Morris Feldstein! What could he have going on? Nice guy, but I mean, c'mon. You stick two Mets tickets in my face, I practically beg you to take me, and you say no? What is that?*

Which is why she spent the night with Tom Hanks.

The lobby to Dr. Kirleski's office was empty and dark. A single window, facing the street, provided as much light as a porthole in a prison cell. Magazines were strewn on coffee tables; their six-month-old pages tattered by the germ-infested fingers of patients. Mismatched couches and fabric chairs were propped against the walls. And those walls! Those walls had always annoyed Victoria. It was Dr. Kirleski's idea to plaster them with meditative landscapes, which he thought would lull his patients into a relaxed state, as if staring at a Sonoran Desert sunrise would make it more pleasant to have a stick scraped against the enflamed recesses of a strep throat. The scenic montage was interrupted with dire skull-and-crossbones warnings from the Centers for Disease Control. There, above a couch, was a photograph of turquoise waves lapping against an untouched Caribbean beach, then the dazzling greenery of an Amazon rain forest, then a startling display of skin-rash patterns associated with Lyme disease.

A small television was mounted on a corner shelf. She turned it on with a remote to see footage of President Bush and some geeky-looking guy who was about to become head of the CIA. She turned it off.

Every time you turn on the TV they scare you half to death, she thought. *With the color-coded warnings and Iraq and Afghanistan and car bombs. Who needs it?*

She plunked her purse on the desk behind the glass partition. Prepared to sit, she heard rattling sounds coming from Dr. Kirleski's rear office—the familiar opening and closing of drawers and the shuffling of papers. *There he goes,* she thought, *looking for something that's probably right in front of him.* A brilliant diagnostician, they said of him. Just not able to identify his own nose. She marched through a darkened corridor, past Exam Rooms 1, 2, and 3, past the heavy metal cabinets where years of chicken-scratch records were filed and medical samples were stored. She entered Dr. Kirleski's tiny office. He sat behind his desk with a perplexed expression, scratching the few white wisps of hair left on his scalp.

"Oh, Victoria. Good. Have you seen the file on Mrs. Johanson?"

She approached the desk and picked the file from under the morning *New York Times.* "Aaaaahhh," he said, as if he were opening wide for his own throat exam. "Thank you, Victoria. You're a lifesaver."

"Sure, Doctor K."

He cleared his throat, a signal of more to come.

"So . . . how was the Mets game?"

Ucccchhh. He had to ask. Bad enough I didn't go, but now my pathetic little life has to be his business. "I stayed home. Wasn't in the mood."

"Stayed home? By yourself?"

No, stayed home with the Mets. They all came over after the game. "Yes. By myself."

Dr. Kirleski stared at her, as if diagnosing some horrible disease. Terminal loneliness, she assumed.

"Well, Doris had an idea. We met someone last night. At the

charity dinner. She thought you might like to meet him. I have his card. Here, somewhere."

Oh God, Victoria thought as Dr. Kirleski raked his fingers through the jumble of papers on his desk. Another find by Doris Kirleski. There was Romance.com, Cupid.com, Match.com. And there was Doris Kirleski. As if the divorce from Jerry made Victoria some kind of charity case. To be pandered to and pitied, to be made Doris's pet project. With that condescending voice, assuring Victoria, "Don't worry. I'll find someone for you. You're special." Pronouncing *special* as if she really meant "pathetic."

And the matches this matchmaker made!

The multiple divorcées; the massive bellies; the balding scalps and comb-overs; the open shirts blossoming thick tangles of chest hair; the heavy cologne and clunky jewelry; the "father types" who were on the fast track to an assisted living facility; the "such-a-nice-guys" with the clammy handshakes and mumbled conversations; the players who never missed an opportunity to peer down her blouse; the loners, the losers, the louses. Either they were barely a step ahead of Jerry or barely a step behind. Ucccchhh.

"Here it is!" He squinted at the business card in front of him. "Doris thinks this one is perfect."

Doris thought the "small businessman" who picked me up in a taxi was perfect. His small business was driving the taxi.

"You're making that face!" Dr. Kirleski warned.

"What face?"

"The face when you scrunch up your nose and curl down your lips. Like you're swallowing bad medicine."

"It's just that—"

"Victoria. I met this guy myself. I wouldn't steer you wrong. Call him. One date. What do you have to lose?"

She unscrunched. "I'll think about it, Doctor K. Your first appointment is almost here."

By the time she returned to her desk, she'd thought it over. She looked past the glass partition and out the waiting room porthole, toward her car, where the two unused Mets tickets sat, souvenirs of her loneliness. And she thought of another night, watching *Sleepless in Seattle* again, in that ratty "feel-sorry-for-myself" robe, with her fingertips saturated in popcorn oil.

She picked up the card and read it:

RICARDO MONTOYEZ

Chairman of the Board

VON ESCHENBACH'S SYNDROME FOUNDATION.

Victoria D'Amico prided herself on her cynicism toward men. It was born and bred out of her marriage to that-bastard-Jerry-who-screwed-the-slut-behind-the-counter-and-kicked-me-to-the-curb. Still, she thought, cynicism may have been the armor that protected her from being hurt again, but it made a lousy companion.

At some point Doris Kirleski's inventory of damaged goods has to be exhausted. Somewhere, there has to be someone for me. My one true love.

She cradled the business card in her palm.

THE TOWEL ATTENDANT II

WEDNESDAY, AUGUST 11, 2004

Hassan could sense trouble. It smelled of suntan lotion and sounded like heavy chains clanking around someone's neck. It always began the same way:

"Can I get anuthuh towel?"

From his unfortified station at the towel hut at the Paradise Hotel and Residences at Boca Raton, Hassan braced himself and said: "Sorry, sir. Only two towels per guest." He pointed his olive-skinned finger to the large sign above him that said: TOWEL LIMIT: 2 TOWELS PER GUEST. THANK YOU.

"It's faw my wife. She'll be down in a minute. C'mon dude, gimme a break."

"I'm sorry. Two towels per guest. When she comes—"

"I'm paying four hundred freakin' dolluhs a day and you won't give me a freakin' towel? Aw you freakin' kiddin' me? Lemme see yaw supervisa, moron."

"Her name isn't moron. It's Clareesha—"

"No, she's not the moron. Yaw the freakin' moron. Why can't you freakin' people learn how to speak freakin' English!"

"I'm sorry sir. Only two towels per guest."

The tourist stormed away, his belly undulating with every step, his multiple gold necklaces clanking violently around his neck.

Hassan squinted after him. Even in the late afternoon, as shadows extended their reach across the beach, the sun seemed strong. The chlorine tingled his nostrils and irritated his eyes. And he could feel that familiar pain building in his groin. The longer the summer, the worse the pain. He would try the tricks they had taught him in training camp. Focus on the mission, Hassan. Think only of the seventy-two virgins that await you in Paradise, Hassan. Before you know it, your cell will be activated, your mission complete, and you will join those seventy-two virgins and the pain will go away. Forever.

Forever. That's how long it seemed since he had been placed in America. Without a word from the home office in Tora Bora. Abandoned to the infidels, to the hordes of tourists with their incessant demands for more towels, to the temptations of the flesh.

Waterboarding is not torture, Hassan thought. *Waiting is torture.*

How much longer? How many more towels and arguments over towels?

That morning, Hassan had sent yet another coded e-mail to his control officer. Just to remind him that he was there. With the others. Ready to strike. Waiting for the seventy-two virgins in Paradise.

"Can we get tix to the concert?" said the e-mail.

The answer was the same as all the others he had received for years. "Not tonite."

Don't call us, we'll call you. Meanwhile, wait. The seventy-two virgins aren't going anywhere.

THE BLIND DATE

WEDNESDAY, AUGUST 11, 2004

Victoria D'Amico had a theory about men. A theory that was formulated, tested, and validated by eighteen years with Jerry. Men were either good for nothing, or too good to be true. There was nothing in between. Nothing.

She brought that theory into the dark-mahogany interior of Murphy's Steakhouse in Manhasset, on the first blind date of her brand-new life without Jerry. And dared Ricardo Xavier Montoyez to disprove it.

He wouldn't.

In the first place, Murphy's Steakhouse was a little too good to be true. Not exactly the finest dining—filled with loud Long Islanders bellowing at each other as they chewed their steaks and gulped their wines—but at least two or three stars above Jerry's favorite pizza place. Whenever a decision had to be made on where to eat, where to vacation, where to shop, Jerry would groan. When she suggested a trip to Paris, they ended up at Carlsbad Caverns. When she asked about "someplace exotic, like a Caribbean island," he reminded her about the horrible sunburn he had contracted at the local beach. Instead they spent a week with his mother in Utica. And when they would go someplace that appealed to Victoria, like the annual Financial Planning Conference in Orlando, Jerry would crane his neck at every passing woman half his age, and flirt with the waitresses at restaurants. If only they knew, Victoria would think, that his favorite game at home was shooting spit-saturated, teeth-crushed pistachio shells from his lips into an ashtray, and letting her clean up "the missed three-point shots."

And then there was her date, who approached her from a corner of the bar, where he had been waiting. Too good to be true.

It was as if central casting had dispatched him. A baritone voice laced with a silky, Ricardo Montalbán Spanish accent; short gray hair, swept to the back of his scalp with a sheen; and a wisp of a moustache that seemed carved into his deep olive complexion. An island of civility among turbulent waves of Mets, Yankees, Islanders, and Rangers jerseys, in orange and blue, and black and white, crashing up against the bar and clamoring for "anuthuh."

"I am Ricardo Xavier Montoyez," he trumpeted, clasping her hand while executing the official US Department of State Guide to Official Protocol six-inch bow. "I have a table reserved and have already ordered some wine. A Pride Claret. I hope you like it." He swept his arm forward, indicating that he would follow her. A refreshing change of pace from Jerry, who would walk six paces ahead of her at all times.

The maître d' led them on a zigzag pattern between the crowded tables, to the sounds of silverware clanking against plates and chairs scraping against the wood floors, frequent eruptions of laughter, and boisterous outbursts of Lawn-Guylish:

"Dat's awwwwwsum!"

"Dya wanna go tuh 'thuh mawwl tuhmawruh?"

"Waituh, we need maw bread he-uh."

They settled into their chairs, and Ricardo looked as if he was pre-paring to deliver the six o'clock news. His long fingers smoothed a silk tie against his chest. He tugged on the back of his herringbone blazer so that it snapped snugly against his shoulders. He pinched each shirt cuff, coaxing it down his wrist until his gold cuff links peaked from his jacket sleeves. He folded both hands on the table, conducted a visual inspection of his manicured nails, leaned forward, and fixed his attention on Victoria.

"Now. Tell me about yourself. I must know everything."

And that was it. He sealed his lips under the thin moustache, withdrew his hands to his lap, and listened.

What do I do now? Victoria asked herself. She knew how to listen, but not how to be listened to. With Jerry, a tête-à-tête was mostly just tête. She wasn't accustomed to a two-way conversation with a man in which more than one of the conversants actually showed signs of life.

She was careful to avoid any talk of Jerry, because the words *bas-tard, creep, friggin', lyin', cheatin'*, and *son of a bitch* seemed inappro-priate for a first date. So she spoke in generalities about her job with Dr. Kirleski, which seemed interesting to Ricardo. His eyes didn't glaze over, and he didn't yawn like a moose, and he didn't bellow: "Holy crap, is this going to go on much longer because I'm starving over here!"

When she finished, it was time to put him to the test. To establish whether he was good for nothing or too good to be true. She fixed on his eyes. They seemed amused, as if he were about to tell a joke.

"So now it's your turn," she said, leaning forward as if to depose him.

If eighteen years with Jerry left Victoria with any benefit what-soever, it was that she had become a five-foot, six-inch, blond-haired, one-hundred-and-twenty-pound lie detector. She could sense evasions, excuses, and lies of all types: falsehoods and half-truths, fabrications and deceptions, and complete and total bullshit.

"I am in global health care," he replied, in a tone normally reserved for "I'm a CPA."

"What kind of health care?"

"The von Eschenbach's Syndrome Foundation."

"Never heard of it." She knew her tone had all the grace of a chat at the Guantánamo prison. But that's what men deserved. Never the benefit of the doubt. Because when you gave them the benefit of the doubt, they took it, and also took Angela, the countergirl at Paventi's Pizzeria, and the Volvo, too. You gave them the benefit of the doubt, and they gave you the cable bill, the landscaping bill, a bad credit report, and eighteen wasted years.

"Von Eschenbach's Syndrome," he repeated. "It is an orphan disease. In remote areas of Africa."

"Oh my God. A disease that only affects African orphans? How horrible."

"No, no. Not a disease affecting orphans. An orphan disease. There are some diseases, like von Eschenbach's Syndrome, that affect so few people that they are abandoned by the medical establishment. They don't represent enough profit potential to justify the investment in a cure."

Ricardo's fingers, strong and prominent, now seemed to be attacking a cocktail napkin, shredding it into pieces that crumbled around his wine glass. "AIDS, malaria, cancer—they get all the attention. And all the money. Von Eschenbach's Syndrome? Nothing." He stared vacantly for a moment then shrugged. "We hired a publicity consultant. 'Have a telethon,' he told us. 'Like Jerry Lewis.' We tried. But it is impossible to get an A-list celebrity for a C-list disease. All the good ones are taken. We ended our efforts when Howie Mandel turned us down."

"What are the symptoms?"

"It depends on the strain."

"The strain?"

"Well, of course. Von Eschenbach's Syndrome comes in many strains."

Of course, thought Victoria. *Everyone knows that!*

"The most prevalent would be von Eschenbach's Strain A. It begins with irritability and restlessness. Then lethargy, fatigue, disorientation, and nausea."

A night out with Jerry, she thought. "Oh my God! So there's no cure? At all?"

Ricardo's olive cheeks twitched. He seemed to be gritting his teeth. And then he sighed. A long, troubled sigh. "That is what angers me so, Victoria. Our laboratory—in Côte d'Ivoire—is so close to a vaccine. But our work is slowed by the lack of medical supplies. No one wants to send medical supplies for research of an orphan disease in Africa."

"Horrible!" she agreed, with just a scent of reservation. "What kind of supplies do you need?"

"What do you have?" he asked, almost urgently.

"Excuse me?"

There was an awkward silence. At a nearby table, someone bellowed, "Wait-uh, we need maw caw-fee heuh!"

"I'm sorry," Ricardo stammered. "I should not have asked that. Sometimes my work for the foundation interferes with other priorities. You should be my priority tonight, Victoria. Not seeking medical supplies for sick and dying children in Africa."

Something inside of Victoria flashed a warning. Like a blinking yellow light. Warning her that if any man was either too good to be true or good for nothing, he was sitting right across from her, doing his best Ricardo Montalbán imitation, trying to lure free medical samples out of the metal cabinet in Dr. Kirleski's office. And maybe trying to lure Victoria into bed as well.

She considered disregarding the warning. Not out of weakness or naïveté. Victoria was the type who sped up at yellow lights. She knew she should stop. But she would race through anyway. Maybe she was in a rush for companionship. Or maybe she was intrigued by the possibility that he was acting dishonestly with her. She could do the same; they would use each other for a night, and then resume their separate lives. Maybe this is what liberation from eighteen years of captivity was about. Beggars become choosers.

Or maybe there was a possibility that von Eschenbach's Syndrome was afflicting remote villages in Africa, and she should try to help.

Or all of these things.

And then she noticed something. The usual type of creep at the bar. Gawking at her. Only this gawk was different. Usually, Victoria's gawkers would stare at her, then stare at their drink then stare back at her again. Usually there was a nauseatingly suggestive smile. Sometimes even a ridiculous wink that may have been learned back at the junior prom. Not this guy. This was a tight-lipped, no-blink, comatose-frozen stare. And it unnerved her.

"Ucccch," she said, scowling.

"What is it, Victoria?" asked Ricardo.

"Guy at the bar. Staring like that. I hate it!"

Ricardo turned slowly. And when he saw the man at the bar, Victoria noticed his moustache seem to twitch, and his eyes seemed to fall cold. He swung his head back. "Yes, that is rude of him."

"Whatever. I get it all the time. Should we get menus?"

"Yes, of course. But would you excuse me for a moment while I make a phone call?"

As he left the table, Victoria thought, *This is the part where he's lying to his wife about why he won't be home tonight . . . or calling in a cure for cancer.*

Ricardo Xavier Montoyez was doing neither.

THE FDA

THE SAME NIGHT

In a blue sedan in a dark corner of Murphy's parking lot, Special Investigator Anthony Leone slumped behind the steering wheel, thinking, *Tell me how crime doesn't pay? Lucky bastard's inside having a steak dinner with the blonde. Me? I'm stuck out here all freaking night.*

Then he saw Montoyez emerge from the restaurant and present a stub to a parking valet.

"Holy shit. Holy shit, holy shit," he repeated as he fumbled for his cell phone then panted into it, "Subject's leaving. Subject's leaving. Alone."

"Stay with him," a voice crackled.

"What about her? The woman?"

"Cooper will keep his eyes on the woman. You follow Montoyez. Stay . . . with . . . Montoyez."

"Roger. Follow Montoyez."

• • •

Two hundred and fifty miles away, in the Washington headquarters of the Food and Drug Administration William Sully thought, *Stand by. Stand by. That's all I do with Ricardo Xavier Montoyez. Stand by. Until he escapes. Then find him again. And . . . stand by.*

Sully pressed the tips of his fingers against a pain that throbbed deep between his eyes. He had been up most of the night, staring into a bank of computer screens. Now the images grew blurry. There were fuzzy black-and-white images of various Long Island neighborhoods, brought to Sully courtesy of the Nassau County Police Department's Neighborhood Block Watch cameras. On another screen was Murphy's Steakhouse. An electronic map of Long Island flickered on a third screen, its coastlines streaks of blue against a black background. Red orbs pulsated in the vicinity of Murphy's.

He sat in the Situation Room of the Food and Drug Administration Counterfeit Drug Investigation Division, surrounded by the video screens, speakers in all shapes and sizes, tangles of cables and wires, and an assortment of discarded soda cans dented from his grip. Four special agents stood behind him, on loan from the FDA Division of Sugar Substitutes–Office of Testing, Evaluation, and Compliance. Sully was building an investigative empire, plucking assets from the bowels of the federal government, where nobody would notice they were gone. He had become the master of the "Intra-agency Reverse Lateral Detail," a little known bureaucratic maneuver that allowed employees to be transferred from one office to another "temporarily." In Washington, that means forever.

Ricardo Xavier Montoyez might be able to evade the law, but Sully could make federal employees vanish and then reappear in his budget lines. Now you see them, now you don't.

When he began his career in federal law enforcement, Sully never envisioned he would end up at the FDA. He was once a rising star at the Central Intelligence Agency. But he became impatient with the obsessively cost-conscious, low-bid budgeters there. The ones that preferred green eyeshades to night-vision goggles; who insisted that you could conduct an effective surveillance op with equipment that came off the discount table at Crazy Harry's Electronics Warehouse.

And the micromanagement! Christ, you allocate a couple hundred million dollars to a satellite surveillance technology that accidentally snaps a picture of some Senator and his girlfriend naked in a backyard hot tub and suddenly they make a federal case out of it—literally. They summon you to congressional committees with words like "oversight" and "investigation" in their titles. They start poking their noses and their subpoenas into your budgets. People start knowing who you are. And if they know who you are, they'll soon know what you're doing. And then tell you not to do it.

Sully needed a place where he could work without being watched. A place dark and deep within the bureaucracy, where he could grow his empire like mushrooms. One morning, his CIA colleagues showed up for work, and Sully's cubicle was empty. Picked-clean. He had vanished. Except for a triplicate copy of an Office of Personnel Management Authorization for Voluntary Reduction in Force pinned to the fabric divider.

Sully had fired himself. And then rehired himself at the FDA.

Technically his occupational specialty was leading a task force to investigate the influx of counterfeit drugs into America's medicine cabinets. Not exactly tracking Taliban suicide bombers. But who at the *New York Times* or the *Washington Post* cared about the investigative techniques used by a division director at a backwater agency sworn to protect and defend America's aspirins? He could toil in obscurity. Just the way he liked it.

Sully reached for a tattered manila folder on the counter in front of him and opened it. Again. It was like a book he couldn't put down. The Life and Times of Victoria D'Amico. Employee of Dr. Richard Kirleski (whose life and times were contained in another file within arm's reach of Sully). Recently divorced from one Jerome D'Amico.

Owner of a mortgage at 88 Algonquin Lane (with a recent frequency of sixty-day-late mortgage payments); lessee of a Volvo SUV (also some late payments). Vices? An addiction to the shoe departments at Bloomingdale's and Nordstrom, the jewelry counter at Fortunoff, and credit card purchases that seemed to bob up against her limit. *A well-worn plotline,* Sully thought. *Man leaves woman for a much younger woman. Man leaves older woman with stretch marks and a plummeting credit score.*

All routine, except for this twist: Victoria D'Amico, medical secretary with access to a treasure trove of pharmaceuticals, consorting with Ricardo Xavier Montoyez, known pharmaceutical counterfeiter.

Or "Rx Rick," as he was better known, who was creating the medical equivalent of two-dollar bills. He was part of an extensive and profitable enterprise that purloined pharmaceutical shipments from manufacturers, diverted them to secret locations, where they were diluted, tainted, relabeled, or copied as cheap facsimiles before being reinserted in the supply chain and delivered to your local pharmacist. Taking medicine for your chemotherapy? That vial may be filled with water. A tablet for your blood pressure? Chalk. Your doctor prescribed twenty milligrams? You were taking only five. And you didn't even know.

He was the lowest of the low. So low that every major terrorist organization on earth—with one exception—rejected the practice as inhumane. If there were a Geneva Convention for terrorist groups, counterfeiting medicines might be the only entry. "Are you out of your mind?" one terrorist leader screamed at a subordinate in a Baghdad safe house. "Counterfeit cancer medicines? Our mothers take this stuff."

Twenty minutes after Ricardo Xavier Montoyez left Victoria, she peered at a bill for two steak dinners that were never served, one bottle of Pride wine, and a mountainous portion of Murphy's Original

Famous cheesecake. She had ordered the cake because, she reasoned, the night shouldn't be a total loss.

He had left her. Left her at Murphy's, in the company of the imbecile at the bar with the frozen stare. Left her in the midst of a crowd that occasionally turned toward her with sympathetic curiosity. Tears stung her eyes, and she worked to blink them back. *I will not cry. Not here. Not all by myself at a table at a restaurant. No way!*

She dug into the cheesecake.

Asshole, she thought. *Every man's an asshole. It's just that simple. They either leave you for a slut at the pizza parlor, like Jerry, or they just vanish into thin air, like Ricardo. They're either good for nothing, or too good to be true. No exceptions. Nothing in-between. Nothing.*

For the first time since her divorce, Victoria D'Amico felt truly, hopelessly alone.

And not even Murphy's Original Famous Cheesecake could stop her tears.

"I can't believe this!" Sully pounded the table.

I cannot keep doing this. Losing Montoyez. Finding him. Losing him again. I can't keep up with him with what I have. They want me to bring down a global medical counterfeiting empire with a dozen FDA inspectors trained in the war against trans fats. Armed with beakers and food scales. Gotta get more. More, more, more.

He planted his elbows on the console, cupped his hands, and cradled his chin. He ran his fingers across his cheeks, and felt the coarse stubble, the result of a dull razor he was too busy or too careless to replace. Deep waves of documents covered the table, lapping toward his torso: multicolored file folders crammed with loose papers, maps of Long Island neighborhoods, and satellite photographs in halftones of gray, sections of newspapers pulled apart and strewn in all directions, and an assortment of light reading including the *Guide to Federal Pharmacy Law*, *Lange Q&A: Pharmacy*, *Pharmacy Law Digest*, and Delmar's *Pharmacy Technician Certification Exam Review*.

And one massive book, nearly nine inches thick, sagging under its own weight near a corner of the console.

Sully stretched his arms and struggled to reel it in. It was thicker than a phone book, its pages dog-eared and paper-clipped and decorated with yellow Post-it notes. Its glossy cover bore the official seal of the United States of America.

It was THE FEDERAL BUDGET: EXECUTIVE SUMMARY.

He thumbed it open, and the left-side pages fell with a pronounced thud.

"Let's see," he whispered contemplatively. "Who has stuff they're not using? Let's do some shopping."

He flipped through the book. Line item after line item after line item, an infinite scroll of dotted lines and bottom lines, decimals and denominators. Flowcharts with big boxes connecting to smaller boxes connecting to tiny boxes representing the federal food chain.

His index finger dropped down the pages, lower and lower into the depths of the federal bureaucracy. Until it stopped.

"Ahhhh."

The Department of the Interior

Office of the Assistant Secretary for Fish and Wildlife and Parks

Bureau of Wildlife

Division of Science & Technology

Office of Species Management/Protection/Preservation

Species Management Section

Office of Surveillance, Assessment, & Analysis

Sully imagined some poor receptionist in this place, handling the phones: "Good morning. Thank you for calling the Department of the Interior . . . Office of the Assistant Secretary for Fish and Wildlife and Parks . . . Bureau of Wildlife . . . Division of Science and Technology . . . Office of Species Management, Protection, Preservation . . . Species Management Section . . . Office of Surveillance, Assessment, and Analysis. How may I help you?"

His lips curled into a smile. "Species surveillance!" he

marveled. "Man, they gotta have some pretty neat equipment down there!"

After sending some e-mails to friends in the Department of the Interior, Sully consummated a three-department trade of personnel (including two FDA employees to be named later).

He had one more item of business.

He ordered his staff to leave the room, closed and locked the door, and then logged in to his computer.

YOU ARE ENTERING A RESTRICTED SITE. AUTHORIZED PERSONNEL ONLY.
VIOLATORS WILL BE PROSECUTED TO THE FULL EXTENT OF THE LAW.
PRESS ENTER FOR NICK. PRESS EXIT FOR HOME PAGE.

Sully entered his NICK authorization codes and his password: ASPIRINMAN.

The NICK menu said: ENTER A SUBJECT.

He typed in Victoria D'Amico's name and social security number. With a satisfied sigh he said, "This should do."

EMERGENCY ROOM

THURSDAY, AUGUST 12, 2004

"Is that you, Victoria?" Dr. Kirleski bellowed from his back room. He could hear the rattling of coins and keys in her purse as she plunked it on her desk.

No. It's Miss Universe. I'll be filling in for Victoria today.

She walked into his office.

"You're a bit late, no?"

"I couldn't get parking in the lot this morning. Is someone having a sale or something?"

Kirleski gazed out the window. "Someone must be moving in. Phone company, cable company, power company. Anyway, how was it last night?"

"How was what?"

He seemed disappointed, his smile fading. "Your date! With the guy Doris and I met at the charity dinner. Doris is dying to know!"

Victoria's cold stare informed Dr. Kirleski that Mrs. Kirleski could die without knowing, for all she cared. He withdrew his smile, and said, "Oh. Well then, I'm sorry. Maybe the next one."

Sure, the next one. He's got to be out there. Somewhere.

Kirleski stood awkwardly, jiggling change in his pants pockets, wrestling with his next words. And when they didn't come, he shrugged. "Back to work then, I suppose, eh? Would you call Mrs. Johanson first thing? All night she left her usual life-and-death messages. Will you call her, Victoria? Thank you."

"Sure."

"Oh, and Victoria? There's a strange clicking sound on the phones. Call the phone company and see what it is."

"Sure."

She looked at the accumulated messages. They might as well have been headlined: WHILE YOU WERE OUT, GOD SMOTE YOUR PATIENTS. There were aches and pains, fevers and flu, inflammation and itching. There were stiff necks, tight chests, swollen glands, and light heads. There were hacking coughs, sore throats, cramps, chills, lumps, and hives. That was about half of the message pile. The other half consisted of administrative maladies. Patients fighting insurance companies; insurance companies fighting patients; and everyone fighting Dr. Kirleski. Payment disputes between HMOs and PPOs. Appointments requested, appointments canceled, appointments rescheduled, referrals sought, referrals made.

And a half-dozen urgent messages from Mrs. Johanson.

She thought, *Mrs. Johanson with her brain tumors. Always cancer, never a cold. Always near death, never a sniffle. Never in-between.*

Why can't life be more in-between?

Not the lush waterfalls hanging in the waiting room. But not "You and Your Prostate" either.

Not Ricardo, but not Jerry.

Not Tom Hanks.

Just . . . someone . . . average.

At which point, average walked through the door.

"Hello, Morris Feldstein!" Victoria greeted Morris.

"Hullo, Victoria." Morris drooped his head and stared at his shoes and wondered what to do with his arms. Morris never knew quite what to do with his arms when someone was asking him a question. They seemed rather useless for conversation, almost annoying. He could lock them behind his back, but that seemed too casual. He considered clasping his hands in front of him, but then he became self-conscious about placing them too close to his crotch. Folding them across his chest seemed standoffish. So he let them dangle awkwardly at his sides.

"How'd our Mets do last night?"

"We lost five to four. But we tied it up in the seventh, and if Looper hadn't given up that run in the ninth, I think we would have won. Did you have a good evening?"

"Ucccch, don't even ask. I had the worst date of my entire life. Watched old movies. And then reorganized all my old photo albums. Lucky for you I brought all the pictures in. Thousands of them. Want to see them? The thousands of photos of my life?"

She giggled, but Morris burrowed his hands in his pockets, grinned, and said, "Sure, I would love to see them."

Victoria narrowed her eyes on him, noticing something new about Morris Feldstein. *I bet he would do that*, she thought. *I bet he would stand there looking at a thousand pictures of my life! And I bet he would never get bored.* He had been calling on Dr. Kirleski's office for years, and just now, for the first time, she noticed something attractive about Morris. Not in the Ricardo way, or the way it used to be with Jerry. This sensation was new for Victoria. Morris was . . . different.

She began tapping a pen against her desk.

Where Ricardo projected charisma, Morris projected a belly slightly over his belt. Where Jerry cocked his head and turned up his nose at the world, Morris's face seemed to succumb to gravity.

Except when she spoke to him. Then, he seemed to perk up.

Is this what's between that good-for-nothing Jerry and that too-good-to-be-true Ricardo? Morris Feldstein? All this time, with his bulky case filled with drug samples and Celfex "customer-relations incentives," like the unused Mets tickets, and those Celexpro® glow-in-the-dark Post-it notes.

"Morris," she ventured. "I want to ask you something. Since we're talking anyway."

He bit his lower lip and began swirling loose change in his pants pocket.

"How long have you been coming here?"

"Oh, eight years, now."

"Do you know what your competitors do when they call on Doctor K?"

He stared blankly.

"They invite me to lunch. Or sometimes even dinner. They say their corporate offices encourage that sort of thing. As a customer-relations incentive. What is your company policy on that?"

She accelerated the beat of her pen against the desk, which accompanied Morris's jingling of the change in his pocket. It sounded as if Gene Krupa were performing in Dr. Kirleski's office.

Morris dropped his eyes toward the floor, and mulled the question over as if Victoria had asked for his interpretation of the Internal Revenue Code.

He shook his head and rendered his judgment:

"Well, my district manager, Laurie, always gets a good laugh when I turn in my expense account. I'm not from the big spenders, to tell you the truth. Not big on the wining and dining thing. Laurie says, 'Morris, if you're not spending the company's money, you're not selling the product. And if you're not selling the product, we're not making the money. Take someone out for a drink. You won't bankrupt us.' But who wants a Celfex sales rep talking about products over lunch or dinner? People want to eat in peace. I think so, at least."

"Oh, I don't know. I bet lots of people wouldn't mind getting to know you . . . a little better." *Hello? Victoria to Morris. Do you read me?*

The pen thumping, the coins jingling, Victoria's foot tapping, Morris's heart beating.

"Morris?" Victoria asked.

"Yes?"

Thump-tap-jingle-tap-tap-thump-jingle.

"Never mind. So I guess you want to see Doctor Kirleski now?"

"If he's available. That would be nice. Unless you want to show me the pictures you brought in."

"I don't think we would have time . . . here in the office."

"Sure. Maybe another time then."

"Where?" she asked. *Last chance, buddy.*

"Wherever you want. Here is fine. If it's not any trouble."

Now she banged the pen hard against her desk. "Okay, then. I'll see if the doctor is available." She noticed that her words sounded harsh, even angry. She tried to quell them with a sigh.

"Thanks. I'll just wait on the couch," Morris offered.

And as Morris reached for his briefcase, Victoria couldn't control the words that escaped from her lips. "I was just wondering, was all. I was just wondering why you never invite me to breakfast or lunch. The other sales reps, they always invite me out. And it's not just dinner, by the way! I just thought . . . I thought you and I were kind of friends. That it wouldn't be that big a deal to go have a hamburger at the diner. Just a hamburger at the diner with the rest of Roslyn. You know?"

Morris Feldstein was not particularly adept at nuance. But he had reached a conclusion: *Gottenyu! Victoria D'Amico just asked me out. On a date!*

If Morris Feldstein ever wanted to learn the therapeutic benefits of the entire Celfex product line, he was about to have a crash course. He felt his blood pressure plunge and then surge. He felt his temples begin to throb, his mouth dry up, his knees weaken, and his lungs sink into his stomach. Dr. Kirleski's lobby began a slow spin. When he and Rona used to take the kids to the amusement park, his job was to stand on the ground, guarding the pocketbooks, backpacks, and souvenir bags while the family rode the roller coaster and the Tilt-A-Whirl. Morris wasn't a big fan of motion, especially in places that weren't supposed to be moving, like Dr. Kirleski's lobby, which was now moving pretty fast.

Gottenyu!

Okay. Stop panicking, Morris. Take deep breaths. Inhale . . . exhale . . . inhale . . . exhale. Why is my throat closing up? My tongue is swelling! I'm going to choke on my own tongue. I need a relaxant. They must have some Celaquel in the back. Just ask Victoria for two Celaquel and a glass of water and—Why is it so hot in here? I'm sweating. My face feels like it's on fire! Could you plotz? I'm having a heart attack, a stroke, and I'm dehydrating—right in front of Victoria! And all she wanted was a bite to eat!

He began a soft wheeze.

You know what? On the way to the emergency room Victoria can grab a little nosh in the hospital cafeteria. While they're trying to revive me. That'll be some date. She'll have a nice hamburger, and I'll be on my deathbed.

Stop. I'm not dying. I ain't dead yet. Who said that? I know. Glen Campbell. In True Grit. *On Turner Classic Movies last weekend. I'll miss that channel when I'm dead. Oh-oh. I think I forgot to TiVo* Thirty Seconds Over Tokyo *last night.* Thirty Seconds Over Tokyo. *Nineteen forty-four. Directed by Mervyn LeRoy. With Van Johnson, Spencer Tracy, and Robert Walker. Guess it doesn't matter now. Now that I'm dying. Gottenyu!*

"Morris, are you okay?" he heard Victoria ask.

"Fine—I, just—"

"Oh my God, I came on too strong! I always do that! I'm so sorry! I didn't mean to—I mean—I was just asking about lunch. That's all. Oh God, I'm so sorry. I'm such a schmuck sometimes!"

"No. You're not," Morris mumbled.

"I am!" she insisted.

"Shikse."

"What did you say, Morris?"

"You're a shikse. A gentile woman. Shikse."

She laughed, which made him chuckle. And Morris began feeling better.

RUSH HOUR

THURSDAY, AUGUST 12, 2004

That evening, Ricardo Montoyez drove over the Whitestone Bridge. Following the signs to THE BRONX & NEW ENGLAND, going nowhere in particular. But away from Long Island.

He was annoyed. Not because he had to terminate his Long Island operation. He would be back. But because of the lost opportunity with the blonde. Sitting across from her at Murphy's Steakhouse, he could tell how much she wanted him. He only needed another two hours.

Now, instead of getting laid he had to lay low. He'd spend the day letting law enforcement chase their tails, and now he knew he could leave Long Island. Find a new pharmaceutical front away from Uncle Sam's prying eyes. Where he could continue the free flow of medicines to his processing facilities.

Near the end of the bridge he saw a National Guardsman

clutching an M-16 and eyeing every driver. Looking for the next terrorist who might harm Americans.

Not knowing they should look in their medicine cabinets.

Montoyez rolled down his window. A wave of heavy warm air flowed into the car. The soldier looked at him.

"Thanks for keeping us safe!" Montoyez said as his car rolled past. The soldier nodded.

WELCOME TO THE BRONX, said a huge green sign.

THE SUNRISE DINER

FRIDAY, AUGUST 13, 2004

They ate lunch together the next day, sitting in a red vinyl booth at the Sunrise Diner. The wait staff scurried around them like a circus act, weaving between tables while balancing tire-sized trays of deluxe hamburger platters, turkey club sandwiches, and diet plates heaped with wobbly scoops of cottage cheese and chunks of canned fruit. At every table patrons had to shout above the din. The entire diner sounded like a practice session of Toastmasters.

Victoria glanced at the news on an overhead television and rolled her eyes. "Oh my God, another politician in a sex scandal. What do you think of it all, Morris Feldstein?"

The Feldstein Anxiety Anticipation Index—the one that had hit DEFCON 1 in Dr. Kirleski's office the day before—suddenly nudged. Morris could comfortably carry three types of conversations: Celfex products, baseball, and movie trivia. Any discussion involving words such as *scandal, sex, sexual, sexuality, gay, politics, governor, government, Democrats, Republicans,* or "What's your opinion, Morris?" set off a variety of warning signals exhibited by a nervous tapping of his foot, an anxious biting of his lower lip, a twirling of his pocket change, or in this case, an exaggerated stirring of his coffee. His spoon clanked loudly against the inside of the cup, forming a whirlpool that crested over the lip and flowed down the sides, leaving a messy brown puddle on the saucer.

"Ohhh, I'm not really an expert on these things. I leave that to Rona. And my daughter, Caryn. She's studying documentary film." And then he thought, *Nice, invite your wife and daughter to the table.*

Victoria shrugged. "Guess I'm the same way. So I met this guy the other night."

Morris wasn't sure whether Victoria was telling a joke or not, so he assumed his customary joke-receiving position. He leaned forward, folded his hands on the gray Formica table, widened his eyes in exaggerated anticipation, pasted a smile on his face, and nodded his head eagerly. He had practiced this posture through countless Celfex sales retreats and Men's Club breakfasts. It had two benefits. First, it offered courteous encouragement to the joke teller. And second, it ensured that should the punch line befuddle Morris (a frequent occurrence) he would still be smiling so as not to offend. Morris Feldstein couldn't tell a joke to save his life. But he sure could take one.

"His name was Ricardo," Victoria continued. And the way she pronounced it—a sigh that bordered between forlorn and embittered—demonstrated to Morris that this wasn't turning into a joke at all.

"Ricardo Xavier Montoyez. My post-divorce inaugural one-night stand! We didn't even make it to the cheesecake!" She giggled.

Another nudge of the Feldstein Anxiety Anticipation Index. Morris grasped for something to say. Anything to prove to Victoria that he still had a voice. "Was he a nice guy?" he asked. Which nudged the Feldstein Anxiety Anticipation Index up a notch further. *Because, when you mentioned his name, the look on your face, as if you just*

chugged the curdling milk in the creamer that's been sitting out all day,
could lead me to the conclusion that he was a nice guy.

Victoria shrugged. "Almost too nice. You know what I mean?"

Morris nodded, although he had no idea what Victoria meant.

"You know what my problem is, Morris? I figured it out. After
eighteen years with that son of a bitch Jerry—that's my ex, as if you
couldn't tell—I thought I was owed perfection. I really thought I
would meet my knight in shining armor. But that's just too good to be
true. Don't you think?"

For some reason, Morris thought of Cornel Wilde in *Sword of
Lancelot*, and how he directed and starred in the film, which was produced in 1963, and mumbled, "Sure."

"That's my problem," Victoria repeated. "I have to lower my ex-
pectations. Find someone normal. Average. The happy medium."

That's me! Morris thought. *Morris Feldstein.*

The bill for lunch was twenty-two dollars and change. Morris
paid in cash. He and Victoria didn't exchange a single word about
Celfex products, therefore, Morris didn't feel it was proper to ask Celfex to pay the tab. And besides, he thought, twenty-two dollars—plus
tip—was a small price for watching Victoria D'Amico eat a hamburger while listening to her share the intimate details of her love life.

Others were watching Victoria as well, including Agent Fairbanks of
the Department of Homeland Security's Subagency of Intelligence and
Analysis (Melville Branch), and Special Agent Anthony Leone of the
Food and Drug Administration armed with a new cache of equipment,
on loan from the Department of the Interior, that could detect a buck
moth or tiger salamander from miles away). Also crowded into the parking lot of the Sunrise Diner were the unmarked vehicles of the Nassau
County Police Department, the Nassau District Attorney's Office, the
New York State Office of Homeland Security, the Federal Bureau of
Investigation, and several others who had the good fortune of receiving
a tap on the shoulder from NICK about Victoria D'Amico. The parking
lot at the Sunrise Diner was busier than the Sunrise Diner itself.

Leone watched her from his car, which smelled of discarded Styrofoam cups laced with the coagulated remains of ancient coffee. He monitored Victoria's arrival at Dr. Kirleksi's office that morning; he watched her leave for the Sunrise Diner that afternoon when it grew even warmer. He tailed her through lunch-hour traffic. And even when he lost her, he didn't worry. He'd pick up her trail. She lacked the skills of that master of evasion, deception, and disappearance, the Great Montoyez. And even if Leone took his eyes off her, countless other eyes wouldn't. The New York State Police cameras watched her route to the diner. The News 12 Long Island traffic cams stared from poles towering above the highways. The county's cameras dangled from traffic signals, taking automatic mug shots of drivers' guilt-laced faces at the moment of one infraction or other. The various cameras of towns, villages, and other government bodies keeping their eyes on their parks, their water towers, and their maintenance depots. The security cameras at the drive-throughs at banks, convenience stores, and filling stations and, yes, at the Sunrise Diner as well. All wove together like a spider web waiting to ensnare its victims.

All of these eyes, public and private, peering and leering, gazing and gawking.

The old private eye had been replaced by infinite public eyes. That day, Victoria D'Amico was the most watched reality TV show in the noon slot in the New York media market.

Leone sat in the diner parking lot, trying to ignore the discomfort of his thighs sticking to his pants legs and his pants legs sticking to the seat. "Sure, they sit inside an air-conditioned diner, eating the Deluxe Chicken Souvlaki Melt plus a nice bread basket. Me? I'm sitting in a 1984 Ford Furnace with a broken air conditioner!"

When the sweat became unbearable, he left the car and walked across the parking lot. Inside, he reasoned, he would steal a glance of Victoria and whatever criminal mastermind she was meeting for lunch. Plus, he might as well grab a cup of coffee to go while gulping down as much cool air as he could. He pushed against the glass doors. A gust of cool air dried his sweat-saturated shirt. He took a seat at the counter, scanned a glass shelf of pastries, and ordered his coffee. Then he swiveled on his stool until Victoria came into view.

Right there. With a middle-aged, schlubby-looking guy who seemed nervous if not petrified. With wide eyes and thinning hair. Looking more like an oppressed accountant than a possible link in a global pharmaceutical counterfeiting conspiracy.

Now who is that? thought Leone as he walked away from the diner. He returned to his car, sipped for a few minutes, and then wondered why the hell he didn't order ice-coffee on a day like today, a hot, sweltering day in a federal government vehicle with a broken air conditioner. *Sure, you're a crook, a terrorist, a perp, you get your air conditioner fixed one-two-three. You work for the Feds, you gotta fill out a Federal Fleet Repair Request — OMB Form GSA-FFRR-NY/36F/AC and wait till winter for it to get fixed.*

Finally, the two emerged. First Victoria, chic round sunglasses covering her eyes, her blond hair bouncing as she walked. Behind her, Morris, squinting in the sun, shuffling his feet to keep up with her, looking left and right as if afraid to be noticed. On his FDA-issued camera, Leone recorded what he thought was the most fumbled and awkward handshake ever. Victoria leaning into a tentative hug, Morris jutting arms out to shake her hand, Victoria backing off the hug and offering her palm instead, their hands colliding like kids playing patty-cake. Then Morris nodding, Victoria cocking her head and skipping off as her shoulders shook through a giggle. And Morris fumbling for his keys.

Leone prepared to follow Victoria. But first he pointed his hand-held ScanTag-3000 through his windshield, toward the license plate of Morris's car. He squeezed a trigger and heard a soft beep.

"Scanning complete," advised a woman's robotic voice.

"Stand by" she directed.

Then, from the small ridges in the unit, just under Leone's thumb, she confirmed: "New York License Plate K-two-J-two-seven-four."

And the winner is . . . Leone thought to himself.

"License registered to . . . Morris . . . Feldstein."

"Morris Feldstein," repeated Leone.

"File transmitted," the voice announced.

"Mooor . . . iiis . . . feellld . . . steeen." Bill Sully stretched the name as if thinning out each syllable would make Morris more transparent, revealing a hidden danger about the man. "Mister Mooor . . . iiis . . . feellld . . . steeen."

He had just been handed a thin blue manila folder with Morris's name scrawled in black Sharpie across the tab. Sully loved the smell of fresh Sharpie on a coated manila folder. Crisp, pungent, enough to sting his eyes.

He opened the folder.

"Mooor . . . iiis . . . feellld . . . steeen. Let's see what you're all about."

There wasn't much about him. Sully dug through twelve pages of prompt credit card and mortgage payments, driver's license photos, a manageable and modest household budget, a pristine credit report, and a fastidious observance of every law on the books, including parking, speeding, and jay-walking. Taxes paid, refunds made. Not a single bounced check. A model citizen. A loyal American. If not a paragon of virtue then the epitome of boredom.

On paper, at least.

"Can't be," Sully mumbled, pitching his head forward and rubbing his temples. Once your file made it into his hands, you had to have broken some law, committed some indiscretion. Maybe you said something you shouldn't have said; spoken out against the government; acted against the interests of the state. Violated a rule, regulation, ordinance, statute, act of Congress. Or else Sully wouldn't be peering into your file, smelling your name in Sharpie.

So what was it about Morris Feldstein?

Connect the dots, he coached himself. Connect the dots. Like one of those tests for color blindness. Just stare long enough at a jumble of blotches and soon, the real picture emerges.

"Of course!" Sully blurted. "There it is!"

The other agents leaned forward, now hovering over his shoulders.

"Occupation: sales representative. Employer: Celfex Pharmaceutical Laboratories. Of course!"

Dots connecting.

He slapped his palm on the table. The soda cans rattled.

"Morris Feldstein! Employed by a drug company. A drug company that supplies him with shitloads of . . . well, drugs!"

Of course, the agents nodded.

"Observed lunching today with Victoria D'Amico. Victoria D'Amico, the middleman . . . middle woman . . . middleperson in a chain that leads directly to Ricardo Xavier Montoyez!"

Go on, the agents coaxed him silently.

"Ricardo Xavier Montoyez. Prime suspect in a drug counterfeiting conspiracy. A conspiracy that relies on a regular supply of drugs. From Morris Feldstein!"

Dots connected.

An hour later, pieces of Morris Feldstein's life had been copied and pasted onto NICK's vast hard drive, everything up to and including his subscriptions to *New York Mets Inside Pitch* and *Sports Illustrated* (and Rona's subscription to *Home Therapists Journal*).

Until that moment, NICK wasn't particularly aware of Morris Feldstein. But now that they had been properly introduced, NICK wasn't one to forget a file. Morris had found a home on NICK's hard drive, where information about him could be updated, cross-referenced, double-checked, plucked, and parsed. And if there was anything about the file that created the slightest discomfort, NICK would burp, and the computers of law enforcement offices around the world would blip.

Morris Feldstein, whose worst crime to that point was succumbing to a lunch invitation at the Sunrise Diner.

POLL

SATURDAY, AUGUST 14, 2004

"And so my truth is that I am a gay American." From behind his desk in the White House, Karl Rove watched the Governor of New Jersey make the proclamation. He watched it on his VCR. Over and over. Forward and rewind, forward and rewind. "And so my truth is that I am a gay American."

It was music to his ears.

Rove turned to a thick stack of polling data from Ohio, peering at toplines and crosstabs. Digging his index finger into data as if taking its pulse. Concentrating that famous encyclopedic mind of the American political landscape. And not just the landscape as a whole, but specific zip codes. Especially zip codes in swing districts of Ohio.

Ohio was the battleground in this presidential election. Ohio, with its shallow pools of undecided and persuadable voters. Their values were a complicated grafting of incompatible principles. The self-described "evangelical moderate women" in the suburbs of Cleveland; the "national security Democrats" near Youngstown; the "family-values Blacks who support social spending" in Toledo; and the "right-to-life Catholics who oppose the war" near Dayton.

These were the individual swing voters whose decisions could swing a precinct, and that precinct could swing a whole county, and that county could swing all of Ohio, and Ohio would swing the entire election.

Rove rubbed his eyes, as the small print of the poll grew fuzzy. The news hadn't yet seeped into the data. But it would. Over the next few days and weeks, the images of the Governor's announcement— not to mention the relentless footage of thousands of gay people demanding same-sex marriages in San Francisco—would help the undecideds decide. By putting a giant God-fearing, gay-bashing, gun-loving wedge between them and John Kerry.

And that would seal the deal, he thought.

Fear. Fear was the ultimate wedge issue. And who was tapping on their shoulders in the dark, reminding them of the dangers that gathered and lurked around them? The terrorists, who threatened their survival and the gays, who threatened their marriages. *Boo!*

Rove was satisfied that Kerry's post-convention bounce was easing. It was coming back to earth. An earth infiltrated by gays and terrorists and illegal immigrants. Which made Rove smile.

Down the corridor, in the Vice President's office, Dick Cheney suppressed a frown.

"Secretary Ridge is reluctant to raise the Homeland Security alert at this time," Jon Pruitt had just reported.

"Reluctant?" Cheney repeated, lifting his eyebrow. He glanced at Scooter Libby, who sat stiffly in a Queen Anne chair.

"There's no credible justification at the present time. We already raised the alert for various financial institutions without any supporting intelligence. We can't keep doing that." He sighed, almost painfully.

Cheney remained silent. Libby would do his work for him:

"How about the suspicious foreigner videotaping the Brooklyn Bridge?" Libby asked.

"His hobby is photographing bridges. Wants to publish a coffee table book. Not blow up a bridge."

"That group of foreign students taking out books on nuclear fission from the library in Boston?"

"Students at MIT."

"Okay, what about those guys who pulled out that prayer rug at the airport and started praying toward Mecca before getting on their plane!"

"We checked it out. Evidently the airport chapel was already taken. By Baptists who were praying before getting on their planes."

"Still . . ."

An uneasy quiet settled on the Vice President's office.

Libby broke the silence. "Let me be clear. We go into our convention in two weeks. We need the right atmospherics on this."

Pruitt said, "I think we have the right atmospherics. Tell the voters we don't need to raise the threat level! Why? Because the Republicans are keeping you safe. Period."

Libby nodded his head in protest. "If people feel safe, they'll start paying attention to other issues where we may be . . . soft. Which means they just might elect Kerry. Who will make this country less safe. And expose us to an attack by our enemies."

Good boy, Scooter! Cheney thought.

"As counsel to the Secretary of Homeland Security," Pruitt said as officiously as he could, "I simply do not have the comfort level to advise him to increase the threat level based on . . . political considerations."

"Political considerations? Who said anything about that?" Libby snapped.

"Not me," said Cheney. And he cast a glare that sent a searing pain through Pruitt's stomach.

16

CHINESE TAKEOUT

SUNDAY, AUGUST 15, 2004

"What's wrong with the ribs, Morris? You're not eating your spare-ribs."

Morris chewed on his Kung Pao chicken from the Great Neck Mandarin Gourmet, but he wanted to bury his face in his hands and moan, "Leave me alone for God's sake!" That, of course, would be unprecedented behavior for Morris. And it would upset Rona. So, to keep the peace, he feigned a slight smile, and said, "It's fine. I'm just full." And continued chewing. Through gritted teeth. The food was bland. *Bland like my life*, he thought. Another Sunday night. Same take-out order from the Mandarin Gourmet, same white cartons and silver handles with the brown sauce overlapping the brims. Same fortune cookies and tiny plastic packets of duck sauce; same comment from Rona about eating more ribs. Same dark room dimly lit by the chandelier from Fortunoff. Same beige walls with washed-out portraits of Jeffrey and Caryn as children. Reminding him that his life had never been updated.

Except for one thing: Morris had never felt this way before. His lunch with Victoria had changed everything.

Ever since that lunch, a restlessness coursed through Morris's veins. Nothing satisfied him. Not even the Mets one-run win over the Diamondbacks on Saturday. He couldn't even concentrate on Turner Classic Movies' weekend tribute to Claude Rains. Victoria intruded on almost every minute of the past forty-eight hours. How she crinkled her nose when she chewed her food, how she swept loose wisps of blond hair behind her ears, how her dress swirled above her knees when she walked.

How she laughed.

He had spent the entire weekend considering the contrast between that scintillating one-hour lunch with Victoria, and the bland and unsatisfying totality of the rest of his life.

The lunch with Victoria was a curve ball in Morris Feldstein's infinite extra-inning game of no runs, no hits, no errors.

"Are you sure you're full?" Rona asked, chewing through her Special Chicken and Vegetable in Garlic Sauce. "You hardly ate! Have another sparerib. You love spareribs, Morris."

"No. Full."

"Have another, Morris."

The sign outside on their lawn said: RONA FELDSTEIN, CSW. Just down the hall, in her small office at the end of the house, she probed and peeked at the innermost anxieties of imperfect strangers. And here he was, just at the other end of the table, married for thirty-four years, and what is her professional evaluation? Have another sparerib, Morris.

He felt a twinge in his chest; in a place he estimated was roughly where his heart should be. Just like the feeling he had in Dr. Kirleski's office. Only now it seemed worse.

That was the other thing about the past few days. The anxiety attacks. The chest pains. The signs of a midlife crisis halfway through a crisis-free life. *Is that my heart beating faster?* he thought. *Or, does it always beat this fast but now I'm overly sensitive to it, which is causing anxiety that's making my heart beat really, really fast until it will stop altogether? Gottenyu—is it hot in the room, or is it the Kung Pao? Stay calm,* he coached himself. *No need to panic. I'm Morris Feldstein. Bad things don't happen to me (or good things, for that matter). I'm not the type to have heart attacks or panic attacks or any kind of attack. People who jump out of planes—they have* mishagas. *Risk takers and workaholics. Not pharmaceutical salesmen who don't make waves. We just go on. And on . . . and on . . . and on. No runs, no hits, no errors. No anxiety, no ecstasy.*

He felt better. More relaxed. More like himself. He was ready to attack the evening with a newfound energy. He would plunge into the RoyaLounger 8000 and watch the ESPN Game of the Week.

And then Rona asked, "Were you going to watch a game tonight, Morris?"

"I was. But if you—"

"No, it's okay. If you want to watch the game, we'll watch—"

"What do you want to watch, Rona?"

"Nothing. It's just the Summer Olympics. In Athens. Look, what's the big deal? I can miss them. They'll be on again in four years."

And the pain returned.

"CHECK, PLEASE"

THURSDAY, AUGUST 19, 2004

That day, sitting across from Victoria at the Sunrise Diner, Morris's eyes kept investigating the way her blouse clung to her chest and her skirt clung to her hips; how her forearm muscles bulged when she brought a drink or a fork to her lips; and how other men in the diner took mental snapshots of her.

So Morris was mentally unprepared for Victoria's question:

"Morris, how come you never talk about your wife? Tell me about her."

He shrugged his shoulders and said, "Rona." Because that pretty much said it all.

"That's it?" Victoria giggled.

Morris felt a slight nudging of the Feldstein Anxiety Anticipation Index and began tapping his foot. Then he fidgeted with his wine glass, moving it from one side of the plate to the other and watching the streak of moisture it left. "What do you want to know?"

"What does she look like? Do you have a picture?"

A *picture*, he thought. He couldn't remember the last time he looked at the picture of Rona buried in his wallet. He fumbled through his inside jacket pocket, unfolded the wallet, and produced the only three photographs it contained: two high school graduation pictures of Jeffrey and Caryn, and a photo circa the 1990s of him and Rona taken at a dinner function he couldn't remember. Someone's bar mitzvah or wedding. Or maybe one of those Celfex Employee Appreciation dinners he hated. They sat at a table cluttered with plates and glasses and a huge floral centerpiece. His arm was extended across the back of Rona's chair. She assumed her standard pose: her head cocked at an odd angle, her eyes widened. In that photograph, her auburn hair fell below her shoulders. More recently, it was cropped, and assumed an unnatural red sheen.

He passed the picture to Victoria, who studied it closely. "Awwww, you're cute."

"Who, me?"

"Yes, you."

"No. I'm not cute."

"Well I think so."

Victoria returned the picture, pressing it into Morris's palm. And when she did, she let the tips of her fingers rest there, just for a moment. But long enough to send a jolt through Morris's body, as if she had rubbed her feet on carpeting on a cold winter's day and shocked him. So that he felt the hairs jump on the back of his neck and a tingle pass straight down his back and into his groin.

"Rona's okay. But you know how it is."

"I know. Jerry."

"You drift apart."

"Eighteen years. That son of a bitch."

"You run out of things to say."

"But you never stop fighting."

"We don't fight," said Morris.

"You will."

"She just doesn't . . . understand me anymore."

"Jerry never listened. Never."

"You develop separate interests."

"Like a pizza girl. That—"

"It becomes . . . boring."

"Painful."

"Suddenly you have nothing in common. Nothing. Rona loves to watch the news. I love watching the Mets."

"Let's go Mets. Doubleheader tonight. Benson is pitching. Bad trade, I think. How about you?"

That was it. That was the moment. A question about Rona, with a follow-up question about the Mets' pitching rotation. Marking the one time that Morris could not keep his feet reliably on the ground. Because Victoria D'Amico had swept him off his feet. Rona didn't know the difference between Benson and Leiter. And here was Victoria—not exactly *The Bill James Baseball Abstract*, but she understood Morris. At his most primitive level. The Mets.

As they drank the last of their wine, Victoria looked at her watch and exclaimed, "Oh my God, Morris, we've been here so long we can go right to dinner. Or skip the diner and go right to the Bayview!" And giggled.

The Bayview was the Bellmore Bayview Motor Inn. It was also known as the "Pay-Per-View Motor Inn," the "Bellmore Bordello," and "Schtups-R-Us." And if you were slinging back a beer at Flanagan's Pub, which was just adjacent to the Bayview, you would here this joke:

"Question. How many people does it take to screw in a lightbulb at the Bayview?"

"I dunno. How many?"

"Two to do the screwing and—hold it—since when does the Bay-view have lightbulbs! Ha!"

Unfortunately for Morris—or fortunately, depending on how one looks at it—when Victoria made that crack about skipping dinner and going straight to the Bayview, he wasn't in his joke-receiving position. He was in no position at all to defend against a joke, now that he had lost his footing. So he responded, "Yeah, we sure could."

To which Victoria curled her lips devilishly and said, "Oh, and don't you just wish." Which also verged on humor in the playful, flirtatious "I-could-be-kidding-but-maybe-not, let's-just-see-how-you-respond" kind of way.

But Morris didn't receive that as a joke, either. He looked at Victoria seriously, even sadly, and said, "I do wish."

Which even caught Victoria off guard. *Oh my God! Did he just say what I thought he said? He just crawled out on a limb? Now what do I do? Saw off the limb? That would be some reward for being honest. And look at those puppy dog eyes!*

Victoria had a soft spot for honest men, puppies, and international drug counterfeiters.

The Feldstein Anxiety Anticipation Index began its inexorable ascent, forcing Morris to blurt out, "I'm kidding," and then laugh, as if he were only kidding. He tried to regain his joke-receiving footing, like a staggering fighter who had just taken a sucker punch.

But it was too late.

"Let's go!" Victoria declared.

Now, Morris had to retract his retraction, otherwise he would have caused irreparable offense to Victoria and lost an opportunity to see her naked. So he promptly said, "Okay!"

And then there was the ritual diplomacy and negotiations that often accompany such arrangements:

"I mean, if you would, I would," said Victoria.

"Do you want to?"

"Do you?"

"If you do," Morris offered.

"When?"

"I have three more appointments—"

"I have to get back to Doctor Kirleski—"

"Oh."

Silence.

"Tonight?" Victoria suggested.

"You mean *tonight*—as in when today ends?" asked Morris.

"No?"

"No?"

"I mean," stammered Victoria, "yes. I was asking 'no' as a question. I would go. After work. Only if you can, Morris."

"I can."

"Me too!"

"Waitress! Check, please!"

When the check came, the formerly good and decent model citizen Morris Feldstein reached across the depravity line. So flummoxed was he that he grabbed the first credit card in his wallet that his thumb touched, which just happened to be his Celfex-issued American Express card.

It was so unused that he hadn't even signed the back.

THE BAYVIEW MOTOR INN

THURSDAY, AUGUST 19, 2004

Bill Sully had a front-row seat from the FDA control room in Washington and Agent Leone sat nervously in his car in the Bayview parking lot. Tom Fairbanks monitored a bank of television screens in Melville. And Agent Russell fidgeted in his vehicle under the flickering neon of the BAYVIEW MOTOR INN sign. One video surveillance system affixed to a satellite in geosynchronous orbit five hundred miles above Bellmore assisted them. In addition, six Sanyo digital binocular cameras with 5x telescopic lenses and high-speed shutters; two Nikon Infinite-Range Day Color/Night Black-and-White video cameras with 5-50 mm adjustable telephoto zoom lenses; two Hitachi long-range parabolic listening systems with pinpoint accuracy to one-thousand yards; one Toshiba laptop-based digital video recorder with 72x CD-RW, a 120 fps, 320x240 recording system, and 360GB storage capacity; and dozens of AAA batteries stuffed into the glove compartments of the small fleet trailing Victoria and Morris to their less-than-secret rendezvous that evening.

All watching Morris Feldstein and Victoria D'Amico. Watching and waiting for them to do something. To do anything.

Nu? So what am I waiting for already? Morris asked himself. He practiced his breathing exercises. The windshield was fogging heavily and almost everything outside was fading from view: the dim light fixtures hanging in front of every room of the Bayview, the passing headlights on Merrick Road, even the garish neon from the shopping center across the street. Then, fearing that Victoria might disappear as well (in a sudden rubber-burning, brake-squealing, panicked recognition of the mistake she was about to make), he whined, *"Gottenyu"* and pushed open his car door.

A warm breezed brushed his face, and he could taste the salt air from the Atlantic. He gazed for a moment at the second-floor balcony. Every room had two windows facing the parking lot. A curtain was drawn across every window. Some of the rooms were pitch black, and others flashed tantalizing columns of light where the curtain fell short of the window frame—a peep show that didn't offer much of a peep.

Morris dug his hands in his pockets and walked to Victoria's car. Every step was weighed down by the gravities of doubt, self-loathing, and fear. But those forces were matched by another force that pushed Morris forward. An irresponsible force that drowned out the cautious voices in Morris's mind. It exclaimed, "Soon I'll see Victoria naked!"

Which is exactly what kept him going, until he arrived at her car and heard her window hum open.

"Hello, Victoria," he said. He sounded as if he were greeting his tax accountant.

"Hi, Morris!"

"So how was the rest of your day?" he asked.

"Fine. And yours?"

Cars swooshed past on Merrick Road.

"Fine. Just . . . did a few things," reported Morris, and then jiggled some change in a pocket.

"Yes. Me too."

Refined social graces are imperative in the moments before skulking into a motel room for some primitive grunting. It lends a certain air of decorum.

"So," Victoria sighed. "Do you want to get a room?"

"A room? Of course. A room. Should I go to the front office now?"

Victoria giggled. "Or I can go. If you want."

"No, I'll go. Should you wait here? In the car, I mean?"

"Okay. Unless you want me to come with you."

"You mean go together?"

"We could."

"At the same time?"

"Or I can stay here."

From his seat, Sully dropped his head into his hands and moaned, "Christ, it's like they're negotiating troop positions in a cease-fire!"

Morris raised his palms. "No. You stay here. I'll go get the room. Then I'll meet you back here. At the car."

"Okay. I'll wait here." And then, eyeing the nondescript sedans idling in the parking lot, Victoria said, "Wow, it's crowded here, isn't it?"

Morris turned toward a sign that flickered OFFICE in dim red letters against a white background, dropped his head as low as his chin would allow without denting his chest cavity, and hurried through the lot.

In the front office, a lonely, overworked fluorescent bulb struggled to do its job, and a clerk stood behind a chipped Formica counter, dressed in a wrinkled black shirt and a carelessly knotted yellow tie. His eyes were locked on a small television that sat at the edge of the counter. To Morris's discomfort, the clerk seemed to be watching a selection from the Bayview's extensive "Discreet In-Room Adult Pleasures Library." Unless "Oh yes, yes, there, uh-huh, right there, yeah, yeah, yes, yes, ooooooh" accompanied by the warbled twang of a guitar was a new Food Channel special featuring Rachael Ray basting a turkey. Which was possible.

Just next to the television was a wobbly Lucite brochure holder, stuffed with helpful tourist tips, as if to lend the Bayview a sense of respectability. Because it was a good bet that after sex so illicit and so depraved that it had to be conducted in a cheap motel room, one would feel the sudden urge to "Visit Sagamore Hill, the Bucolic Estate of Theodore Roosevelt, our Twenty-sixth President."

Morris had developed two scripts for this moment. There was "A horrible fire just destroyed my home but thank God my loving family is visiting relatives down in Trenton so I need a room just for the night" or "I'm an electronics salesman and I'm too tired to drive all the way home to Trenton so my loving wife suggested I take a little nap here because she thinks I'll fall asleep at the wheel on the New Jersey Turnpike. Women are really something, aren't they?" But before he could say a word, the clerk gave him a look that said, "Save your breath because I've heard them all and don't give a damn." Then, after returning his eyes to the moaning and groaning of the Food Channel or twenty-four-hour-sex network, or whatever it was, said to Morris, "Standard room forty-nine dollars plus tax. Deluxe, seventy-nine plus tax. Theme room ninety-nine plus tax. Honeymoon special, one forty-nine plus tax."

Now what? No one told him there would be a menu.

"What's the difference between the standard and the deluxe?"

"Jacuzzi. And the Throbomattress five thousand."

"Standard! Please!" Morris plunked down three twenty-dollar bills and waited for the clerk to fish out his change and a key.

Meanwhile, from a control room at the FDA, William Sully was canvassing screens and snapping his fingers as if directing a live television reality show. He pitched his body toward the console of monitors and snapped commands for close-ups and wide shots. He listened to the transmitted chatter of agents reporting on every motion of the stars of their show: Morris Feldstein and Victoria D'Amico.

"Subject B exiting front office. Returning in the direction of Subject A. Over."

"Subject A exiting her vehicle. Walking in the direction of Subject B. Over."

"Both subjects proceeding on foot toward middle staircase. Over."

"On stairs . . . proceeding up stairs . . . both subjects now on balcony of floor two. Repeat. Now on floor two. Over."

"Unit Three: I got 'em. Subjects proceeding north on balcony. Passing room two-zero-three . . . two-zero-five . . . two-zero-seven . . . two-zero—hold it! Stand by . . . stand by . . . subjects now reversing . . . you see them, Unit Two? Over."

"Unit Two, roger. Two-zero-seven . . . two-zero-five . . ."

Sully watched as Morris fumbled with the key in front of room 205.

"Now entering room two-zero-five. Repeat, two . . . zero . . . five. Over."

The door closed, and Bill Sully smiled.

The door closed, and Morris Feldstein felt nauseous.

It wasn't the room that sickened him. The décor was surprisingly pleasant, like the floor display in a furniture showroom. It was dominated by a king-sized bed draped with a pink-and-black floral spread and a mountain range of oversized pillows that might require a dynamite charge to remove. There was a gray carpet with signs of dropped cigarettes, a spilled drink, or the rubbing and chafing of bodies. And the walls featured gold-framed abstract art that represented— depending on your powers of observation and your insight into Freudian psychoanalysis—either the twin forks of Long Island or a woman in a pre-coital recline.

It wasn't even the unique odor of the room that nauseated him—a sharp blend of antiseptic cleansers, furniture polish, stale tobacco, and cheap air freshener. What made Morris nauseous was the distance—about ten yards—between where he stood and the bed Victoria now occupied. She had made the trip, it seemed to Morris, the way a runner on first base steals second—charging without hesitation. Once there, she had draped her hair over the front of her shoulders, and flashed the most inviting smile that anyone had ever flashed at Morris Feldstein.

That's what made him nauseous. And it wasn't the mild, light-headed queasiness that one can manage with a few deep breaths of air and a gentle rubbing of the stomach. No, Morris sensed that this nausea could lead to the spewing of entire body organs. Which is why he conditionally accepted Victoria's inviting smile by whimpering "Be right back" and turned into the bathroom with his lips sealed.

The faucet squeaked when he turned it, and a resistant dribble of tepid, rust-colored fluid trickled into his palms. Then, after several belches, the faucet spurted an unpleasant combination of stale air and brackish water, which turned after a few spurts into a cool and consistent stream. He splashed his cheeks and ran his wet palms behind his neck and under his collar. And when he looked in the mirror he could barely recognize himself. His skin was flushed and his eyes uncertain. His face shimmered from either tap water or sweat, he couldn't tell. He wasn't even certain who he was looking at. Was it the Morris Feldstein that he had stared at every morning for fifty-seven years—the one whom he could reliably depend on not to make waves? Or was this a new, lascivious, corrupt Morris Feldstein? *Like that* Star Trek *episode*, he thought. *The one where the transporter malfunctions and accidentally divides William Shatner into the meek Captain Kirk and the maniacal bloody-lipped Captain Kirk. God, I think I forgot to TiVo that one, too!*

He stared hard into the mirror. *What am I doing? Who am I?*

Nothing but the sound of water falling from the faucet and splattering against the sink.

He turned off the faucet and wiped his face with a towel, which he noticed was stained with faint splotches of brown and yellow. It had a musty scent. And just as he reached for the door, having accepted the humiliation of explaining to Victoria that he could not have sex with her because he was too nauseous and didn't want to upset his long-standing record of not throwing up before, during, or even after sex, he heard a voice.

It was the last voice he thought would come to him under the circumstances. A voice from so far back in his life that it took him a moment to remember.

"Assistant Rabbi Kaplan?" he asked.

It was. Assistant Rabbi Marc Kaplan, who had coached Morris through his bar mitzvah forty-four years earlier at the Hillel Torah Hebrew Academy of Bayside. Then, as now, the voice was heavy and solemn, suffused with years of accumulated rabbinic study.

Assistant Rabbi Kaplan's voice said:

"Class, today we will study the teachings of Judaism's vision of the ideal human. The great scholar and ancient Rabbi, Rabbi Hillel. Who taught *tikkun olam*, the repair of an imperfect world. The Rabbi said—and repeat after me, class—'If I am not for myself, who will be for me? If I am not for others, what am I? And if not now, when?'"

Morris repeated the words, watching his lips move in the bathroom mirror.

"If I am not for myself, who will be for me?" he whispered.

"And if not now, when?"

"That's correct, Morris!" Morris looked in the mirror and saw the ethereal reflection of an ancient figure, dressed in black, with a long white beard cascading down his chest like a frothy waterfall.

"Is that you, God?" he asked.

"Sure. God appears as a burning bush to some people, and in the bathroom mirrors of seedy motel rooms to others. No, I'm not God. But close. I'm Hillel. Rabbi Hillel."

"This is a dream," Morris mumbled.

"Dream. Vision. Prophecy. What's the difference? My question is this: Are you going to go through with it? With the shikse outside? If not, why not? If you are, when already?"

"You think it's okay?" asked Morris.

"Whoa! Not up to me. That's a higher pay grade. I'm just saying—your whole life has been about not making waves. Not causing trouble, right?"

"Well, that's how I feel sometimes."

"Sometimes? This is Hillel talking. From a bathroom mirror. It's kind of hard to put one over on me, Morris. My point is that you shouldn't feel guilty when you feel the need to do something for Morris, Morris. You know, show a little chutzpah. Stand up for yourself. Make a wave every now and then!" Rabbi Hillel gave Morris a thumbs-up in the mirror, which is something Morris never would have imagined the great scholar doing.

It was a sign.

Prayer heals. And at that moment, Morris's communing with the ancient sage cured his nausea and strengthened his spirit. He opened the bathroom with a click of the latch, and headed straight for Victoria, across the ten-yard expanse that had earlier sent him scurrying in the opposite direction. A *journey of many miles begins with a single step*, he thought. But he was certain that didn't come from Rabbi Hillel.

"Are you okay?" Victoria asked from the bed. Her hands were folded on her lap, and her knees and lower thighs peeked out from under her skirt. Morris noticed that her lips had a fresh gloss, her hair had been brushed to a lustrous sheen, and her cheeks had a pink glow. This transformation had happened while he was in the bathroom, studying Hillel.

"Do you want to sit down, Morris?"

"Yes. I'll sit," he said, with all the officiousness of a diplomat accepting his chair on the United Nations Security Council. As he pressed down on the mattress, it caved in with the fatigued squeak of some springs, and the laws of physics pulled Victoria's body against his. "Oooops," she giggled, as she scrunched up against him.

Now what? he thought. The last time he was in similar circumstances was with Rona, two years before they got married. It was after their fifteenth, or maybe it was their twentieth, date. They had been roller-skating. Or bowling. Or it might have been the movies. *Well, it doesn't matter*, he thought. All he could remember was that he had forgotten all the rules of the first kiss. And even if he had remembered, Morris reasoned, it wouldn't make much difference. Rules change. It's not like baseball, which you could have watched forty years ago, then watched again forty years later, and understand the intricacies of every play. Except for the designated hitter rule. *But now is not the time to debate the designated hitter rule*, thought Morris.

Now what? Should I just kiss her? Do I ask permission? Is there a disclaimer? A fair warning? Do I say, "Now I am going to kiss you but you have five seconds to opt out?" Is there a form? Maybe we should talk first. Or maybe turn on the TV. That would be a good icebreaker. Turn on the TV and find the Mets pregame show. Except that I'd probably have to flip through all the porn channels to get there. How awkward would that be? I mean, if you're gonna watch porn with someone on a motel bed you might as well just kiss her . . .

Victoria could tell Morris was nervous. She gave him a gentle pat on his thigh and cooed, "Are you sure this is okay?"

Where lovemaking is concerned, men like Morris—hesitant men, insecure men, but ordinarily decent men—require clear and unmistakable signals. Aggressive, insensitive men believe the appropriate signal is that a woman is breathing and her pupils aren't dilated. Morris, however, needed something more explicit.

He now had three such signs.

First, Victoria was leaning against him in a demonstration of "joined at the hip" in a motel room. On a bed.

Second, Rabbi Hillel had blessed it. It was the Rabbi himself who preached to Morris, "If not now, when?"—a rabbinic way of saying, "Go for it, dude."

And third, Victoria's hand patted his thigh, in the geographic center between his knee and his crotch.

The convergence of these signs lit Morris up like a firecracker. His instincts took over, hijacking his body from his good senses and sending it into a frenzy. *Whoooooa*, his mind screamed, but his arms didn't listen. They wrapped themselves around Victoria's shoulders like a snake around its prey. Morris had experienced the pleasure of having his arms around only one other pair of shoulders in his life, Rona's. These seemed narrower, and sturdier. And as he adjusted to this change in circumstances, he screamed at himself a second time: *Wait!* But his fingers moved through her silky strands of hair, and then down her neck.

And before he could summon the strength and the discipline to stop, Victoria was falling into the mattress, and pulling Morris with her.

Gottenyu, he thought.

Earlier, as he walked to Victoria in the Bayview parking lot, Morris had learned that there are forces that propel men to do things they will regret. And now, with Victoria's skirt somewhere in the vicinity of her knees and heading south, he learned that there are forces even more powerful. Supernaturally deflating forces.

Like guilt. Guilt, when dispensed in the circumstances Morris occupied, is the anti-Viagra. It is what some people call "a mood killer."

He felt his body grow limp (like one of those high-speed films of a flower wilting). But he wasn't sure whether he and Victoria had finished what they had started out to do. He was pretty sure nothing had happened to him. He thought he had detected a satisfied moan from Victoria. And so he looked at her, smiled, and offered a polite "Is everything okay?"

She narrowed her eyes, bit her lip as if to chew over the question, and whisked some stray blond hairs away from her face. "Yes. That was nice. It was very nice."

Which didn't tell Morris much of anything, except that whatever "that" was, or wasn't, it was nice.

Victoria pulled herself up from the bed. Morris tried not to stare at her while she pulled her blouse down and her skirt up. He distracted himself by staring at the artwork on the wall and wondered if it was indeed a map of Long Island, where Great Neck was. That's where Rona was waiting for him.

"The bathroom is right there?" Victoria asked.

"Yes," Morris said. And then thought, *If you meet Rabbi Hillel in there, don't listen to him!*

Morris made the bed.

Maybe it was a nostalgic tribute to Rona, who was obsessive about prepping their hotel rooms for the maids each morning. ("Why are you bothering, Rona, let the maid do that," he would insist. "Why should the maid see our filth? What would she think?" was her response.) Or, it might have been a guilt-induced homage to his wife: "Yes, I did go to bed with another woman, but don't I get any credit for making the bed when we were finished? Isn't that what you would have wanted?"

Whatever motivated Morris to neaten the bed was irrelevant. Neatness counts, but in this case it would count against him.

Sully checked his watch and smirked. Twenty-two minutes. It took twenty-two minutes for Subject A and Subject B to enter room 205, occupy it, exit it, return to their vehicles, engage in an awkward and hesitant hug, and drive, as fast as seemingly possible, in opposite directions on Merrick Road.

Twenty-two minutes.

Sully had spent an entire career observing criminal behavior and the darkest possibilities of human nature. He could time his watch to fifty separate felonies. He knew how long it took for a person to be murdered, a drug deal consummated, a politician bribed, a currency forged, an illegal substance smuggled. Any of these could be performed easily within twenty-two minutes.

But sneaking into a motel room and having sex? Not so fast.

Not at $49 for an entire night.

This encounter was not about pleasure, Sully thought. *This was business.* And if his hunch was correct, this little meet and greet in the Bayview Motor Inn could lead to multiple charges of drug dealing, money laundering, and tax fraud, and ultimately lead him directly to the king of medical counterfeiting, Ricardo Xavier Montoyez.

NICK was aroused. He purred with curiosity.

He may have been the triumphant integration of microcircuits and silicon wafers, but NICK understood human nature better than any human being. Show NICK a covert stay in a cheap motel, and NICK's programming could show you a behavior pattern that could turn against the interests of the United States government. A reckless pursuit of self-gratification. A vulnerability to blackmail. A predictor of even greater perfidy. So, once Morris inserted the key in the motel door, NICK unlocked his grand sweep of keywords embedded in websites that Morris may have visited, movies he may have rented, novelties he may have purchased.

And it was all a matter of record.

A subject of interest to NICK may have accidentally and innocently visited www.buxomcoedcheerleaders.com on the way to, let's say, www.nationalpublicradio.org. They may have visited that site in the blink of an eye and a frantic and embarrassed click of the mouse, but that fleeting moment was forever recorded in NICK's hard drive. A hotel pay-per-view title might, as promised, "not appear on your room bill," but it was permanently burned into NICK's memory.

Not Morris Feldstein. NICK couldn't find a single salacious website visited. No wicked pay-per-view titles ordered. Not even sex at the Bayview Motor Inn.

Morris Feldstein. Rated G.

Hmmmmm, gurgled NICK. If Feldstein wasn't guilty of adultery at the Bayview Motor Inn, what was he doing there? What was Mister

Clean doing with the girlfriend of a known medical counterfeiter?

Suspicious, NICK calculated. And then NICK upgraded the threat assessment on Morris Feldstein.

Agent Russell pitched forward in his seat, hugged the steering wheel to his chest, and watched the sudden evacuation of the Bayview parking lot. The groaning of engines and the burst of headlights. D'Amico's car rolling forward, then turning left into the harsh glare of Merrick Road. Feldstein turning right. Then the black sedans, pulling away like a presidential motorcade. A covert convoy, leaving the old neon BAYVIEW MOTOR INN sign behind, winking knowingly at them in the steamy August night.

BREAKING UP IS
HARD TO DO

FRIDAY, AUGUST 20, 2004

"Morris! Morris! Are you sick?"

Morris heard Rona, and he felt her hands shaking his body in bed. "I'm fine," he grunted. But he wasn't fine. Not at all.

As his eyes opened, a heaviness pushed him into the mattress. It tightened around his throat and fell into his chest, it pressed against his heart and squeezed at his stomach. Morris wanted to bury his head in his pillow. Bury it along with the shame and guilt from the prior night.

"Morris?"

He didn't want to get out of bed. He didn't want to shave or dress. He had no interest in reading the *Newsday* sports section or eating his bagel. And the thought of getting in his car and making his first sales call—to Dr. Kirleski—tightened his chest even more.

The clock on his nightstand blinked 7:30.

He wanted to stay right there. In the safety of his bed where there was no tempting receptionist and cheap motel, no cheating on Rona and fudging Celfex expense reports. No waves. Or maybe sit all day in his RoyaLounger 8000. Watching those comforting black-and-white movie classics. Maybe some musicals or screwball comedies. And if there happened to be a movie that contained tsuris, Morris could simply mute it or change it or even end it with the press of a button on his remote.

Call in sick, he thought. *Call my district manager, Laurie, and tell her I've caught something. Why not? What's one more crime in my new life of crime?*

Morris had never improperly taken a sick day. That would upset the people who depended on him. But today—

"Morris," Rona groaned into her pillow, and nudged his shoulder again.

Sure, take a sick day. Stay home all day. With Rona. Trying to look into her eyes. Without looking guilty.

He swung his legs out of bed and shuffled to the bathroom. Each step was like a step on death row. Like Cagney in *Angels with Dirty Faces*. When he looked back at Rona, cocooned in the blanket with one arm flung to the now-empty spot next to her, all he could think was, *How did this happen?*

There was plenty of excitement blaring from Morris's car radio on the drive that morning. While Morris had been—or maybe wasn't—schtupping Victoria at the Bayview, the Mets had stomped the Rockies in a doubleheader in Denver. And while sweeping a doubleheader in August didn't mean a World Series, for Mets fans it did produce a similar euphoria. It was a new sign of hope.

For Morris, there were no such signs. Just the same shopping centers and Starbucks. Intersection after intersection, block after block, as he crept closer to the Roslyn Medical Arts Building, which was as bad as the crime scene. It was where the crime was hatched.

Morris drove to Dr. Kirleski's on the same route he always took, but it was an entirely different course. The smooth and level ride that had been Morris Feldstein's life was now bumpy, and it rattled him. The straight center lane was now twisting, and Morris couldn't see around the next curve.

He stopped at a red light. *What do I say to Victoria? And shouldn't I say something to Rona? If I do, what? And when? Where is Rabbi Hillel when I need him? I could use a miracle. Like the Mets doubleheader last night.*

Morris was so lost in thought that he didn't notice the light turn green, until every driver behind him was angrily pounding their horns.

He stepped on the gas and peered into the rearview mirror, cringing at the angry line of cars behind him.

I will tell Victoria that she is a wonderful, wonderful woman and I am flattered that she finds me attractive but I am married to Rona so we must never, never do anything like this again and I'm sorry I hurt her but let's just be friends and that she is welcome to any future Mets tickets which Celfex provides.

And as he turned into the parking lot, he knew this act would certainly create waves with Victoria. But it had to be done. Now.

"Hello, Morris," Victoria said with a nervous smile from behind the glass partition. She tapped a pen against her desk.

Morris jammed his hands into his pockets and jingled some coins. "Hullo, Victoria."

Jingle-jingle. Thump, thump, thump.

The lobby was empty. Which relieved Morris. Because this breakup, which might rival the Clark Gable-Vivien Leigh scene in *Gone with the Wind*, didn't need a live audience.

"Morris. We need to talk."

"Yes, we do."

"Follow me."

She led him through a dim corridor, into Exam Room 1. The sharp scent of disinfectant stung Morris's nostrils. He was comforted by the industrial-size tissue box that sat on a stainless-steel counter. That would come in handy to absorb Victoria's tears.

Victoria positioned herself on the examination table, the disposable white paper crinkling under her. When she crossed her legs, and her floral summer skirt crept above her knees, Morris thought, *This conversation is going to be very hard, letting Victoria down. So maybe we should go out one more time. To get it out of our systems. Then never again. Ever!*

"Are you okay?" she asked.

He said, "I'm fine. Are you okay?"

Her lower lip projected slightly and her voice quivered as she spoke. "Oh, Morris, you're such a good guy. And I had a nice time. But . . ."

But?

"But I think we should be friends. I mean, you are an incredibly sensitive guy, and I'll never forget what happened. Or didn't happen. But to tell you the truth, Morris . . . I-need-some-time-to-get-over-my-divorce-from-that-SOB-Jerry. And-it's-not-you-it's-me-Morris-so-please-can-we-be-like-really-good-friends?"

She stretched out her hand to consummate the arrangement with a brisk handshake. As if they had just agreed to sell a car instead of end their romance.

That was that.

After awkwardly writing up several orders for Celfex refills, Morris left Dr. Kirleski's office. Into the scorching sun. His shoulders dropped. His chin slumped into his chest.

He was not rid of the guilt over briefly cheating on Rona. But now he was experiencing the pain of Victoria's rejection. Like losing a doubleheader. Like the Rockies last night.

I do not know if I can take any more of this, he thought.

He opened the trunk and stared at the case of medical samples, glittering in soft pastels. Beckoning him to help himself. Literally. He reached toward the Celaquel. *Just one. To lift me out of this funk. To smooth out the waves.*

But that would be a flagrant violation of *Our Prescription for a Long Career: The Celfex Pharmaceutical Employee Code of Ethics.* As well as a possible federal crime. So he got in his car. Drew in the hot, oppressive air. And exhaled it with a long and labored "Oyyyyyyyyy."

THE DISTINGUISHED TERRORIST FROM MASSACHUSETTS

FRIDAY, AUGUST 20, 2004

"This is not funny!" Jon Pruitt growled into his phone from his office at the Department of Homeland Security. A group of senior DHS officials stood around him, nervously shifting their feet.

He heard the uncontrollable squealing of Scooter Libby on the other end. "It's actually hilarious! You couldn't make it up! I'm about to brief the Vice President and he'll love this! He needs a good laugh!"

What Libby found funny was that day's disclosure that Senator Ted Kennedy had been detained at airport security five times because his name was on the terrorist watch list. Which, in some quarters of the White House, was not a snafu. It was probable cause. This was Ted Kennedy, after all.

Pruitt felt that twinge in his stomach as if Cheney's mysterious grip on almost everything in Washington somehow included his intestines. He wondered whether this was an innocent mistake or one of those Cheneyesque power plays. *If we can't beat Ted Kennedy at the polls, let's strip search him at the Delta Shuttle!* He took a breath, scanned his desk for some Tums, and sought to control his voice. "I don't think you appreciate the problem here. This reflects poorly on our entire system. The American people must have confidence in the ability of their government to tell the difference between a Senator from Massachusetts and a terrorist from Afghanistan."

Same difference, thought Libby. But he saw Pruitt's point. "Okay, okay. So what do you propose we do? Maybe the President should ask for a Joint Session of Congress so he can formally apologize to Ted Kennedy. Is that it?"

"No. But Asa Hutchinson will apologize. Publicly. Today."

Libby was fine with that. Hutchinson was a former Republican Congressman from Arkansas who jumped from anonymity in the House to anonymity at the DHS. His title was Undersecretary, so as a matter of Beltway protocol, this wasn't actually an apology. It was an under-apology.

"Hutchinson's fine. Just make sure he reminds the American people that we are trying to protect them from the enemy. Terrorists. Jihadists. Liberals!"

The last thing Pruitt heard was a burst of laughter, and the click of the phone.

PART TWO

THE SHIVA

THURSDAY, AUGUST 26, 2004

Judaism's traditional period of mourning, the shiva, is seven days. But God created the world in six. So it was that Rona Feldstein mourned for a full six and a half days after Morris confessed the death of their marriage.

After the confession, an angry storm had settled into a desolate silence punctuated by curt exchanges of necessity. For example, "Take out the garbage, Morris." The week had featured news reports about high-level American military leaders who permitted torture in an Iraqi prison. The prison was named Abu Ghraib. While Morris paid little attention to the news, this topic interested him. He felt as if he were living in solitary confinement, broken only by Rona's spontaneous sobs, and her deep and heavy sighs, and her refusal to accept his apology. There was also the matter of the Mets. They had swept the doubleheader on the night of Morris's visit to the Bayview. But then dropped six of the next seven. As if God were sending Morris some kind of sign. Through Hillel. Morris sinned and the Mets suffered.

Then, on Thursday night, the mourning ended. Shiva was over.

They sat in the dining room, listening only to the scraping of their forks against plates containing take-out from the Great Neck Greek Palace.

Then Rona broke the silence.

"Morris. I made a decision, Morris." Her voice was heavy and strained, as if she were about to render either the death sentence or mercy for the husband who betrayed her.

Morris lifted his head from his plate. This moment was the first time he had made prolonged eye contact since he had returned from the Bayview. And it was the first time that Rona seemed to show her age. Her slender body was slumped in her chair. Her hair, normally fiery red and cropped close to her head, was tousled and fading into a bland orange. Her lips usually formed a slight overbite that accentuated every syllable; now she pursed them as if she was sucking on every word. And her eyes were puffy from a week's worth of crying.

He was grateful to hear more than an angry grunt from Rona, but wary of what would be said. He tried to swallow his food, but felt his throat begin to tighten and his stomach gurgle.

Rona sighed. "I don't want to end our marriage, Morris." The words came laced with anguish. "What you did was wrong. Terribly, completely, unforgivably wrong. You made a promise to God and broke that promise. And not just to God. But to Jeffrey and Caryn."

It was a direct hit, and Morris winced.

Rona continued. "But maybe I bear some responsibility."

"No, Rona—"

"Ah, ah, ah, ah, ah," Rona sputtered as she waved her index finger. "Let me finish. Maybe you're bored, Morris. Maybe we have a boring life. You sell pharmaceuticals all day. You come home. We bring in dinner. We eat. You go to the den. You watch your sports. Day in. Day out. That's our routine.

"You know something, Morris? Guess what. I'm bored too. How do you like that?" She slapped a hand on the table and the containers and plates of Greek food jiggled. "Of course, I would never find a man and cheat on you to relieve the boredom, God forbid. For me, watching Wolf Blitzer is just fine, thank you very much.

"Anyway, I think we need a change. We're suffocating, Morris. Our marriage is stifling."

"What kind of change? What do you mean?" Morris asked, the words catching at the back of his tongue. "Maybe a nice vacation?"

"Not a vacation, Morris. Vacations don't save marriages. They kill time. We did the Alaska cruise. Big deal. You schlepped me to Europe. We froze in Canada. We *shvitzed* in Israel. And we came back, to what? Did those vacations make you happy with our marriage? Obviously not. You had to go to a motel with Vanessa—"

"Victoria."

She glared.

Morris felt his chicken souvlaki sitting in his stomach, with a generous heaping of guilt.

"We need something more than a vacation, Morris."

"What?" he asked helplessly.

For dramatic effect, Rona pushed her plate forward. "Morris. I want a change of scenery. I want a place in Florida." There, she said it. Those were her terms, laid out on the dining room table, right there along with the aluminum containers of pita and hummus and souvlaki.

"You want us to move? To Florida?"

"No. I want to buy a second home. I want to go to Boca. For long weekends. And winter. With a golf course—"

"Since when do we play golf?"

"God forbid we should learn something new. God forbid we should go to Boca, like the Deutsches, the Sterns—"

"I thought we don't even like the Sterns. We always like it when they leave for Boca. And leave us alone here in Great Neck."

"But they're happy, Morris. They're happy! Who the hell stays in Great Neck after Yom Kippur? It's like Anatevka here. A wasteland. A barren wasteland. No wonder our marriage . . ."

Her lips began to tremble and Morris felt panic. "Rona. Rona. Okay, I didn't say no. We'll research it—"

Rona reached under her chair, and then plunked an oversized high-gloss folder on the table. It unfolded into an accordion display of slick photos: a diversity of smiling, happy, white-teethed couples on a beach, in front of a sunset, swinging golf clubs, ordering at a restaurant, sipping frozen drinks at a pool, even cooking meals in gleaming kitchens.

"Listen to this," Rona said, perching her reading glasses on her nose and clearing her throat. "'Now you're home in Paradise. The legendary Paradise Hotel and Residences at Boca.'"

Rona Feldstein, certified social worker, therapist, and victim of her husband's infidelity, became the best salesperson that Paradise Global Ventures LLC ever had.

"'The hardest part of visiting a Paradise Hotel and Residences is leaving,'" she read, enunciating every word as if reading Morris the directions on how to connect the TiVo. "'Until now. Because now, you are home at Paradise. Announcing The Residences at Paradise at Boca. Fifty-two highly anticipated luxury condominiums. And a world-class resort at your doorstep.'" She raced through the background on how fifty-two units at the sprawling Paradise Hotel and Residences at Boca had been converted to full-ownership condominiums; how each proud owner receives all the privileges of resort membership. Then she slowed down, highlighting for Morris the key selling points.

"Four lifestyle swimming pools, Morris. Four. 'The Main Pool. Plus, Meditative, Fitness, and Family Fun. And a golden private beach,'" she read.

Since when do we go to the beach? Morris thought. *She hates the sand.*

"'A twenty-four-hour, state-of-the-art, world-class fitness center,'" she read.

We've never been to a fitness center. Why do we need one open twenty-four hours?

She looked up at him. "Now, Morris. There's bad news and good news. I'll give you the bad news first. They're sold out. I called a few days ago."

"Ohhhhh. That's too bad." Morris mustered as much disappointment as he could.

"Ah, ah, ah, ah. Now the good news. The girl called me today. The designer model they sold—it fell through. So it's available. It's fully furnished, Morris. We wouldn't have to buy a thing. Listen to this . . ." She pulled a glossy eight-by-ten from the folder and began reading again. "'. . . Emeril Signature gourmet kitchen . . . cherry-wood cabinetry . . . subzero freezer . . .'"

Since when does she cook?

"'Walk-in closets . . . breathtaking ocean view . . . thirty-two-inch wall-mounted plasma television with satellite service—'"

"What did you say?" Morris asked, suddenly intrigued. "It must cost a fortune."

"It won't cost us a thing to look. It's free."

"How could that be?"

"They faxed me a 'VIP Invitation to Paradise.' For qualified buyers only. All we have to pay for is the airfare. They even pick us up at the airport. We get to stay at the resort. A private VIP tour, a free VIP dinner-slash-briefing at the . . ." she peeked inside the brochure, "at the top-rated Paradise Grille. Breakfast buffets. And, we get a 'free gift bag.'"

"And everything is free?" Morris asked.

"The whole weekend. This weekend, Morris. It's a beautiful weekend package. We leave tomorrow and come back Sunday night."

"Tomorrow? It's Friday. I have to work. I can't—"

Rona's face began to fall. "So you'll call in sick. For once. What's the difference?"

"Call in sick? I've never done that. It's not right—"

"Not right?" She looked at him, first with an angry flash, and then her eyes seemed to fall and her lips trembled and her nostrils began to quiver. She tapped her fork against her plate and her eyes glistened. The silence that had tormented Morris for a week returned.

"They have satellite TV?" he asked.

And there was peace.

THE THREE-DAY WEEKEND

FRIDAY, AUGUST 27, 2004–SUNDAY, AUGUST 29, 2004

That Friday morning, Morris screwed-up his courage, called his district manager at Celfex, and lied as best he could about "a stomach flu or something, some kind of bug I must have caught. Maybe something I ate." Then he and Rona drove to LaGuardia Airport.

Morris lugged two suitcases, some light reading, and an excessive amount of guilt over calling in sick to Celfex. The terminal echoed with the plunking and rattling of plastic bins and the occasional beeping protests of metal detectors, the barks of TSA agents for "bag check" and "male secondary" and the repeated and urgent directions on the basics of air travel. Because in a nation of frenetic multitaskers, a nation derived from restless immigrants who managed to leave their villages and cities and cross vast and roiling oceans a world away, today's Americans have trouble removing their shoes, placing their belongings on a conveyer belt, and walking ten feet through a metal detector.

Morris was not a nervous flyer. But when he arrived at the small podium at the front of the line, and saw the strange reaction to his boarding pass by the guard from the Transportation Security Administration, his nerves activated, bringing small beads of sweat across his forehead. The guard's eyes widened in seeming alarm the instant he saw the boarding pass. They darted from Morris's flushed and perspiring face, to the driver's license, and back to the boarding pass. Which made Morris sweat even more. Which made the guard sweat also.

Something's wrong, Morris thought.

"Uhhhhh, Mister Feldstein, I'm going to need to call my supervisor over for a moment," the guard reported.

Supervisor? Morris hated supervisors. They were authority figures, and authority figures intimidated him. It didn't matter whether it was a Celfex district supervisor, or a supervisor at the Bloomingdale's shoe department when Rona returned merchandise, or a TSA supervisor. When a supervisor was called into a situation, there was a situation.

This particular supervisor happened to be about seven feet tall, with broad shoulders that seemed to extend about the length of three airport gates, and a scalp so cleanly shaven that it refracted the bright overhead lights, making Morris squint. And when he examined the boarding pass, Morris could swear he saw some frothing on his lips.

His voice was deep and officious. "Sir, we're going to need you to step aside for secondary screening."

Secondary screening? Terrorists get secondary screening! Criminals! Not Celfex employees who tell white lies about a stomach flu.

"Male secondary!" The supervisor bellowed. Which fingered Morris to the entire line in back of him. Like a picture in the post office.

He was mortified. And behind him, Rona whispered, "Oh my God, Morris, now what did you do?"

Something told him to turn around, right then and there, and go home. Go home and pick up the phone and tell Celfex, "I am feeling much better now, it must have been a twelve-hour thing, and I'm starting my sales call right this second." He wanted to drop his luggage and relieve his guilt and forget the free weekend vacation offer at the Paradise. But he couldn't, because the hulking TSA agent had already clasped his humongous fingers around Morris's elbow and tugged.

The supervisor led Morris to a screened-off "privacy area," which offered all the privacy of the stage at Radio City Music Hall.

Morris Feldstein was a highly private man. Men who guard their privacy generally don't like removing articles of clothing in public, having scanners waved in front of their genitals, and then feeling the palms of strangers pressing and squeezing against the insides of their thighs. But Morris did what he was told: standing and sitting, holding his arms outstretched and resting them at his sides. He watched as they swabbed his luggage to test for explosives.

Finally, he was freed. "Have a nice flight," said the supervisor. Morris detected a tone that said, "We're watching you, Feldstein!"

As he and Rona rushed to the gate, Rona said, "I heard on the news that Senator Kennedy got stopped five times at the airport because his name was on one of those lists. Maybe you're name is on one too, Morris." *That's what it must be*, she thought. A no-fly list of terrorists, United States Senators, and adulterers.

The plane lifted off the runway. Morris craned his neck and watched the vague outlines of Long Island slip away. He felt relieved. As if he was leaving the tsuris behind.

Later they arrived in the Palm Beach International Airport terminal, searched for the luggage carousel, got lost, and found their way; met a cheerful young man with bronze skin and blond hair in a yellow shirt and khakis holding a sign that said, WELCOME TO PARADISE, MR. AND MRS. FEINSTEEN; drove with him in the yellow Paradise Resorts courtesy van; settled into their room; watched TV until they fell asleep; woke up on Saturday to a complimentary VIP breakfast at the

Paradise Grille; watched a ten-minute *Welcome Home* video; boarded a yellow golf cart and enjoyed a private VIP tour of the grounds followed by a sales presentation at dinner. On Sunday they inspected the designer model, peered into the subzero freezer and cooed at the walk-in closets; nodded their approval at the twenty-four-hour world-class gym; tentatively dipped their toes in the lapping turquoise waves of the Atlantic, sat for two minutes under a yellow-and-white Paradise Residences beach umbrella, and wiped the sand from Rona's sweater; repacked their bags, which now included a yellow-and-white complimentary Paradise Resorts carry-on; flew back to LaGuardia, and drove home to Great Neck.

And when they plunked their luggage down in the front hall, they were the proud new owners of nine hundred square feet of paradise, with a nice view of the ocean and the Major League Baseball upgrade on satellite television.

THE DEPARTMENT OF SPECIAL PROGRAMS

SATURDAY, AUGUST 28, 2004

"As if Saturday morning with Cheney isn't creepy enough!" Jon Pruitt sighed when he saw Scooter Libby and Karl Rove rushing toward him in the darkened West Wing corridor fronting the Vice President's office. Since it was Saturday, the White House tempo was relaxed. But those two made up for it with their determined march.

"You see this!" Libby excitedly waved a bunch of newspapers at Pruitt. "They're questioning the President's record in Vietnam! This is the Democrat playbook. To distract the American people from al-Qaeda with smear attacks on the President's military record! His military record! It's over the line!" Libby slapped the newspapers against his palm for emphasis.

"We can't go into the convention with this story!" warned Rove. "We need to change the focus back to our sweet spot."

Fear, thought Pruitt. *E pluribus petrified.*

"So what's our status with an upgraded threat alert?" Libby asked.

"Again, I'm unaware of any specific intelligence that justifies an increase in the threat alert."

Libby rolled his eyes then whispered, "Are you going to the Vice President's Special Programs meeting?"

"What 'Special Programs' meeting? I don't know anything about that."

"Oh, that's right" Libby cooed. "You're not authorized to attend the 'Special Programs' meetings. Too bad."

Pruitt felt a twist in his appendix. "I'm here because the Vice President asked me for a homeland security briefing on the Republican Convention." And then asked, "What 'Special Programs'?"

"Really can't say. Evidently you're not authorized to know."

"I'm Special Counsel to the Secretary of Homeland Security. I should know."

"If you should know, you would know. Since you don't, you shouldn't."

Pruitt's momentary confusion was interrupted by a secretary informing them that the Vice President was waiting for them.

Behind his desk, Cheney sat like a statue. Same cool texture. Same frozen expression. Same blue suit and red tie even on a Saturday morning in August. On an opposite wall, three muted television screens showed helicopter footage of a mass of pre-convention protesters in New York. An undulating blue line of cops was attempting to contain them in a fenced-off area, like trying to get thousands of charging bulls into a pen.

"Sit down," Cheney instructed. Rove and Libby sat together on a couch, and faced the Vice President. Pruitt remained standing.

"What's our status?" Cheney asked.

"Mr. Vice President, we've increased the threat assessment in the vicinity of the convention."

Libby said, "The whole country should be put on alert. I mean, look at that!" He pointed to the televisions.

"Half of the protesters are undercover," Pruitt said. "The other half are exercising their constitutional rights."

"I'm sorry," Libby sneered. "I didn't realize you dropped out of the Federalist Society and joined the ACLU."

"Would you like a free copy of the Bill of Rights?"

"Want to compare my degrees from Yale and Columbia with your degrees from . . . exactly which public college did you go to?" asked Libby.

"Hold it." Cheney raised his hands to impose order. And let the silence work on Pruitt's nerves. "Do you have anything else?"

"Yes, sir." Pruitt gulped hard. "What 'special programs' do you meet about?"

Cheney simply stared, as if the question hadn't been asked.

"Does the White House counsel know about these special programs? Justice Department? Anyone?"

"That's none of your business!" Libby snapped.

"I am bound by my constitutional oath—"

"Here we go again," muttered Libby. "With the Constitution."

Cheney raised his hands again. "Mister Pruitt, don't take my lack of response to your question as a confirmation or a denial. As for your constitutional obligations, I am the Vice President. A constitutional officer, elected by the people, just like the President. With certain rights and responsibilities. Invested with certain authorities. Some of which you may be aware of. Some of which you may be unaware of."

"We don't know what you know. We don't know what you don't know." Rove snickered.

Cheney continued, folding his hands in front of him. "Now, as to the matter at hand. If DHS is of the opinion that there are no threats justifying an increased alert level, the DHS is entitled to its opinion. But it is only an opinion. We will use every means to assess threat and respond accordingly."

The words "every means" made Pruitt wince.

"Have a good day," Cheney said. Which, Pruitt concluded, was

Cheney's way of saying, "Have a nice life." He stood, convinced that he had just submitted his resignation from the Bush Administration. Or his death warrant. He wasn't sure which.

"All right then," Pruitt said. It wasn't the dramatic exit line that brought down the curtain. It wasn't exactly Nathan Hale, regretting that he had only one life to give for his country. It was just the best he could come up with. "All right then."

After he left, Libby blew an angry gust of air. "Those guys at DHS just . . . don't . . . get it!"

"It really doesn't matter," Cheney replied. "We don't need DHS to advise us on threats. We can put other oars in the water."

NICK, thought Libby. Cheney's "Special Program."

Cheney fixed his eyes on the television screens. The NYPD was moving against the demonstrators. But every pressure point created a surge somewhere else. Like squeezing a water balloon.

Those poor, naïve people, he thought. *Who have no idea how the world works. Who want to read Miranda rights on the battlefield to people plotting to blow up more of our buildings. The Blame-America-First crowd. The Bush-haters. The idealists and anarchists. With their bandanas and their bicycles. The ACLU and MoveOn and the Audubon Society. Carrying their signs with one hand and a Starbucks Mint Chocolate Chip Frappuccino with the other. The coddled and the cushy. Who get their news from NPR instead of the CIA. Those frighteningly naïve people. Without the slightest idea just how dark and messy and bloody it is out there. In the caves and mountains and the mosques. Where the enemy watches and waits. Buying, trading, selling the components for the next attack. Or attacks. Killing and beheading and dismembering . . .*

Cheney felt his heart thumping.

Go ahead. Protest us. Picket us. Keep whining. Every day you remind America about how unsafe we'll be if you get your way. How the Democrats will take the global War on Terror from the battlefield to a UN cocktail party. How the biggest army in America will be the Legal Aid lawyers representing enemy noncombatants.

Cheney looked at the morning newspapers that he had read earlier, piled on the far corner of his desk.

In four days I will remind the American people what really counts. Their survival. In four days.

Until that one moment when all hell broke loose, Caryn Feldstein's video camera was documenting a party. They chanted and sang. They clasped hands and waved their arms and hoisted their signs high above their heads. They embraced and laughed in common cause.

She stood near the front of the crowd. She wanted to arrive early to establish a sense of place and find the perfect angles. She left her studio apartment at ten, wearing denim shorts, Nike sneakers, and a red IMPEACH BUSH T-shirt. Carrying her Canon High Definition camcorder with 24-105 mm lens (equipment that required a considerable number of overtime hours at the Gap, where she worked as she planned her career as a famous filmmaker). She took the subway to Penn Station, emerging into a circus atmosphere. Thousands of delegates milling around, their convention credentials tangled with camera straps around their necks. Vendors with thick New York accents hawked souvenirs: Bush-Cheney coffee mugs, Bush-Cheney T-shirts, and official Republican National Convention 2004 refrigerator magnets. American flags were everywhere, and in every form, stenciled and silk-screened. The delegates believed that the Constitution of the United States should be amended to protect the flag from desecration. With a waiver for certain undergarments and glow-in-the-dark flyswatters.

Caryn found the protesters in the official protest area, close enough to the convention site to avoid an ACLU lawsuit on First Amendment grounds, but distant enough so that they wouldn't inconvenience the delegates. Because those who attended the convention to support the Administration's fight for freedom around the world shouldn't have to encounter freedom around the block. There's a place for freedom. Preferably out of the angles of network cameras.

She pushed her way into the crowd, in order to draw her audience into the scene. To capture the moment with close-ups.

Then things got too close.

She felt that first shove from behind. Not too forceful, just enough to bend her knees and loosen her footing. "Whoah!" she complained as she tried to hold her position and her camera at the same time. But the pressure only increased, like a wave gathering in strength.

She felt her grip on the camera loosen. It fell from her hands, swallowed in the crush of people. It bounced off bodies until she heard the sickening sound of metal and glass hitting pavement, and crunching under countless feet.

Her arms and legs were locked with other arms and legs, as she was swept forward. The smell of perspiring bodies, compressed under a warm sun, choked her. The feel of her flesh against other flesh nauseated her. Her ears thundered as helicopters seemed to roar down on them, to the cries of "Stop pushing!" and "Quit shoving!" Then the rogue wave began breaking—toward a distinct blue line of police.

Later, the conspiracy theorists would insist the whole affair was instigated by moles inserted into the crowd to discredit the protests, placed there by a cabal consisting of the police themselves, the CIA and FBI, the International Monetary Fund, and "Corporate America."

But at that moment, as Caryn Feldstein and her cohorts were in a wave crashing toward the New York Police Department, conspiracy theories were irrelevant. Physics was operating, the physics of mass and velocity and momentum. Caryn tumbled forward, trying to break the momentum by planting her feet, watching through flailing limbs as she hurled toward that blue line.

Caryn Feldstein, proud former candy striper at North Shore–Long Island Jewish Hospital, cofounder and copresident of the Great Neck High School Vegans' Club (incessantly mocked by fellow students as the Great Neck High School Virgins' Club), member of the

Brandeis University Environmental Justice Student Organization, and current employee at the Gap would now have a new biographical entry. For the rest of her life, when she filled out an application for employment or credit, where it says, "Have you ever been arrested?" she would have to answer "Yes." Of course, she could go on to append the form: "But the charges were dropped. And it wasn't really anything bad. I was filming a protest. At the Republican National Convention. Using my lens to uncover the role of government in suppressing dissent in a free society. For a documentary I was going to call 'Gag Rule.' It's not like I robbed a bank." But most forms didn't offer space for such explanations.

Later, scuffed and bruised, sniffing back sobs, Caryn hurried across Thirty-Second Street, toward the Hudson River, to get as far away as she could from the sounds of the sirens and helicopters and the indignant chanting of the remaining protesters. The farther she walked, the quieter it became. Until all she could hear, strangely, was the soft voice of her father, whose advice, she now realized, may have some merit after all: "Why make waves?"

Hungrily, NICK consumed the news. Absorbing the police reports from New York, the names and fingerprints and photographs.

Caryn Feldstein. Twenty-three. Daughter of Morris and Rona. Morris, person of interest for his known association with Victoria D'Amico. Victoria D'Amico, a known associate of medical counterfeiter Ricardo Xavier Montoyez. All believed to be involved in a drug conspiracy to finance terrorist operations against the interests of the government of the United States.

This Morris Feldstein was beginning to piss NICK off.

NOTHING TO FEAR
BUT FEAR

WEDNESDAY, SEPTEMBER 1, 2004

"Four more years! Four more years! Four more years!"

Vice President Cheney soaked in the deafening roar at Madison Square Garden. He tried to wave as practiced, but his stiff movements made him look as if he were swatting at the audience. A towering graphic of an American flag sparkled behind him.

Seventy-one years after FDR calmed the nation by assuring them there was nothing to fear but fear itself, it was now up to Cheney to make his prime-time national audience shit in their pants with fear.

When the chanting subsided, the Vice President proclaimed, "Mister chairman, delegates, distinguished guests, and fellow Americans: I accept your nomination for vice president of the United States!"

"Four more years! Four more years! Four more years!"

Cheney grew impatient, thinking, *Let me get to the point.*

He marched through the early parts of his speech. Ticking-off the obligatory references to domestic issues as if they were irrelevant distractions.

Then he pronounced "September eleventh, 2001." He felt the words heavy on his tongue but also deep in his chest.

"On that day we saw the harm that could be done by nineteen men armed with knives and boarding passes. America also awakened to a possibility even more lethal: this enemy, whose hatred of us is limitless, armed with chemical, biological, or even nuclear weapons. . . ."

The hall was now still and silent.

"The fanatics who killed some three thousand of our fellow Americans may have thought they could attack us with impunity, because terrorists had done so previously. But if the killers of September eleventh thought we had lost the will to defend our freedom, they did not know America, and they did not know George W. Bush."

He waited for the applause to die down. It seemed like hours.

He pushed through, his impatience growing. Reminding Americans about the hundreds of al-Qaeda members killed or captured, the terrorist camps destroyed, the weapons of mass destruction secured. Kind of.

Now, he was approaching his target. A few more passages. Just around the next rhetorical turn. Right . . . there: John Kerry.

The words tasted sour in Cheney's mouth as he spat them. "Senator Kerry began his political career by saying he would like to see our troops deployed 'only at the directive of the United Nations.'"

Angry boos thundered through the hall.

". . . Senator Kerry opposed Ronald Reagan's major defense initiatives that brought victory in the Cold War."

"Booo!"

". . . Senator Kerry voted against Operation Desert Storm!"

"Booo!"

Cheney paused. The way the speech coach suggested. To shift gears. To bring the audience to a different place.

"Even in this post–nine-eleven period, Senator Kerry doesn't appear to understand how the world has changed. He talks about leading a 'more sensitive war on terror.'"

Derisive laughter echoed in the hall.

". . . As though al-Qaeda will be impressed with our softer side."

More laughter.

"He declared at the Democratic Convention that he will forcefully defend America after we have been attacked. My fellow Americans, we have already been attacked!"

The audience erupted in applause. Cheney heard a few spontaneous chants, then more, until all of Madison Square Garden was booming, "USA! USA! USA!"

He continued: ". . . Senator Kerry also takes a different view when it comes to supporting our military. Although he voted to authorize force against Saddam Hussein, he then decided he was opposed to the war, and voted against funding for our men and women in the field!"

"Flip-flop! Flip-flop! Flip-flop!"

Cheney hated giving speeches. But this speech was almost fun. And almost over.

". . . We all remember that terrible morning when, in the space of just one hundred and two minutes, more Americans were killed than we lost at Pearl Harbor. We remember the president who came to New York City and pledged that the terrorists would soon hear from all of us."

Applause.

"George W. Bush saw this country through grief and tragedy. He has acted with patience and calm and a moral seriousness that calls evil by its name."

Applause.

". . . When this convention concludes tomorrow night, we will go forth with confidence in our cause and in the man who leads it. By leaving no doubt where we stand and asking all Americans to join us, we will see our cause to victory!"

"Four more years! Four more years! Four more years!"

PART THREE

PART THREE

THE THERAPIST & THE TERRORIST

FRIDAY, SEPTEMBER 3, 2004

The days were growing shorter, the pain in Hassan's groin sharper.

After an entire summer of flesh, Hassan could barely stand in the towel hut. The pain was worse, like a knife plunging into his innards, twisting and turning. And so he braced his stooped body against the counter, dispensing towels, collecting towels, shuffling like one of those ancient cripples who would sometimes come to the boardwalk, one arm resting on a cane, the other intertwined in the arm of a visiting nurse.

How far he had fallen. From terrorist-in-training at the Abu al-Zarqawi Martyrs of Militancy Brigade to resident-in-waiting at the Dade County Jewish Home for the Aged.

Summer was fading. Another summer without a word from Tora Bora. And thank God for that! If they sent the signal today—activate the cell, Hassan, contact your brothers, take up your arms, mix the explosives, hit the target—he simply couldn't. Not with this pain. Not with the headaches that had dulled his senses and blurred his vision. Unless, of course, the seventy-two virgins were waiting. For the promise of the seventy-two virgins, he could ignore the pain.

Ouch. It hurts.

The recent news—the American elections, a hostage crisis in Russia, bombings in Fallujah—had been eclipsed by special bulletins about a hurricane named Frances. She would smack Florida tomorrow or the next day. There was talk of mass evacuations. Politicians planted themselves in front of television cameras, surrounded by grim-faced emergency services officials, and pretended to be meteorologists. Adding hot air to the coming storm. Meanwhile, plans were being made to defend the Paradise to the last umbrella stand. Hassan's assignment was to dismantle the towel hut and store it in a safe place. When the storm passed, life would continue. From utter destruction, the towel hut would rise again.

Praise Allah for this hurricane and the merciful end of summer. Let these infidels flee, only to be caught by the wrathful winds of God. May it come soon!

It couldn't come soon enough. This was the proverbial calm before the storm, as Paradise guests crowded the main pool to soak in every last ray of sun before the deluge. It was summer's grand finale of intertwined limbs, of jiggling, bouncing, sweating bodies. One final surge of towel-usurping, piña colada–slurping infidels. If Hassan could just manage to get through the next few days, he would pass the test. Hurricane Frances would come, the tourists would leave. The summer would be over. Then Hassan would be nearly alone for the winter, with seagulls swooping on the beach and closed umbrellas standing like lonely sentinels on a forgotten battlefield. The main pool would grow quiet. And Hassan could recuperate. The pain would subside. He would regain his strength. Until winter break.

He was close to a whimper. The last gasp of a forgotten terrorist ending another season.

And then—

"Excuuuuuse me!"

Hassan's thoughts were interrupted by that unmistakable accent, piercing his ears and curdling his blood and heralding the arrival of yet another New Yorker. Hassan's eyes fluttered as the pain burned.

And in the harsh sun that beat on him, he saw a vision.

"Excuse me, if it's not too much trouble, may I have a towel . . . puuleeze?" Rona Feldstein asked.

How could this be, thought Hassan. A woman who asked politely for a towel rather than demanding one. A woman who said "Please."

A modest woman who wore a broad straw hat that cast a deep shadow across her face and oversized sunglasses that shielded her eyes.

And this burka! Hassan marveled. *Okay, maybe not a burka,* he thought, *but it has the same utility.* Layers of black fabric, wrapped around her from neck to sandals. Not an inch of flesh exposed. True, he could do without the blue canvas tote bag she was clutching, stenciled with I MADE IT TO MASADA! UJA NY DIVISION MISSION TO ISRAEL. But then again, this was Boca. What did he expect?

Hassan squinted in the sun. "How many towels would you like?"

Rona seemed frozen. She stared at the towel limit sign, then removed her sunglasses, and read it slowly. Her brown eyes sparkled as they scanned the sign. "It says two per guest. But I only need one."

Allah be praised!

"Morris, my husband, fell asleep upstairs. Watching the Mets, of course. Did you evuh? We buy a place in Florida, and what does he do? The same thing he would be doing if he were home right now! And on such a gaw-jus day. Maybe the last day of sun before the hurricane. You know what, if he should wake up and decide to join me, we can ask for anothuh towel. For now, one will do. Can you help me find a chair?"

Hassan led Rona on a journey for the perfect spot. Far enough from the pool "so I shouldn't get splashed," but close enough "so the people serving drinks can see me if I should get a little thirsty"; not too close to any young families "because I adore children but I have to have my peace and quiet"; but "not near those two, over there, because it's a little uncomfortable sitting on top of people groping each other in public. I mean I'm happy they seem to be in love but do I have to watch their business in broad daylight? Isn't that what the hotel is for?"

Hassan found a spot within eyesight of the towel hut. As he bent to unfurl the towel over the chaise, a wave of dizziness overcame him. He grabbed the back of the chair, steadied himself, and rose slowly.

"Oh. My. God!" Rona exclaimed. "Are you okay?"

No one had ever asked Hassan that question. He was flustered, and embarrassed. As he rubbed his temples, the entire pool seemed to spin around him.

"Are you dizzy? You look a little dizzy to me. Is it the heat? You could *plotz* from this heat. *Gottenyu!*"

"I am fine." He resumed covering the chair, tucking the towel between the vinyl slats, adjusting it, smoothing it. And when he stood again, he did so slowly.

"Thank you. That's very nice," said Rona. Then she peered at the gold nameplate pinned to his yellow polo shirt, glinting in the sun, just above the stenciled PARADISE HOTEL logo. "Hass-in. Is that your first name?"

"Has-saan."

"I'm Rona. Rona Feldstein. It's a plesh-uh to meet you."

"Here's a little something for you, Hassan. Thank you." She pressed a dollar into his hand.

He nodded in protest.

A camera snapped nearby.

"Ah, ah, ah!" Rona said, wagging her finger. "You take this, Hassan." And as she pushed the crinkled bill into his palm, she asked, "So where do you live? From around here?"

"Yes. I live nearby."

"Me too. We just bought right here. In The Residences. Our other home is in New Yawk. Great Neck?"

A *question or a statement*, Hassan wondered. He nodded.

"You've heard of Great Neck? About a half hour to the city. Unless there's traffic on the LIE, of course. Which there always is. And that Queens–Midtown Tunnel. Aaaach, you could suffocate in there. We just bought here. A designer model! Everything else was sold out. And we're here now because it's Labor Day weekend. Morris—that's my husband—had so much vacation time coming to him. God fuhbid he should use his vacation time. He's a sales representative. For a drug company. But it's not what you think. He's not a drug pusher. He supplies doctors' offices. For Celfex. Celfex Pharmaceuticals? Maybe you've heard of it? Anyway, then we'll come again for the Jewish holidays. We're not that religious, to be honest. As far as I'm concerned, people are people. What difference does it make what you are? What do you think, Hassan?"

No one had ever asked Hassan what he thought. Either they told him how to think, or told him what to do. *Bring more towels, Hassan. Clean up those towels, Hassan. Destroy the infidels, Hassan.* "I think—"

"Do you think the hurricane will hit soon? Just our luck, Morris and me, to buy a condo just when the storm of the century is coming! Did ya evuh?"

"Yes. No."

"Well, I'll enjoy it while it lasts. No biggie. There are some things we have no control over and the weather is one of them. Right, Hassan?"

"Yes."

"Let me ask: Do a lot of the owners rent their units when they're not here? Morris thinks that's what we should do. To recoup our investment. Look, we're not the Rockefellers, if you know what I mean. So maybe some rental income would be nice. On the other hand, the thought of dealing with other people's *schmutz* in our unit—it makes me queasy."

Hassan wasn't sure what *schmutz* was. He knew *queasy*.

"So is this what you do full-time, Hassan? Schlep towels?"

"No. I am . . . in school."

"Studying what, may I ask?"

"Nursing." A much better cover than they concocted for the last sleeper cell. Aviation school! Why not just send them to the community college and ask if they offer Terrorist Infiltration 101? What were those imbeciles in Tora Bora thinking?

"Nursing? Ooooooh, how nice. I'm a CSW."

Hassan stared at her.

"That's Certified . . . Social . . . Worker." Her voice underlined each word, but just to make sure she used her index finger to draw lines in the air. "I have a small therapy practice. In my home. In Great Neck. Just a few clients. Stress reduction. Anxiety issues. Meditation. For example, I can tell something about you Hassan. I know something about you already."

Hassan stiffened.

"Do you want to know what it is?"

He looked into her eyes, as he was trained to do. "Please," he said. "Tell me."

"Something is wrong."

"No. Everything is—"

"Ah, ah, ah!" Again the finger wagging. "I know it when I see it. And I'll tell you what I see. . . . You have a headache. Don't you? A terrible headache. Am I right or am I wrong?"

How did she know about the headache? he thought. *I hope she doesn't ask about the groin pain.*

"You can tell me, Hassan. I can see it in your eyes. I'm trained to recognize stress signals. Let me guess. It's at the back of your eyes, and in your temples, right?"

"Yes."

"And you've had it for weeks. Yes?"

"It won't go away," Hassan stammered. And just by getting the words out, the pain seemed to ease. As if talking about it relieved it.

"And does it spread? Through your sinuses, down your whole face?"

"Yes. Yes it does."

"Uh-huh!" she said confidently. "And the dizziness. Does it blur your vision?"

"Yes. Sometimes."

"Sure!" Rona exclaimed. "I knew it. From the moment I saw you I knew it. Here, I have something that may help."

She plunked herself on the chaise lounge next to the one Hassan covered, and using her arm as a crane, lifted the giant United Jewish Appeal tote bag and tipped it forward. A waterfall of medicines cascaded out. Above the sound of pill bottles, cellophane, plastic, and cardboard containers clanking as they hit the chair, Rona said, "My husband works for Celfex, but my friends say I'm a walking pharmacy. And why not? God forbid you're in the middle of nowhere and need a little something!"

Her "little something" was more like a pharmaceutical manufacturer's delivery truck. Everything from aspirin to zinc. Hard candies and softgels, tablets and caplets, drops and pills, lotions and creams. In greens and blue and pinks and silver. The pile grew with Cold-Eeze and Sleepeaze, Dayquil and Nyquil. There was Advil and Alka-Seltzer. There was Bayer ("Just in case Morris gets chest pains, it could save his life,"). There was Benadryl, Blistex, Claritin, Dramamine ("Look, I get a little queasy on the plane."), Excedrin, Imodium, Kaopectate, Motrin, Pepcid, Pepto-Bismol, Sine-Aid, Theraflu, and Tums ("You don't know what they're serving you in some of these places!"). And Tylenol, Tylenol Sinus, Tylenol Extra Strength, and Tylenol PM. And Visine and Vaseline and Zantac. All mixed with little clear bottles of hand sanitizers and tiny pink aerosol cans of Lysol disinfectant. Plus, what looked to Hassan like enough Kleenex tissues to clean an oil spill.

And then, topping off the pile, like gravy, was the assortment of brown pill bottles filled with Celfex products procured from the black bag that Morris stowed in his trunk. Harmonex for occasional anxiety. Digaflex for nausea. Lunaflex to help Rona sleep at night, and Vasoflex to elevate Morris's good cholesterol levels. Finally, the last stubborn bottle dropped from the bag and plunked into the pile.

Hassan watched as Rona picked through the pile as if she was searching for gold. "Got it!" she puffed, and retrieved a single pill bottle, like one of those arcade claws that dips into a pile of stuffed animals. She looked around, almost suspiciously, opened it, and let a single pink pill slip into her hand.

"Here. This should help. It's my Migramize by Celfex. An absolute lifesaver, I can tell you. Take it now. If it doesn't help, you'll come see me."

She deposited the pill into his palm. "Be sure to take it with a full glass of water. So you shouldn't get a stomachache. You understand, Hassan?"

The camera snapped again.

"Yes. Thank you."

He could feel the sweat of his palm on the pill, and when he opened it, a soft spot of pink appeared.

"You know what?" she said. "Come to think of it, I think I feel a headache coming on. Sure, you go from air-conditioning to heat, heat to air-conditioning in this place. Achhh, you could *plotz!*" She popped a pill into her mouth then grabbed a bottle of water she had brought down from the condo, and sipped it.

Hassan returned to the towel hut, took the pill, and washed it down with an entire bottle of water. He studied Rona from his perch, watching and waiting for two things to happen.

First, he waited for the pill to poison him, to bring him to his knees. He would grope at his throat, and then die amidst the towel pile. In which case he could just forget the virgins in Paradise. Dying before suicide rendered the whole event null and void, according to the contract he had signed with the Abu al-Zarqawi Martyrs of Militancy.

Second, he waited for Rona to do something that ended his fantasy of her. Maybe peel off the burka to reveal an immodest bikini. Or walk right up to the towel hut and say, "What was I thinking? Gimme three towels!"

Neither occurred.

In fact, within an hour, the crushing pain had abated, as if someone had connected the pool pump to his temples and sucked out all the tension. For the first time in weeks, he could think clearly.

He could see clearly, too.

There was Rona, across the pool, almost shimmering like a mirage. Rona Feldstein: performer of medical miracles, abider of the two-towel-per-guest rule, guardian of her own purity. Even when the sun rose high overhead and forced everyone into the lukewarm pool, Rona remained on the chaise lounge, one leg fused to the other, covered by that black robe, fanning herself with her magazines. All the other women at the pool, with their flesh exposed and their breast implants, read magazines plastered with exposed flesh and implanted breasts. But not one of Rona's magazines even hinted at such immodesty. Not the *Psychology Today* or *Ventilate: The Public Opinion Journal For Social Workers* or the *Hadassah Magazine* with its banner headline:

JAKE GYLLENHAAL IS JEWISH?
HADASSAH'S TOP TEN CELEBRITY MINYAN!

Hassan often heard Jews talk proudly about famous Jews. It confused him. In training camp, he had learned how the Zionists owned all the world's banks and controlled, among other enterprises, the United Nations, the United States, the military-industrial complex, Exxon-Mobile, Saudi Arabia, all the 7-Elevens, and everything between Wall Street and Hollywood. So why the ecstasy when they learned that some famous or quasi-famous personality was Jewish or half-Jewish, or married someone who was Jewish or half-Jewish? Or, in the case of Madonna, studied Kabbalah? And if the Jew just happened to be a professional athlete! Forget Moses with his Ten Commandments. We have Art Shamsky, who played outfield in the 1969 World Series!

When the heat overcame Rona, she unwrapped the robe, self-consciously darting her eyes, until she revealed a one-piece bathing suit that stretched from just below her neck to just above her knees. No *flaunting or flashing*, thought Hassan.

Just like what his grandmother, Fatimah, wore on the rare visit to the ocean in Gaza.

When the heat became too strong for her, Rona stood. She kept her hat on her head and her sunglasses perched on her nose, wrapped the towel around her narrow waist, and stepped toward the pool, like she was approaching the edge of a high cliff.

How she immersed herself! thought Hassan. The others hurled their bodies into the pool or rolled in like great whales, spraying waves of pool water mixed with tanning lotion, tiny wisps of grass, brown specks of beach sand, and flakes of peeling skin everywhere. As if they owned the pool; as if they were the only ones in the pool. How typically American.

Rona's entry was like a delicate minuet. She dipped the toes of one foot, lifted them from the water and shook them gently, then repeated the action with her other foot. Once acclimated to the temperature, she clutched the rail and eased herself down each step. Slowly. Hesitantly. And when the water lapped at her knees, she bent forward as if to dive, cupped her hands, and sprinkled a few drops on each shoulder. Next, she rubbed her wet hands down her neck, and across the top of her chest. And climbed out of the pool, panting.

She had "spritzed" herself, which was the Rona Feldstein equivalent of the fifty-meter freestyle in the Summer Olympics.

Throughout the day, Hassan ventured from the towel hut. Gathering used towels and replacing them with fresh ones, adjusting towels on chairs and lounges, folding and refolding towels, fluffing towels, turning towels, patrolling for any loose or errant towels. Sometimes, when he would pass Rona, she would peer over her sunglasses, raise her palm, and wiggle her fingers so that her bracelets jingled and flashed in the sun. No one waved at him, unless they were beckoning him to do something for them. *Bring me a drink, Hassan. Adjust my umbrella, Hassan. Another towel, Hassan.* Embarrassed, he spun his head in a different direction and walked past Rona. As if he didn't notice her waving. Checking on him.

When the sun turned burnt orange and cast long umbrella-shaped shadows across the pool, Rona lifted herself from her lounge, gathered her belongings, and then began folding her towel, from end to end, smoothing the layers as she folded. Then she brought the finished product to the towel hut. "It was nice meeting you, Hassan. I'm going up to get ready for dinner with Morris. Get a good night's sleep and tell me how you feel tomorrow."

"Yes, Mrs. Feldstein. Tomorrow."

"And Hassan. Next time when you don't feel well you let me know. Remember, I'm trained, Hassan. As a therapist, and as a mother!"

The camera clicked one last time.

26

THE VOYEUR

FRIDAY EVENING, SEPTEMBER 3, 2004

Alonso Diaz didn't mind Friday night shifts, when his colleagues emptied out for the weekend. He preferred to be alone with his photo collection, hundreds of images glowing on his computer. Peering into the lives frozen in the click of a shutter, examining their forbidden secrets, peeking beneath whatever layers they had wrapped around them.

Diaz was a voyeur. Employed by the Federal Bureau of Investigation Boca Raton Field Office. Tonight, he was annoyed. The hurricane was threatening to rip across his region within days. Hurricanes weren't good for the terrorist surveillance business. Terrorists tended to stay indoors in bad weather. Out of the reach of Diaz's cameras.

He sat in the cluttered cubicle they called his "work station," enveloped by a soiled beige fabric partition plastered with Miami

Dolphins stickers, curling and faded photos of family fishing trips with his family, and an array of bureaucratic memos.

He leaned into his computer monitor, rubbed his eyes, and studied the latest photos. In the War on Terror, Alonso Diaz's weapon of choice was a fast shutter—capturing images of men and women suspected of suspicious behavior, questionable associations, and un-American activities. Agent Diaz connected the dots by building a massive database of pixilated images. Surveillance photos of taxi drivers and fast-food workers, college students and maintenance crews. In black and white. But mostly olive.

Some were suspected terrorists, some were suspected of knowing someone who knew someone who just might be a terrorist, and most just happened to have stumbled within Diaz's depth of field. It didn't matter. He often thought, *Show me a picture of anyone and I will show you a story to be told, a secret to be outed, a lie to be exposed.* It was all so . . . scintillating! The blemishes of human nature just waiting to be developed. Like in the old days in the darkroom. You exposed the image to some light, immersed it in a chemical bath, and before long, patches and blotches appeared. Subtly at first, until a vivid picture emerged.

Today's collection, for example. Hassan Muzan appeared to be just an overworked towel boy at the Paradise Hotel and Residences. And his conversation with that redheaded woman wasn't exactly destined for *Top Ten Crime-Scene Photos* on the Discovery Channel.

But these days, appearances were deceiving and deception appeared everywhere. Diaz had a collection of informants bothered by aspects of Hassan Muzan's behavior. His strange habit of purchasing and discarding cell phones. His periodic meetings in Little Havana with three suspicious men. His belligerent behavior when asked for too many towels.

So he—literally—became the focus of Diaz's attention. Framed, shot, pixilated, and uploaded over the past few weeks, a face among the other faces in Alonso Diaz's Rogues Gallery.

With a cameo appearance by Rona Feldstein.

Soon something would develop from these photos. Maybe not a plot against the United States, but something. Diaz had a hunch.

As Diaz was fond of saying: "Cameras don't lie. People do."

MONSOON OVER MIAMI

SATURDAY, SEPTEMBER 4, 2004

The next morning, Rona suggested to Morris that they go to the pool. Morris looked out the window at dark clouds roiling over the ocean, and watched as gusts of wind rattled the palm trees and blew errant papers across the patio. Yesterday the ocean was turquoise and placid. Now, it was gray and frothing.

There was tsuris ahead, Morris knew.

"The storm is coming," he said.

"No biggie. Why should we lose a whole day of our weekend, Morris. Let's sit by the pool while we can."

No biggie? They are evacuating half the state of Florida and she wants to sit outside? This from a woman who didn't like sitting too close to the field at Shea Stadium because "God forbid a foul ball can take somebody's eye out"?

What's happening? thought Morris.

Once, I sat safely in my RoyaLounger 8000 and watched my Turner Classic Movies. Now I'm about to reenact the tornado scene in The Wizard of Oz.

Even with the wind blowing and waves swelling, Paradise guests converged on the main pool, hoping to cram in a few hours before the hurricane drove them inside.

Rona led Morris to the towel hut, clamping her hat to her head, against the wind.

"Hello, Hassan! This is my husband, Morris. Oh my God, this storm looks like it will be something!"

Hassan smiled, half glad to see Rona and half giddy at the approaching Armageddon where God would wipe out the infidels. "Hello!"

"Thank you again for the towel yesterday! The pool was very refreshing."

For thirty-four years Rona had guarded her body from the transmission of germs from "other people's *schmutz*." Morris found it implausible that Rona would insert a single body part into a public pool, no less dry the polluted water from her skin with a towel used by strangers and washed with other towels in a communal laundry.

A few drops of rain began to fall, and Morris said, "I'm going back inside, Rona. Are you coming?"

"I'll be up soon, Morris. There's something I want to discuss with my new friend, Hassan."

As he walked back, Morris had no doubts that Rona had befriended Hassan. Rona befriended everyone within her peripheral vision. If you were standing beside her at the supermarket checkout, or eating at an adjacent table at the diner, or sitting near her on an airplane, it wouldn't be long before you were hearing about her childhood, or flipping through pictures of her children. There was no escape.

Rona leaned against the counter:

"*Nu?*" Rona said.

Hassan turned away, toward the towels.

"Hassan?"

"You asked for a new towel. I'll get one."

"No. Not new! *Nu!* As in 'Hey, what's happening?'" Rona began a cackle deep in her throat.

"So, are you feeling better?"

"Yes, Mrs. Feldstein. I slept all night! And awoke with no pain! Thank you!"

"Don't thank me. Thank Migramize. By Celfex. When you go to your doctor, you'll tell him: Mi . . . graaa . . . mize. By Celfex. He'll write you a little prescription."

Hassan's smile faded.

"What's the matter, Hassan?"

"A doctor is expensive in your country."

"*Gottenyu!* What these Republicans have done to health care in America. You could bust a gut. And if you did, who could afford the surgery? It's a national *shonda!*"

"Yes, Mrs. Feldstein. A *shonda.*" Hassan entered the word into his ever-expanding mental dictionary of Yiddish phrases that should be memorized by every sleeper cell terrorist.

"Look. You'll give me your address. When I get back to Great Neck, I'll mail you some samples from Morris's trunk. No biggie."

"Thank you, Mrs. Feldstein."

"You have to take care of yourself, the way you schlep towels all day! Running around like that. You could get heat stroke, God forbid. I hate to sound like your mother. But you do need to be careful. Where is your mother by the way? Where does she live?"

Hassan Muzan was well trained to resist most interrogation techniques, including beatings, threats, seduction, frothing dogs, solitary confinement, electric prods, simulated drowning, and Twisted Sister's

"We're Not Gonna Take It" played at ear-bleeding volume. Defending against a Jewish psychotherapist asking about his mother had not been part of his training.

"She lives in Kuwait," he stammered. It was a lie. And now he felt something strange and new: a pang of guilt.

"Aaaaach. So far away. It must be lonely. You should call your mother, Hassan. She must worry about you. Being so far away. And with this hurricane coming. It would eat out my *kishkas* to have a son so far away and not hear from him."

He thought of the last time he had seen his mother.

He had arrived home and sat at a wobbly table in the kitchen, to report his decision. Over the din of the congested and dusty street outside, the babies wailing and the children screeching and the muezzin's calling, he told his parents he would drop out of college and join the jihad—specifically, the Abu al-Zarqawi Martyrs of Militancy Brigade, which offered, among other perks, a signing bonus, training, a chance to see the world, a gun, and the seventy-two virgins in Paradise.

His mother wailed at the news. "Why are you doing this? Why?"

"To end the Zionist occupation. To protect my homeland."

Hassan left out the part about the virgins.

"Stop this foolishness!" she said, as if Hassan had revealed that he wanted to become an astronaut or a cowboy. "Let the troublemakers blow themselves up. You will go into the orange-exporting business. With your father and uncles. And Cousin Qassim. It's settled."

"It is not settled! It is my life and I will decide how to live it!"

His mother narrowed her eyes. "That troublemaker Abdul put you up to this, didn't he? I told you to stay away from Abdul. Why can't you be more like Cousin Qassim! Qassim is going places. In the orange-export business!"

Hassan would not listen. And his mother would not shut up about Cousin Qassim this and Cousin Qassim that, and how Cousin

Qassim would save the world one crate of oranges at a time. Soon she was shrieking and clenching her fat fists in the air.

Meanwhile, his father sat impassively under the crooked framed photograph hanging on the wall, the photograph of Cousin Qassim with his moronic grin and ill-fitting American suit. He watched his wife and son battle in the detached way he watched everything. As if watching one of those silly soap operas on Israeli television.

Then his mother did the unthinkable. She turned to his father, pointed a puffy finger at him, and screeched: "You are to blame. You. You I curse!"

She had humiliated him. Right there. In front of Hassan. So loudly that the neighbors had to hear it.

His father fidgeted through his rough beard nervously, and his heavy, sad eyes connected with Hassan's. Weak, pleading, helpless eyes.

Eyes that said, "Go. Escape this woman. Now."

That night, Hassan took one last look at his young sisters, Adiva and Ameerah, and stroked their black hair against the pillows in the bed they shared.

The next morning Hassan set out on his new life. A life which, if he studied hard and did everything right and mastered his trade, would end with his blowing himself up.

Final destination, martyrdom.

With a layover at the Paradise Hotel and Residences.

"Look," Rona said. "I think a mother should hear from her son. My Jeffrey moved to Chicago. Maybe not as far as Kuwait, but it may as well be. Still, every Sunday he calls. At six on the dot. Before our Chinese food. You and your mother are none of my business, I know. Morris says I can't help myself. So what's such a sin? So shoot me, why don't you."

Not you, thought Hassan.

A gust of wind blew in from the ocean, etching determined

currents in the pool and bending palm trees. Guests shivered and wrapped towels around their bodies.

"Oh my God," Rona exclaimed. "I better get inside. Do you think the hurricane will be bad?"

Hassan thought, *If there is a merciful God, yes. It will destroy everyone and everything. It will be the mother—the mother—of all hurricanes.*

ELDERCARE

SUNDAY, SEPTEMBER 5, 2004

Even at the age of ninety-six, Minny Schwartzman had a crush on that nice man who visited her room twice a week. He would sit next to her bed as she watched *The Price Is Right* on the wall-mounted television. He studied the family photographs that littered her room. He nodded with interest at the stories she shared about her life. He helped her eat her favorite Melba Toast snacks and made sure she took her medications. And how handsome he was! With that Clark Gable mustache and the Charles Boyer voice.

Having escaped the surveillance of federal authorities on Long Island, Ricardo Montoyez found a new home—specifically, the Bella Abzug Home for the Aged in Riverdale, New York. He volunteered there to provide people like Minny companionship in their incredibly old age, posing as a retired hedge fund executive who wanted to give something back. And take a few things in the process.

The Abzug Home was like a pharmaceutical gold mine, a treasure trove of medications that kept hearts ticking, blood creeping, bowels moving. From Avodart for prostates to Xarelto for blood. Drugs for brittle bones and drugs for foggy brains. Drugs to keep every overworked organ functioning for at least another day. Twenty, thirty, forty pills a day. Scooped and shoveled out of plastic cases that looked like fishing tackle boxes. Inserted through ancient lips, washed across toothless mouths, and choked down grizzled gullets.

All those medicines. Under the watchful eye of Guadalupe, the flirtatious pharmacy assistant with the butterfly tattoo rising from her chest. Not exactly Ricardo's type, but here in the mausoleum romance wasn't difficult with someone who still had her own teeth and didn't forget her name.

He thought sometimes about the blond receptionist he jilted on Long Island.

I've gone from Victoria with those sexy legs to Minny with one foot in the grave. Aaaaah, the sacrifices I must make.

But it was worth it. He was stockpiling medications, delivering them to a safe place on Long Island where they were soon watered down and chalked up. Then they were resold into the retail market and stocked on the shelves of America's drugstores. True, people were dying. But he was making a nice living.

He learned one thing at the Bella Abzug Home for the Aged: We all die, sooner or later. Or in the case of Minny Schwartzman, way, way later.

CALL YOUR MOTHER

SUNDAY, SEPTEMBER 5, 2004

You're kidding, right? Hassan asked God.

The hurricane had come. And it had gone. Barely scuffing the Paradise Hotel and Residences. As if God Himself, in one of His infinite mysteries, decided to spare Boca. Florida's orange groves—those He destroyed. The Zionists, the infidels, the occupiers of lands and towels, they escaped His wrath. Again.

You've got to be kidding!

Balancing on a stepladder, Hassan returned the TWO TOWELS PER GUEST sign to its place. A cart containing dozens of laundered towels was parked next to the hut. Hotel workers raked the beach and swept the grounds to erase any sign of the hurricane. An early-morning sun glowed on the horizon, winking at an ocean that seemed to sigh with relief.

Hassan stepped off the ladder, bent toward the cart, scooped the first pile of fresh towels, and placed them on the shelves in the hut.

Then he heard it:

"So *nu*? You're back in business?"

Like the call of the muezzin, a sweet beckoning to Hassan.

"Good morning, Mrs. Feldstein! You survived the storm, thank God."

Rona waved dismissively. "*Gottenyu*, all that hype! Morris and I were fine. His biggest crisis was when we lost the satellite TV. As if he didn't already know the ending to *Meet Me in St. Louis*. Did ya evuh?"

"I nevuh, Mrs. Feldstein. May I give you a towel? Or two?"

Rona turned, and her shoulders drooped.

"Is something wrong, Mrs. Feldstein?"

"No towel today, Hassan. I'm afraid my pool days are over for now. Morris and I going home. To Great Neck. Morris has to get back to Celfex and I have my clients."

Hassan felt his stomach tighten. Who would give him medicine if his headaches returned? Who would mother him?

Rona interrupted his despair. "Hassan, I have something to say."

She cleared her throat, as if summoning the words from inside, bit her lip, and said:

"Hassan, I've given it a lot of thought. I'll be very concerned about you when I leave. So I want you to keep this. For when you need it."

Hassan felt a thin slab of metal attached to a crumpled card pressed against the palm of his hand.

"It's the spare set of keys, Hassan. To our unit. You can keep an eye on things for me while we're away. And God forbid, while you're checking on everything, you put on some air-conditioning . . . watch some satellite TV . . . make yourself a little nosh . . ." Her voice lifted the last word of each phrase into the air, as if singing a jingle about the amenities of her condo.

"Oh no, Mrs. Feldstein. I couldn't. What about the *schmutz*?

Remember what you said about other people's *schmutz* in your unit—"

"Oooh, pul-eeeeze, Hassan. I've seen how you fold towels! You're very professional. And you're not like other people! You're like family! I'm your surrogate mother, Hassan. Your surrogate Jewish mother from Great Neck, New Yawk! How many Arabs can say that!"

Probably not that many, Hassan thought.

"I wrote down my cell number. I want you to call me. When you want to schmooze. When . . . when you need someone to talk to, Hassan. Promise you'll call me, Hassan."

"I promise, Mrs. Feldstein."

"Good. Now, we're going to make a little deal, you and me."

"A deal, Mrs. Feldstein?"

"Yes. You can use our unit. But don't breathe a word to Morris. It's our little secret."

I can keep secrets, Hassan thought.

"And one more thing I want you to do."

"Yes, Mrs. Feldstein?"

"I want you to call your mother."

Reflexively Hassan pushed the keys back to Rona. And just as reflexively Rona held up both hands.

"Ah, ah, ah. I am not taking no for an answer! I'm a professional. I'm trained to pick up certain clues. You don't think I noticed how you reacted when I asked you about your mother? The clenched fists? How your face shriveled up like a day-old Danish?"

Hassan lowered his eyes.

"Don't be embarrassed, Hassan. The mother-son dynamic is complex. Entire books have been written on the subject. Have you read *Chicken Soup for the Oedipal Male Soul?* No? I'll send it to you. With the Migramize. I'm trying to help, Hassan. Call your mother."

The sweat of his palm now covered the key. "I cannot . . ." His words were course and heavy.

"Hassan. I'm not asking you to call your mother in my

professional capacity as a certified social worker with a degree from Long Island University. I'm giving you this advice . . ." she paused in a futile effort to keep her voice from trembling, ". . . as a mother myself."

Hassan noticed Rona's lips begin to quiver. "I have two precious children. My Caryn wants to be a filmmaker. Documentaries. Have you seen *Fox News Fascists*? On YouTube? That's Caryn."

"Now my Jeffrey, he's another story! Whatever you think your mother did to you, you've punished her enough. No, you've tortured her, Hassan. Because when a mother loses a son, it's torture. God knows my Jeffrey and I had our differences. I wanted him to go to law school. I begged him. But no. Stocks, he said. Did you evuh? One day they're up, the next day they're down.

"'Jeffrey,' I said, 'you want to earn a living on a roller coaster, you should go to work at Disneyland.' So we fought. Like cats and dogs. But I cannot imagine how it would be if Jeffrey stopped talking to me. Fighting I can deal with. Silence? It's like torture. Tor . . . cha!" Rona bit her upper lip, removed her sunglasses, and wiped her glistening eyes with a fresh Kleenex she retrieved from her tote bag.

Hassan felt an uncomfortable stirring inside. Rona managed to do what no CIA interrogator could hope to do: She got inside his head. Dredging the muck. Starting a flow of submerged thoughts. Eroding his willpower. And Rona knew where to pull the pin of the emotional grenade: in that part of the brain where guilt resides. That was the sweet spot. Rona knew it, as did all the Jewish mothers and the Italian mothers and the Irish mothers and even Hamidah Muzan, a Palestinian mother in Gaza. They could be their own category in the Geneva Convention prohibitions against cruel and inhuman punishment; but no one wanted to upset them by suggesting it.

Still, Hassan knew that calling home—just for a moment, just to hear his mother's voice, just to let her know he was alive—could compromise the entire operation. *One call from my cell phone and the next thing I know, a B-52 drops a five-hundred-pound bunker buster and there's a crater where the towel hut used to be. No thank you, US Air Force!*

"Perhaps another day, Mrs. Feldstein."

"Take it from me, Hassan. Take it from a mother."

Resist, Hassan!

"I will write to her, Mrs. Feldstein."

"Writing is always nice . . ."

Excellent, Hassan!

"Assuming your mother gets the letter, of course. Acchhh, who knows with the mail these days? You'll write a letter to her and God only knows when she'll get it. Or if she'll get it. But I'm sure she can wait. After all, she waited all this time to hear from her son. What's another few weeks. Or months? Or evuh?"

Hassan thought: *Plus, she could open the letter, get a paper cut and blood poisoning, and that's that!*

"Here." Rona extended her cell phone to him. "You can borrow my cell."

"Yes, Mrs. Feldstein."

NEWS BREAK

TUESDAY, SEPTEMBER 7, 2004

That night, in Morris and Rona's Great Neck dining room, the negotiation of what to watch on television commenced over some Italian food from Luiggi's Ristorante.

Morris surrendered early.

After all, the Mets had dropped nine in a row. Morris was tired of losing. The only thing better than watching another agonizing Mets loss was watching the agonizing news.

He sat in the RoyaLounger. Rona curled up on the couch. And the dramatic CNN overture filled the room.

Wolf Blitzer began with a report of a deadly battle between US troops and Shia forces in a place called Sadr City. And Rona bit her lip.

Then Blitzer reported a grizzly milestone: the one-thousandth American death in Iraq. Rona let out a long, quivering sigh. Or cry.

This is why we shouldn't watch the news, Morris thought. *It's always bad, these days. And there's nothing we can do about it. So why bother?*

On the couch, Rona felt the lump in her throat grow. And couldn't help but liken it to the lump on that chair. *Staring at the television as if it were just one of his classic movies, as though he could just change the channel instead of trying to change the world.*

THE SAFE HOUSE WITH LOX

WEDNESDAY, SEPTEMBER 8, 2004

"This is Paradise."

"No it isn't."

"It seems like Paradise."

"Then where are the virgins?"

"Maybe no virgins. But it's got the Emeril Signature kitchen, satellite television, and look at that ocean view!"

"You are a fool."

Hassan cradled his head in his hands as his cell members bickered in the Feldstein living room at The Residences at Paradise.

Azad was sprawled on the Berber carpet, leafing through a *People* magazine. He wore his favorite designer jeans, which annoyed Hassan. They must have cost Azad a month's pay mowing lawns at the landscaping company.

Achmed napped on the couch, snoring through a gaping mouth.

He was constantly tired from his night job cleaning jets' cabins. Achmed was the cell's explosives expert.

And Pervez. On the battlefields of Afghanistan, he was famous for uncoiling on his enemy like a venomous snake. Now he seemed stitched into a green microfiber recliner. He was bloated from the employee discounts he received as a counterman at McDonald's.

Gleaming marble, sparkling glass, and textured wallpaper with extravagant pastel streaks surrounded them. Hassan's nostrils tingled from the scent of the recently installed Berber carpet.

Almost as soon as Rona and Morris returned to New York, he had relocated the cell from a hovel in Little Havana. It seemed like a sensible idea at the time. The Residences at Paradise was the last place the FBI would be on the lookout for global crime (unless they were investigating an international mahjong ring). And the relocation would improve the cell's morale, which was just as low as his own, at least prior to meeting Rona. Here, they could plan their attack, and when fatigue set in, they could take a break, have a little nosh, and watch the gigantic plasma television mounted on a wall.

Hassan stared at the screen. CNN was regurgitating a comment the Vice President had made earlier in the day: "It's absolutely essential that eight weeks from today, on November second, we make the right choice. Because if we make the wrong choice, then the danger is that we'll get hit again and we'll be hit in a way that will be devastating from the standpoint of the United States."

How did he find out? Hassan thought.

Achmed awakened with a grunt. "I am sick of CNN," he said. "Turn on Fox News!"

Azad protested: "I refuse to watch Fox! I want to watch *That '70s Show!*"

"But we had a deal!" insisted Achmed. "Your shows on odd-numbered days. Fox on even days. Today is the eighth. We watch Fox. Right, Hassan?"

Before Hassan could take a side, Pervez chimed in. "Excuuuuuse me! Someone is trying to read here!" He was now leafing through a copy of Rona's glossy coffee-table book, *Marc Chagall: Masterpieces*.

"Shut up, Pervez!" Azad yelled.

"Enough!" Hassan said. He grabbed the television clicker from the coffee table and stuffed it into his shirt pocket. The gesture caught everyone's attention. They trained their eyes on him, not quite ready to confront the authority that befalls one who possesses the television clicker.

Hassan stared back, making sure to fix his eyes on each one. They wouldn't challenge him, he knew. They couldn't. They were too lazy. Draped around the room like discarded clothing.

This terrorist cell would bring the West to its knees. Right after Larry King on CNN.

Hassan clapped his hands like cymbals. "We must stay focused!" he demanded.

"Focused on what, Hassan?" Pervez grumbled. "It's been thirty months. And still we know nothing about when we will attack, where we will attack, who we will attack, or even if we *will* attack! I thought I would be in Paradise by now. Instead I just got my fourth raise at McDonald's and I'm up for assistant manager. I can't keep waiting. Maybe I'll apply to al-Qaeda. I hear they're expanding."

"Then go to al-Qaeda," said Azad. "Whine to them. See how fast they take you!"

"I will go, Azad. But first I will cut out your tongue," Pervez snarled. There was a time, Hassan reflected, when that threat would have petrified Azad. The first time that Hassan saw Pervez—at the Abu al-Zarqawi Army of Jihad Martyrs of Militancy Brigade training camp—he immediately requested that headquarters assign him to the South Florida cell. That snarl would come in handy at the right moment. It would strike fear into someone's heart. But Pervez's transfer to America required him to change his appearance to blend in. His beard came off, and after he started at the McDonald's, the pounds went on. His jowls grew puffy, and his once-fierce jaw drooped with wobbly flesh. Now, his snarl was no more threatening than the annoyed expression of a McDonald's employee toward a customer who took too long deciding on which value meal to order. And it's hard to effectuate a good snarl when your lips are orange from Doritos crumbs.

They were looking, acting, more like the Weight Watchers Club of Boca Raton than a terrorist cell, Hassan realized. Thirty months was just too long to maintain unit cohesion and discipline.

What is Tora Bora waiting for? How long can they expect me to keep everyone motivated without even giving us a hint of our mission? How many towels must I fold? How many Happy Meals must Pervez serve, lawns must Azad landscape, planes must Achmed vacuum, before the order comes to activate the cell?

A string of commercials droned on the television, broken by some gentle piano notes. A woman stared through a window at a slightly falling rain. And then this: "Sometimes, even your depression medicine isn't enough. That's why there's Enhancify. Prescribed by your doctor, Enhancify gives you the added tools you need to make it through the day. Every day." In the next scene, the woman walked with her husband, under an umbrella with the bright-yellow Enhancify trademark.

"This I do not understand," Azad commented. "They give you depression medicine for your depression medicine?"

Which gave Hassan an idea.

Rona. The surrogate mother/therapist. With her UJA tote bag full of kaleidoscopic pills and tablets.

The words were recorded slowly and methodically. The voice heartened Hassan.

"Hello. Thank you for caw-ling Row-nuh Feldstein, C-S-double-yuuuuuu. I am unable to come to the phone at the present time. But if you leave yaw name, phone numbuh, day and time of yaw call, I will return it as soon as possible. Please. You should wait for the beep. And then tawk."

"Hello, Mrs. Feldstein? So, *nu*? Please call me. It is important. Good-bye."

Please call back soon, he thought.

The call was intercepted by Alonso Diaz of FBI–Boca. He plugged into his computer the New York phone number that Hassan had called. Leaned back. And waited.

His monitor flickered with information about the recipient of Hassan's call: Rona Feldstein of Great Neck, New York. He scrolled through her driver's license number, her social security number, her current address (19 Soundview Drive), her previous known address/ addresses ("none"), her employer ("self-employed"), her husband's name, social security number, and employer, her record of arrests and infractions ("none"), and miscellaneous details about her life that had all the intrigue of a PBS series on the Blue-winged Warbler.

He clicked the icon on his photo gallery and found the images of Hassan and Rona at the Paradise. It brought a delicious smile to Diaz's lips.

The camera doesn't lie. People do.

What turns ordinary people into secret agents, skulking in the shadows, disguising phone records, and creating clandestine greetings like "So, *nu*?"

"Sometimes a cigar is just a cigar," he liked to quote Freud. It was the only Freud quote he knew, but it seemed to explain most of the entries on the "persons of interest" list.

Lust.

Take Hassan and Rona. How perfect! Not only was a middle-aged Jewish woman from New York cheating on her husband, but she was doing it with an Arab! What could be more dangerous? More arousing? Less kosher! Talk about mixing milk with meat!

Diaz got excited just thinking about it.

Still, he had a job to do. His supervisor—Mr. Terrorist Behind

Every Tree—would demand an update about the people under Diaz's watchful eyes.

He pecked at his keyboard until this message flashed on his screen:

YOU ARE ENTERING A RESTRICTED SITE. AUTHORIZED PERSONNEL ONLY.
VIOLATORS WILL BE PROSECUTED TO THE FULL EXTENT OF THE LAW.
PRESS ENTER FOR NICK. PRESS EXIT FOR HOME PAGE.

After typing a succession of passwords, authorization codes, and secret answers to secret questions, he arrived at his file on the Network Centric Total Information Collection, Integration, Synthesis, Assessment, Dissemination, and Deployment website.

"FELDSTEIN, RONA, he typed. He added her social security and phone number, and, just for good measure, he typed the name of her husband.

While NICK contemplated, Diaz daydreamed over one of the pictures hanging on his partition. He and his wife were posing on the deck of a cruise ship, the sun setting at their backs.

The monitor flashed:

NICK ALERT NICK ALERT NICK ALERT

AMBER WATCH UPGRADE

NICK HAS FOUND MULTIPLE THREAT PATTERN[S] FOR FELDSTEIN,
MORRIS SOLOMON

DATA FILE: 30/5/NYLIFO/1527HRS/0-14-1051-1455-R

DECLARED POTENTIAL PERSON OF INTEREST

FILED BY DC HEADQUARTERS

FIELD OF INTEREST: LONG ISLAND, NY

SEE LINKS:

D'AMICO, VICTORIA ELLEN

MONTOYEZ, RICARDO XAVIER

FELDSTEIN, CARYN—ARREST

FILE # PPI-FELD136-NY-4268-7010(a)

Then NICK blinked, and added the latest news reported:

UPDATE THREAT PATTERN

DATA FILE: 12/08/FLFTL/1725HRS/3-22-150M-4320-F

INQUIRY

FILED BY FLORIDA HQ, BOCA

FIELD OF INTEREST: FT. LAUDERDALE, FL

SEE LINKS:

MUZAN, HASSAN

FELDSTEIN, RONA JANET

FELDSTEIN, CARYN—ARREST

FILE # PPI-FELD136-NY-4268-7010(a)

NICK ALERT NICK ALERT NICK ALERT

UPGRADING FELDSTEIN, MORRIS S. TO:

AMBER WATCH

AMBER WATCH

AMBER WATCH

:/

Amber watch! That was about five colors away from a SWAT team kicking down a door somewhere. NICK had always blown him off, with nothing but a blank stare from the monitor.

Now, amber!

Maybe this isn't just another cigar, he thought.

Goddamn amber watch! In Florida! Why me? Why does this always goddamn happen to me?

Agent Fairbanks felt his neck muscles tighten as he glared at his computer screen. It was taunting him with the news of Rona and Morris Feldstein. From Florida. Fifteen hundred miles south of Fairbanks's Long Island jurisdiction. Florida. Where all the action was. The Feldsteins, the terrorists, the Feds, the Jews, the Cubans, the suspicious elections, the suspicious persons of interest, NICK's goddamn amber alerts.

Calm down, Fairbanks coached himself, trying to remember his anger-management sessions.

The Feldsteins were now on Long Island, having brought back their weekend sunburns, their sacks of Florida oranges, and the various federal agencies that trailed them. Resuming their life of crime and their consorting with counterfeiters and terrorists and other enemies of the State. And now that they were back in Fairbanks's jurisdiction, he was ready for them. He would kick in their doors and elbow out his law-enforcement rivals. He would assert his authority and stand at the press conference and feel the warm glare of the klieg lights and the thankful embrace of the media and announce the arrest of Morris and Rona Feldstein for heinous crimes against the government of the United States.

What those crimes were, however, he didn't know at the moment. But, sitting at his desk, his neck muscles pulsating, he resolved to find out.

He would need proximity. Someone to watch the Feldsteins' every move.

He punched at his phone. Agent Russell answered.

"Go pay a visit to that nut, McCord," Fairbanks ordered. "It's time to tighten the noose."

In Washington, Bill Sully dug his thumbs into his temples and nodded his head in disbelief. He had gathered assets from every available federal agency, department, division, bureau, and office in his pursuit of Ricardo Xavier Montoyez. And what happens? Some local yokel in Boca Raton blows the whole thing wide open with an amber watch on NICK. Like one of those tests of the federal emergency broadcast system. Buzzing throughout the entire department. Setting off lights and sirens in the darkness that he craved. Inviting everyone with a colored windbreaker and stenciled acronym to join the investigation. His investigation. They would push in and crowd him out. Assert their jurisdiction. Point him back to his place at the bottom of the law-enforcement food chain. He could already hear the condescension: "Leave this to us, Bill. We're the CIA. You go back to where you belong. To the Meat, Poultry, and Egg Security Division."

I refuse to go back. I've come too far. Built things up. This is my bust. My moment. All I need is some help. A little more help!

And so it began. Bill Sully's quiet but urgent search for

reinforcements. Calling in favors and redeeming chits dispensed across an entire career in the federal criminal justice bureaucracy. Contacting old friends at the Food Safety and Inspection Service and the Animal and Plant Health Inspection Service. Pleading with the boys at the Grain Inspection, Packers and Stockyards Administration, and the Plant Variety Protection Office. Cajoling his human resources contacts at the National Drug Intelligence Center, the INTERPOL-US National Central Bureau, the National Counterintelligence Center, the National Credit Union Administration, the National Crime Prevention and Privacy Compact Council, the Office of Special Counsel, and even the Federal Navigable Lake Ship Inspection Service. Then, just to be sure he had what he needed, Sully reached deep into the Indian Arts and Crafts Board, the International Joint Commission on the US and Canada, the Marine Mammal Commission, and the Susquehanna River Basin Commission. Trading and swapping, loaning and borrowing, transferring and detailing. Moving people from countless boxes on dozens of flowcharts, like a frenzied game of bureaucratic hopscotch. Where everyone's feet landed in Bill Sully's box.

At the FDA.

THE BUSINESS TRIP

THURSDAY, SEPTEMBER 9, 2004

Morris Feldstein drove down Soundview Avenue. In-ground sprinklers hissed and pulsated and sputtered on every lawn. Air conditioners groaned from steel cages next to every home. Stately Tudor homes lined the street, with dark wooden moldings and high-pitched roofs. A canopy of maple tree branches splattered odd-shaped patches of sun on the pavement. Landscaping trucks sat on the sides of the road like infantry vehicles in an army of occupation, a foreign legion of immigrants impressed into lawn-to-lawn combat in the global war on dandelions.

He approached his house, and felt a twinge of nervousness. This time of day there was a good chance of crossing paths with Rona's last appointment. There were, in fact, two paths on the Feldstein's property. One curved from the driveway to the front porch. Lined with evergreen bushes, it wrapped around a chipped aluminum light pole that leaned at a slight angle and bore a sign that said THE F LD-STEINS. (Morris had been meaning to reattach the missing E since it fell off, sometime during the winter of 1987.) The second brick path originated at the separate entrance to Rona's office at the side of the house, then cut straight across the front lawn and terminated at the curb. Rona had wanted to plant a sign on the curb that advertised:

RONA FELDSTEIN, CSW
FAMILY & INDIVIDUAL THERAPY

With one of those bright-yellow happy faces. But Morris knew that the village zoning board frowned upon happy faces on people's curbs.

It was always possible that when Morris came home, one of Rona's patients could be walking down the side path, only thirty feet away. ("Please don't call them patients!" Rona scolded Morris. "That stigmatizes them. They are clients!")

To Morris it seemed the unstigmatized clients walked out of Rona's office as if they were walking the perp line at the county jail. They bowed their heads, hastened their pace, and avoided eye contact. Maybe they thought he was casting judgment on the frayed marriages, the midlife crises, the family feuds, the panic attacks, phobias, and foibles that sent them up and down that path. But Morris didn't stand in judgment of anyone—with the possible exception of the Mets' pitching rotation. He just felt guilty for violating their privacy. So he pretended not to notice them—feigning an urgent fascination with the contents of his trunk, or how the grass was growing next door at the Schiffs'.

Morris drove slowly, craned his neck, and blew a sigh of relief when he saw no car.

He had planned a busy evening. First, there would be the matter of deciding between take-out Mexican, take-out Greek, or take-out kosher deli. After dinner, he would descend into the basement, sit at his junior desk and complete his Celfex Daily Report by pecking at a keyboard with two fingers and e-mailing it to corporate headquarters. Then, he would settle into his RoyaLounger, and watch the game he had recorded between the Mets and the Marlins. And if he still had it in him, there was the possibility of joining Spencer Tracy and Katharine Hepburn on Turner Classic Movies later in the evening.

He pulled into the driveway and saw his across-the-street neighbor, McCord, on his usual vigil, standing like a sentry at the foot of his immaculate blacktop driveway, protecting it from terrorists, criminals, or windswept leaves.

Lately, McCord seemed to be on a heightened state of alert. Watching Morris. Surveilling him in the early mornings when Morris retrieved his newspaper from the curb, and when he left for work and returned home. One night, Morris thought he heard raccoons rummaging through the trash cans at the side of the house. When he opened the front door, he could have sworn he saw McCord dart across Soundview Avenue in night camouflage.

McCord's paranoia, Morris realized, was making him paranoid. He rushed up his brick walk, avoiding eye contact with McCord.

He opened the door and saw two bulging pieces of Rona's luggage, planted smack in the middle of the front hall.

Tsuris. To go.

He heard Rona's urgent footsteps clacking against the ceramic kitchen tile. She appeared in the hall, holding a variety of take-out menus, splayed like a deck of cards.

"Morris? You're home already? How was your day?"

Morris was silent.

"What would you like for dinner? I was thinking maybe Greek."

Morris looked at the luggage and back at Rona. *It seems like a lot to pack just to get some Greek takeout. Unless you're going to take it out from Greece.*

Rona caught the surprised look in Morris's eyes. "Morris, guess what? I'm going back to the condo! On a business trip!"

The Feldstein Anxiety Anticipation Index edged up.

In thirty-four years of marriage, the only "business trip" Rona made was to that little office at the side of the house.

"Remember my Arab friend from Boca? Hassan? He has some friends who need counseling. Persecution complexes I think. Accchhh, all the racism they must experience. I'll do some group therapy. Maybe teach them to meditate. Who knows, maybe I'll open a practice down there! Rona Feldstein. CSW. Florida Office!" She cackled.

Sure, Morris thought. *That's Rona. Counseling Jews in Great Neck and Arabs in Florida. Rona Feldstein. Counseling the world.*

A slight twitching in his stomach overtook his appetite for chicken souvlaki.

"But, Rona. We just got back. Last weekend."

"I know! Isn't it wonderful? A three-hour plane ride and we can come and go as we please. Besides, it's only two days, Morris. I'll leave first thing tomorrow morning and be back Saturday. Just in time for dinner."

"Can't this wait?"

"Well," she said as she puckered her lips, a warning sign that a guilt zone was just ahead, "next week is Rosh Hashanah so that won't work. And the week after is Yom Kippur. When we atone for our sins."

She pronounced the "atone for our sins" part slowly and distinctly. For the benefit of any sinners in the room who might also be hearing impaired.

"But, if you want me to stay here and not see clients while you watch your baseball games and movies, I guess I'll just unpack."

Rona moved slowly toward her luggage, waiting for Morris to say stop.

Morris felt an unusual sensation. Not the usual anxiety accompanied by the release of acids and fluids. This feeling was a soft burning. Like a flame.

Rona stretched out her arms and bent toward the luggage.

Then it happened. That low flame in Morris's gut erupted. Like a fireball, shooting up his stomach and straight into his mouth. Erupting from his cheeks as a withering:

"I'd really rather you not go to Florida, Rona. Not now."

In almost any marriage in America, such a statement would be a civilized way to raise an objection. In thirty-four years of the Feldstein marriage, the words "I'd really rather you not" had never been uttered. There was "Yes, Rona," "Fine, Rona," and "Okay, Rona." This was unprecedented. A violation of the "peace at any price" treaty signed on the Feldsteins' wedding day. A breach of the diplomatic protocols that kept the waves at bay.

And it felt good to Morris! For the first time, refusing to surrender to Rona. Determined to fight. He assumed a self-righteous posture. Something Clint Eastwood might do. Or Gary Cooper in *High Noon*. His legs spread, both hands on his hips. Waiting for Rona to return a fusillade of high-velocity guilt.

"Make my day!" he thought.

He could anticipate what would happen next: how far Rona would roll her eyes upwards, when she would heave her shoulders, how long it would take her to top off her lungs with oxygen, and the duration of the exhalation.

He predicted wrong.

Rona pulled in her cheeks. Her eyes narrowed into slits. Her face turned almost as red as her Clairol Auburn No. 4. Her fingers clenched into tiny fists, shredding the take-out menus. Then she seemed almost paralyzed, gripped by an eerie wordlessness.

Morris sunk his hands into his pockets and began jiggling coins. He visualized the images in the photos of Caryn and Jeffrey on the walls around him. Wondering what would happen next, frozen not only in time but suspense as well.

Watching Rona glare at Morris and Morris jiggle the coins in his pockets.

It was less than a minute, five seconds actually, when Rona's facial muscles untightened and her lips parted just enough for her to force a few words through them. Her voice was gravelly, and she spoke in a tone that was firm, so that even an imbecile like Morris could understand. And when she dropped her Long Island accent, and began pronouncing her Rs, it was a sign of formality. She said: "Excuse me. I have people who need me. In Florida."

"Really, Rona? What are you, the official social worker for Arab towel boys?"

That was the moment when Morris knew how it felt to be a Mets pitcher who threw a game-losing home-run ball. How desperately that pitcher wanted to reclaim the pitch as soon as it was released from his grip; how his stomach dropped when he realized that something bad was going to happen, and all he could do was stand there, watching as the ball wafted toward the batter, waiting for contact. That's how Morris felt the split second after his lips tossed that little bit of patronizing sarcasm at Rona.

But he couldn't take it back. And so he jiggled the change in his pockets faster, blinked helplessly, and waited for Rona to swing away.

Which she did.

"I'm sorry, Morris, that you find it so hard to believe that there are people who want me to travel to Florida to receive my professional services."

There's a long fly ball . . .

"I'm sorry they seem to believe in me. And you don't."

It's well hit. It's way back, way back . . .

"And one more thing."

Morris is at the warning track . . .

"Why should I ask you who I should spend my time with?"

It's at the wall . . .

"When you didn't ask me what woman you should spend your time with?"

It's going, going . . .

"If you know who I mean!"

It's gone! Rona Feldstein hits a grand slam of guilt!

"Now, go get the Greek food. I have more to pack."

Morris Feldstein loses! Loses again!

There was little talk during dinner. Morris pushed his chicken souvlaki back and forth across his plate, his shoulders in a resigned slump. Rona angrily chewed on her Greek salad. *He has some nerve! He gets to have his midlife crisis, cheat on me, then gives me an attitude about a two-day business trip to Florida! All of a sudden he's found a little backbone?*

You know what? He can sit in that chair for two days. Watching his movies and his Mets and not once will he have to watch Wolf Blitzer! Maybe a little loneliness will teach him something. This will be good for us both.

Still, watching Morris's eyes staring at his plate, Rona couldn't help feel some guilt. Suddenly, in the guilt department, she was getting as much as she could give.

They continued eating in silence. Ignoring the raccoons in the bushes. Or whatever it was.

NEIGHBORHOOD WATCH

FRIDAY, SEPTEMBER 10, 2004

Col. (Ret.) Chuck McCord pointed his camera through a narrow separation in the dark drapes of his living room window. He didn't like what he saw. Across the street, the Feldsteins' lawn was overdue for a mowing—again. And if that wasn't bad enough, now there was the matter of Mrs. Feldstein loading her bags in her car and peeling away—without her husband.

Strange behavior set off the clanking of alarms in the Colonel's hair-trigger mind. Col. McCord spent his military retirement keeping his eyes on things from behind the living room drapes, or scanning the street from his immaculately swept porch, or watching from the foot of a driveway that glistened with an annual application of sealant. He methodically entered his observations in his college-ruled spiral-bound notebook, which, once filled with notations, would join a growing collection placed in chronological order in the safe of his "safe room."

In clear and boxy penmanship he wrote:

"FRI 9/10 0800 hrs. Female suspect departs 19 Soundview Ave. Carrying two bags."

"So now what are you looking at?" his wife asked as she poked her head in from the kitchen. She held her favorite coffee mug, the one from the Colonel's secret retirement party, with a picture of Lenin and the imprint: I BROUGHT DOWN THE EVIL EMPIRE AND ALL I GOT WAS THIS LOUSY COFFEE MUG.

"Nothing," McCord insisted.

"What now, Chuck? Communists at the Meltzers'? Aliens at the Slaters'?"

"How about association with terrorists! At the Feldsteins'!" He swung his body toward her, then back to the window, regretting his disclosure. There was a time when you couldn't get something out of him with a cattle prod. Literally. His discipline was slipping. He was getting rusty. He would punish himself later. With a cattle prod.

"Terrorists. At the Feldsteins'. Oooh-kay, I'm going to watch *Good Morning America*. You keep your eyes on the terrorists."

He had heard that mocking tone before. But history always vindicated his suspicions. Who could see around every corner, think five steps ahead, predict threats, and lay out a response?

Colonel (Ret.) Chuck McCord. Patriot.

He climbed the stairs, the exposed wood creaking under his feet, and entered what his wife liked to call "the bunker," even though real bunkers are underground and this one had a second-story view of the McCords' immaculate backyard. McCord locked the door behind him.

He leaned over a desk, connected a cable between a digital camera and a laptop, and began downloading multiple images. Images of Rona loading the suitcases in her car. Images of the car backing out of the driveway. And one unflattering shot of a disheveled Morris Feldstein, loosely wrapped in a bathrobe, bending at his curb to retrieve his morning *Newsday*. He also e-mailed his summary of the conversation he had overheard the night before, while crouching near the Feldsteins' shrubs.

The Colonel pressed Send and watched as a tiny envelope fluttered before whisking off the screen.

Fairbanks's computer pinged with an incoming message: an e-mail from Spymaster432@li.net. He opened the attached photographs. A broad and uncharacteristic smile broke across his face.

"Jesus, Mary, and Morris!"

McCord's message was received. By now, it had probably been intercepted and processed by NICK. Fairbanks's fingers raced against the keyboard.

"C'mon. C'mon. C'mon!" he hoped as his monitor blinked.

Then:

NICK ALERT NICK ALERT NICK ALERT

YELLOW WATCH UPGRADE

NICK HAS FOUND MULTIPLE THREAT PATTERN[S] FOR FELDSTEIN, MORRIS SOLOMON

UPDATED TERROR PATTERN

DATA FILE: 22/08/NYLIFO/1515HRS/0-14-1827-1452-R

FILED BY HATTTL (HON AGENTS TERRORIST-THREAT TIP LINE)

FIELD OF INTEREST: LONG ISLAND, NY

SEE LINKS:

MUZAN, HASSAN

FELDSTEIN, RONA JANET

FILE # PPI-FELD136-NY-4268-7010(a)

NICK ALERT NICK ALERT NICK ALERT

UPGRADING FELDSTEIN, MORRIS S. TO:

YELLOW WATCH

YELLOW WATCH

YELLOW WATCH

:(

MEDITATION FOR MARTYRS

FRIDAY, SEPTEMBER 10, 2004

They are torturing me, thought Pervez. He sat nervously. His eyes clamped shut. Resisting. Resisting. Gasping for air.

"Gently. Breathe gently," the voice commanded.

They were in a darkened room. They had been placed onto straight-back chairs and ordered to sit with their hands on their thighs, palms facing upwards. Pervez could hear a gentle trickle of water and the soft clangs of a wind chime from audio speakers. He had been trained to resist the ear-splitting torture of hard rock. Not Enya.

He sensed the others around him. Hassan, Azad, and Achmed. Breathing in and breathing out.

"Breathe through your nose. Feel the sensation of air as it gently touches your nostrils. Experience the breath. In and out. Breath by breath."

Pervez fought back. His eyelids fluttered and he clenched his fists and gasped for air again.

"Perhaps you should ask Pervez about his mother," Hassan whispered.

"Shaaaaaah," said Rona. Then: "In . . . out . . . in . . . .out. In. Hold it. . . . Now ooouuuuuttttt. Release the pressures."

Pervez thought of the pressures.

The stinging in his cheeks when his father slapped him for not studying the Qur'an.

The pounding on his door when the Taliban delivered the news that Nek, his older brother, had been killed by the NATO men in Afghanistan. The rage at his father for sending Nek across the border to kill the NATO men even if it meant he might be killed by them. The sensation that he would be the next of Nek's eight brothers to die unless he found a way to stay alive.

The persistent voices of the Taliban promising Pervez's father free tuition and hot meals for Pervez at the madrassa. The hate-filled voices of the madrassa teachers telling him the NATO men and the Jews killed Nek. The hot, dry taste of vengeance in his mouth.

The feel, the sound, the smell of his knives entering the flesh of the animals on which he practiced. Animals he imagined as NATO men and Jews and infidels. The feel of the blade against the tips of his young fingers. Slicing his own skin, intentionally drawing his own blood. To feel the blood oozing from his flesh as his brother must have felt. But also to grow accustomed to the pain and the smell and the feel of blood. So that he would not fear taking it or giving it.

He heard Rona, almost whispering: "Now breathe in. Purifying breaths in. Cleansing breaths."

He inhaled. He could feel the knives but he was in his special place: Paradise. He felt the warmth of the sun on his neck as he bent over his knives. He heard the soft gurgling of the cool river next to him. And the cooing of the virgins who had come to admire his skills. Baskets were spread before him. Overflowing with the luscious fruits of Paradise. Grapes and dates and palms; oversized oranges, lustrous red apples, and giant yellow lemons. And platters of juicy meats. He felt the knives slicing through the fruits, releasing pungent juices that trickled onto his fingers. He heard the rhythmic chopping of his blades. He was an artist. Preparing a banquet for a guest list of seventy-two. Plus himself.

Now he was at peace. Breathing free.

Next to him, he could hear the others. The long, relaxed breaths of Hassan, Azad, and Achmed. In their own special places.

After the breathing exercises, they would have what Rona called "Group." Sitting in a small circle around her. Sharing their feelings. At first they were hesitant. But before Rona arrived at the condo/safe house, Hassan told them three things:

First, sharing with Rona would make them better fighters.

Second, it would help clear their minds and sharpen their concentration.

Third, it was no *shonda* to get some help.

Before long, Azad shared his guilt about the adultery he had committed. He had succumbed to a temptress: America. After all these years living under her skirts, how hard it was to resist her seductions! Laughing at her clever wit on HBO and Comedy Central. Humming her songs tentatively during *American Idol*. Gawking at how richly adorned she was in her malls and on her freeways and billboards. Feeling as if his first love, Yemen, was now stifling and dour. His new mistress was scintillating and open. And free.

Of course, Hassan had instructed them not to share anything about their true purpose in America. Because there was a difference between counseling and confession. Especially if the latter landed them in Guantánamo. Plus, Hassan told them that even though he trusted Rona, she could be a bit of a yenta.

At the end of their session, Rona said she would give them certain tools, using her fingers to punctuate the word *tools* in the air. To help them communicate more effectively, to manage their anxieties, and overcome their doubts. To clarify their thoughts and validate their feelings.

Finally, Rona left. Leaving them with something she called a "care package" that she brought from New York: a cellophane-wrapped chocolate babka from Bruce's Bakery, a dozen bagels, and three little blue boxes of Celfex samples from Morris's basement closet.

PART FOUR

WAKE UP, SLEEPER CELL

SUNDAY, SEPTEMBER 19, 2004

"Your long wait has come to an end, brother. Your patience will be rewarded. In Paradise!"

Fakhir smacked his lips so hard that a residue of hummus oozed from both sides of his mouth. Hassan wanted to offer him a napkin, but such a gesture wouldn't be well received by the Official High Representative of the Commander of the Abu al-Zarqawi Martyrs of Militancy Brigade, who also happened to be headwaiter of the Souvlaki City chain restaurant where they were eating. So Hassan nodded, and watched as Fakhir shoveled another spoonful of hummus into his mouth. His heavy jowls wobbled as he chewed.

"How I envy you, Hassan. To be given a mission of such importance to our Prophet. To be at the door to Paradise."

And how I envy you, thought Hassan. *To be waiting tables in a*

Souvlaki City franchise, making nice tips and gorging on free falafels while I plan to blow myself up.

Earlier that day, Hassan had received a text message instructing him to meet "your old family friend" at Souvlaki City in Fort Lauderdale. That was prearranged code, and when Hassan read it his hands trembled. Sure enough, when he arrived at the restaurant, Fakhir the waiter greeted him, led him to a reserved table in a dark corner, far away from any patrons, and instead of taking his order, took a seat. Being a waiter, it turned out, was just Fakhir's day job. His real career was controlling several dozen al-Zarqawi sleeper cells embedded on the East Coast of the United States.

Rona would have said, "Who knew?" But Hassan chose not to say that to Fakhir.

"You will attack in about two weeks," Fakhir declared. "Make your preparations."

Hassan sat, shredding a napkin. "I do not think two weeks is enough time."

"You have orders, brother. Two weeks." And then, after popping an entire grape leaf into his mouth, Fakhir said, "After so many years on inactive status, I would think you would be anxious to . . ."

Blow myself up? Not really. I mean, there are certain things you don't rush into.

"There are problems. Achmed suffers from separation anxiety disorder. Azad? Antisocial personality disorder. And don't get me started on Pervez."

Fakhir stopped chewing long enough to raise his eyebrows. "You have been watching too many episodes of *Dr. Phil* on American television. What is it with this country, anyway? Every channel you watch has a psychiatrist!"

Hassan thought: *You know who deserves her own show? Rona! Much better than those celebrity shrinks on TV.*

"What will we attack?"

Fakhir pushed his hummus to the side, leaned in, and said softly:

"You will attack the infidels nearby. In Miami."

"What is the target?"

Now Fakhir smiled. "Perhaps if you watched more news and less *Dr. Phil*, you would know. In Miami, on September thirtieth, the Americans will hold an election debate on their national television. Between the candidates for President. You will blow the whole thing up. The whole world will watch, *Inshallah*."

Gottenyu, thought Hassan, but he chose not to share that with Fakhir either.

DROP THE GUITAR!

TUESDAY, SEPTEMBER 21, 2004

Squeezed in at the rear of the White House Situation Room, Jon Pruitt felt like the unwelcome but necessary wedding guest. Every once in a while Karl Rove or Scooter Libby would throw menacing glances his way from their corner of the room. But Pruitt felt protected in his corner, blocked by the crowd of Homeland Security, National Security, Aviation, Immigration, and Customs officials who hovered around him.

The managers of an unfolding crisis sat around a large conference table. The Vice President at the head, his eyes frozen on a large screen; Pruitt's boss, the Secretary of Homeland Security, who responded to every development with a heave of the shoulders; the Attorney General; the heads of the recently reconfigured Transportation Security Administration; US Immigration and Customs Enforcement; US Customs and Border Protection, and the Federal Aviation Administration.

All the deck chairs on the *Titanic*, rearranged in the White House.

The crisis at hand was an incoming threat, traveling hundreds of miles per hour, pointed at the East Coast of the United States.

A United Airlines jetliner was carrying suspected terrorist Yusef Islam.

Or, as he was more commonly known, Cat Stevens. The singer and songwriter.

The man who wrote the words "Oh baby, baby, it's a wild world" was about to understand just how wild a world it was.

"Are we sure about this?" Pruitt had asked the Homeland Security Secretary as they sped toward the White House.

Ridge responded, "Yusef Islam is on the no-fly list. The Vice President wants the plane intercepted and diverted."

"Lots of people are on that list who shouldn't be. This will be awfully embarrassing if we're wrong." Pruitt sighed.

"He converted to Islam. He is accused of financially supporting known terrorist organizations in violation of US law."

"He wrote 'Peace Train.'"

Now, the Vice President commanded the effort that would prove America's willingness to pay any price and bear any burden in the struggle against rock.

"Status," snapped Cheney.

"Fighters are scrambled," someone in a blue air force uniform reported. "The United crew has been ordered to divert to Bangor."

Pruitt was going to suggest the evacuation of Maine, but decided to keep that to himself since Cheney was likely to agree and maybe double-down with Massachusetts. Can't vote for Kerry if you are living in a Red Cross shelter in Vermont.

Next to Pruitt, an official clutching a batch of papers suddenly whispered, "Oh shit. Goddamit!"

"What's wrong?" Pruitt asked.

"You don't know the proper spelling of the name Yusef by any chance, do you?"

"Is it Y-o-u-s-e-f? Or Y-u-s-e-f?"

"No clue. Why?"

"'Cause the Yusef on this flight may not be the right terrorist. It's the guy with an O in his name who's on the no-fly list. Not the guy whose plane we just intercepted."

"Fuck!" said Pruitt. Then, just to make a point, he added, "This is with a U."

"Should I tell them?"

Why, thought Pruitt. *The birds are up in the air. The flight is headed to Bangor. They'll get their pre-election headlines that the Administration stopped another color-coded threat. And maybe in a few weeks, there will be a story on page A20 of the* Washington Post *that they had the wrong guy and no threat.*

Meanwhile, a grateful nation will celebrate stopping a man whose worst crime was the song "I Love My Dog."

LONG DISTANCE

THURSDAY, SEPTEMBER 23, 2004

In the Martyrs of Militancy safe house—also known as the Feldstein family condo in Boca—Hassan found a quiet room away from his comrades. He sat on an edge of the Feldsteins' bed, atop a floral comforter that still smelled new. He could hear the rhythmic chopping of Pervez's favorite dagger against a cutting board in the kitchen, and the drone of *Dr. Phil* on the flat screen in the living room. It was dark, and Hassan whispered cautiously into a phone:

"Hello, Mrs. Feldstein."

"Hassan? Oh my God, are you all right? You haven't called! I thought something happened, God forbid."

That he had called three days before didn't ease his guilt.

"I am sorry. I have been very busy. I—"

"I almost called the emergency rooms to make sure you were okay."

Try calling after September thirtieth, he thought.

"Everything is fine."

"What's wrong, Hassan? I can tell from your voice something is bothering you."

"Nothing. I am—"

"Are you having that pain?"

It was late September, and things were slow at the main pool at the Paradise. No tourists, no bikinis. No bikinis, no groin pain.

"I feel okay, Mrs. Feldstein."

"It's Pervez, isn't it?! Is he taking his Celalax?"

"Pervez is fine. He is chopping up a nice fruit salad in the kitchen right now."

"Tell him not to forget to mix in my secret ingredient."

"He will not forget."

"So *nu*? If it's not Pervez, what is it?"

If Hassan could have, he would have erupted into infantile wailing to his surrogate Jewish mother. He would have cried to Rona about how he was about to execute his mission and would never see her again. He would have blubbered that he did not want to go to Miami, or, after that, in a million pieces to Paradise. He would have admitted that folding towels seemed like a better long-term growth opportunity than a suicide bombing.

If he allowed it, he would have told her about the other night, when he went online and researched the Florida Atlantic University degree program in Hospitality Management, and how just before hitting the SEND ME MORE INFORMATION banner, he felt an overpowering sense of betrayal to the Martyrs back in Tora Bora. He had sat paralyzed at the computer, caught between the guilt of moving forward and the guilt of moving backwards.

But Hassan could not share these things. And so he willed himself to move ahead.

To the presidential debate, in one week, where he would hit a career dead end. Literally.

"I am fine, Mrs. Feldstein. In fact, I have decided to go home. To visit my mother. In Kuwait."

"Ohhhhh, how nice! Accchhh, I'm so proud. Are you surprising her?"

"Yes, it will be a big surprise. To everyone. So please say nothing, Mrs. Feldstein."

"My lips are sealed, Hassan. I'm like a vault. Remember . . . therapist-client confidentiality. When do you leave on your trip?"

"Next Thursday. One week from today. From Miami."

"You know what? I'll FedEx you some rugallah from Bruce's Bakery. You can take it with you."

Nothing like a light nosh before a suicide bombing. So we don't have to blow ourselves up on an empty stomach.

Rona said, "Promise me you will call when you get there so I know you're okay."

"Yes, Mrs. Feldstein."

"Take your pills."

"I will, Mrs. Feldstein."

"And, Hassan, don't forget to tell Pervez about my secret ingredient in the fruit salad. So the fruit doesn't turn brown. It's important."

"Yes, Mrs. Feldstein."

FBI Agent Alonso Diaz listened, rewound the tape, and played it again:

"And, Hassan, don't forget to tell Pervez about my secret ingredient in the fruit salad. So the fruit doesn't turn brown. It's important."

Secret ingredient. Fruit salad. Riiiiggghhhtttt.

Next Thursday, he thought. *Miami. Connect the dots. Think ahead.*

Oh my God, the bastards are going to hit the presidential debate in Miami! With biological or chemical or even nuclear weapons.

Or lemon juice.

TASK FORCE FELDSTEIN

FRIDAY, SEPTEMBER 24, 2004

Even Jon Pruitt, who was generally skeptical about the federal government's threat assessments, was concerned about the intelligence advisory that trickled through the highest offices in Washington that Friday morning. He raced through the West Wing to the emergency meeting that had been convened in the Vice President's office. Inside, standing behind his desk, Dick Cheney was studying the written advisory, sneering at its audacity. The Secretary of Homeland Security, the head of the Secret Service, the FBI Director, and Porter Goss, who had been confirmed by the Senate two days before as CIA Director, sat on two couches. As they read their copies of the intel report, they nodded their heads in syncopated disbelief.

Scooter Libby and Karl Rove huddled in a corner. They could have waved a banner at Pruitt proclaiming WE TOLD YOU SO! But that was unnecessary. It was all over their faces.

Cheney looked up from the report. "The Abu al-Zarqawi Army of Jihad Martyrs of Militancy Brigade. Is this some sort of joke?"

"It's nuts!" agreed Homeland Security Secretary Ridge, slapping his hand on his knee. "How do they expect to target a presidential debate? It's the most protected venue on the planet!"

Cheney responded: "Even al-Qaeda has rational operational thinkers. This," he waved the report in the air, "just doesn't seem credible."

Porter Goss cleared his throat. "That may be the point, Mr. Vice President. We have analysis suggesting an attack against a high-profile event, like the internationally televised presidential debate, is both operationally and strategically rational for the al-Zarqawi network. For two reasons: One, it would be a potentially devastating blow against us if they could pull it off. Which no one believes they can. And two, there is a growing rivalry between global jihadist groups. This would be a powerful, demoralizing blow to al-Qaeda, even if it fails. This would signal to terrorists around the world that the new power in town is . . ." Goss glanced at the report, "the Abu al-Zarqawi Army of Jihad Martyrs of Militancy Brigade, the people with the bravery to attack a US presidential debate."

Sounds like a good television commercial on Al Jazeera, Pruitt thought. *We're Abu al-Zarqawi and we approve this message.*

"So we should not underestimate their willingness to attack the debate next Thursday," Goss finished.

Cheney nodded. "In fact, they have experienced some success so far. Embedding a cell in South Florida. Recruiting a Jewish couple in New York. Running a counterfeit-drug ring to fund their operations. And all under the radar, may I add, with hardly any human intelligence picking them up."

That was Cheney's dig at the conventional intel assets that had failed to detect threats in the past, and a silent homage to NICK.

The FBI Director said, "We have enough to go on to issue arrest warrants and take them into custody immediately. My guys are ready to go."

The Secret Service Director said, "We should reschedule the presidential debate as a precaution."

Cheney scowled. "That is exactly what we will not do. We will not cave in to terrorists by postponing the debate, a premier demonstration to the world of freedom and democracy. It sends an unmistakable signal of weakness. Next we'll be considering rescheduling elections."

Which, thought Karl Rove, *might be a good idea*. But only in certain states.

"And we're not going to make arrests . . . yet. We've got six days between now and the debate. Six days of intel gathering to assess how deep and how far this al-Zarqawi network goes. The American people need to know that they have infiltrated our suburbs, our resort hotels. On Long Island. In Boca Raton for God's sake! So we're going to monitor them for the next few days. Cast a wide net. See who else we catch and where we catch them."

Everyone nodded their heads. Even Pruitt. Begrudgingly.

"As for next week's debate, we won't let them get near it. But we'll let them get close enough to catch them in the act. Announce it the day of the debate. And turn this thing from a televised political debate to 'The Kennedy Center Honors President Bush.'"

Cheney thought about John Kerry's opening statement at the debate. Something like: "Mr. President, let me just take a moment to thank you for saving my ass and once again saving the American people from another mortal threat to our way of life. And now, in my remaining time, let me tell you why you need to be replaced . . ."

And speaking of saving asses, Cheney thought, *let me cover my own*.

"Just to be clear, I am specifically not saying or suggesting or even intimating that we should proceed with the debate if it places the President or any innocent Americans in a dangerous situation. The President is not bait."

And don't read anything into my failure to mention Senator Kerry in the aforementioned statement.

"I am saying we will commence an operation to monitor the al-Zarqawi group's movements to disrupt their plan while gathering as much intel as possible about their network and operations within and outside of the homeland."

The Vice President continued, "I want a joint-agency task force all over the al-Zarqawi cell in Florida. If one of them takes a crap I want our guys dusting the toilet paper for prints. And I want a task force on their New York recruits: Rona and Morris Feldstein. They are committing treason against the United States. They are aiding and abetting the enemy. Pull in every counter-terror asset we have. Put predator drones above their house if you have to!"

"With Hellfire missile authorization?" asked the newly confirmed CIA Director, maybe not as a joke.

Rookie exuberance, thought Cheney.

"I will have operational control of all decisions made by Task Force Boca and Task Force Feldstein."

"But—"

Before Pruitt could continue, Cheney said, "Under the express authorization granted to me by the President in Executive Order one-five-three-two-zulu-zulu-two." Which had been written by Cheney himself and might as well have been filed under "Things the President Signed But Couldn't Be Told Why."

The Secret Service Director seemed restless. "Sir, respecting your authority, I wish to register my deep concern with placing the President in a situation with a known elevated threat."

Cheney scowled. *What part of the cover my ass part did you miss, asshole?* "We will disrupt and dismember the cell before they come close to being a viable threat. But just to put your mind at ease, you may provide the President with additional personal protection. I'm sure your tech guys have some toys they'd like him to try on. Spend whatever you need."

Magic words in Washington.

"I want every Cabinet department on this task force."

"Everyone? Even the EPA?"

"Okay, not them. But all the others. We should call this the JTFF. Joint Task Force Feldstein." Cheney gave a satisfied smile, knowing that in Washington, nothing said power like a good acronym. With the word *joint*.

Libby said, "Sir, J-T-F-F may get confused with the J-T-T-F."

"What's that?"

"Joint Terrorism Task Force."

"No. J-T-F-F versus J-T-T-F. One has an extra F and the other an extra T. It's clear as day, Scooter. The American people aren't stupid. They know the difference between an F and a T."

"Yes, sir," Libby replied. "I suppose you want the Director of National Intelligence on the JTFF?"

"Yes, but not the Director of Central Intelligence."

"Check. Yes to DNI, no to DCI."

Director Goss's shoulders slumped.

"How about the OIC?" someone piped in.

"Who?"

"Office of Intelligence and Counterintelligence."

"Fine," said Cheney.

"Well, you can't invite the OIC and not include the OIA!" said the Homeland Security Secretary.

"OIA?" asked Cheney.

"Office of Intelligence and Analysis," Libby answered. "At DHS."

"Oh, fine. OIC and OIA. But that's it."

"Actually . . ." Libby sighed.

"What?"

"I just don't see JTFF without ONSI. The Office of National Security Intelligence at DEA. And if ONSI is in, you have to invite the Office of Terrorism and Financial Intelligence at Treasury. How do you have a JTFF with ONSI but no OTFI?"

"That wouldn't be right," someone said.

"Let me think that one over," replied Cheney. "So how many do we have?"

Libby reported: "The DNI but not the DCI. OIC and OIA. ONSI and maybe OTFI. And all the Cabinet agencies. But not EPA."

"Okay. That wraps it up?"

"Well, we should probably add Customs and Border Protection."

"Or maybe Immigration and Customs Enforcement?"

"What's the difference?" asked Cheney.

No one remembered.

"Fine. They can both come. Anyone else?"

Pruitt thought, *What? No room for the Hoover Dam Police?*

Cheney adjourned the meeting.

"Jesus H., now the whole world is watching," Agent Tom Fairbanks muttered as he stared incredulously at his computer screen on Long Island. Agent Russell stood nearby, wringing his fingers and shifting his weight.

All my work, my surveillance, my careful case management. Shot to hell by NICK. Sending urgent threat advisories to everyone from the Agriculture Department to the National Zoo! Introducing them all to Rona and Morris Feldstein. Jesus H., this case was mine. My bust! and I've been shoved aside by a goddamn computer.

Fairbanks sat back in his chair, rocking back and forth.

Now what? Let the others grab the glory? Go back to staring at multicolored pins stuck onto that giant map of Long Island on the wall? Making the world safe for another Starbucks?

No way, he thought. Joint Task Force Feldstein might be all over Morris and Rona Feldstein. But Fairbanks knew how these things worked. All these agencies stumbling all over one another. Dancing the bureaucratic version of the hokey pokey: you put your right hand in, you put your left hand out. Except that the right hand had no idea what the left hand was doing. Meanwhile, Fairbanks had McCord, just across the street from Feldstein, so close he would be able to pounce before anyone else.

This bust will be mine.

After all, one benefit to being ignored by everybody is that nobody knows who you are. Or whom you know.

LAP DANCE

FRIDAY, SEPTEMBER 24, 2004

Ricardo Montoyez loved a good lap dance. Particularly at the Merry-Go-Round Lounge in Melville. After weeks at the Bella Abzug Home for the Aged, it would be a pleasant and necessary diversion.

He had driven from Riverdale across the Whitestone Bridge and back to Long Island. He took the Long Island Expressway east toward Melville. At one point, near a sign that said MANHASSET NEXT EXIT he thought about that restaurant, Murphy's, and the receptionist, Victoria. The memory stirred his groin, which gave him the idea for the lap dance.

But first he would check on some business matters. Business before pleasure.

In Melville, he drove past the steel-and-glass valley of office buildings, including one that was known to house several US government offices. He pulled into the parking lot of a small, squat building painted dark purple with a weather-beaten canopy of fading pink.

Even now, in late afternoon, there were several cars at the Merry-Go-Round Lounge, driven from the nearby offices of accountants, lawyers, engineers, bankers, and even an occasional federal employee taking a titillation break.

The club was dingy and cramped and reeked of stale beer. "Entertainers" prowled the floor in search of a parking spot on someone's lap. Guns N' Roses blared from overhead speakers.

The crowd was sparse. But paying customers didn't necessarily pay the bills here at the Merry-Go-Round.

Ernie, a wiry assistant manager who doubled as a bouncer, approached Montoyez and whispered, "A shipment came. It's in the back."

Montoyez nodded and walked toward a door with an oversized red sign that said, AUTHORIZED PERSONNEL ONLY. He stepped inside.

The room was large and brightly lit. Dozens of plastic picnic coolers, red and blue, lined the walls. Water was puddled on a yellow linoleum floor.

A FedEx carton sat on a table. Montoyez read the shipping label. It came from AAA Pharmaceutical Wholesalers.

Just what the doctor ordered!

He peered into one of the coolers. Hundreds of tiny vials containing low doses of a medication called Epogen were immersed in a solution of soapy water. Their labels had all fallen off cleanly. Soon, freshly printed labels—falsely indicating a higher dose—would be applied to each vial. Cha-ching!

The miracle of modern medicine!

Of course, this markup might cause some inconvenience to the unsuspecting patient who injected the wrong dose into his blood stream: violent convulsions, extreme pain, permanent liver damage. Death.

But, Montoyez figured, *isn't that the cost of doing business?*

And besides, the risk of getting caught was low. Thanks to the lobbying clout of the pharmaceutical industry on Capitol Hill, regulations to keep America's pharmaceutical supplies safe by tracking their movements—through a strip club, for instance—had been thwarted. It was easier to recall a defective toaster oven than a counterfeit medication.

Maybe that will be my next gig, after I'm done profiting from the contamination of lifesaving medications. Maybe I'll become a pharmaceutical lobbyist.

He shuddered.

His business now in order, it was time for pleasure.

As soon as he reentered the club, his sixth sense detected trouble. He looked across the room, past the dancing and writhing Brandees and Stormees, and saw a man sitting by the stage, focusing on two massive and bare breasts approaching his face.

Junior G-Man.

Montoyez could tell by the discount suit, the blue polyester tie rumpled against a bluer polyester shirt. Plus the official identification on a lanyard dangling around his neck.

So much for the lap dance, Montoyez thought as he headed for a back door.

Near the stage, a dancer named Summer Rayne bent toward the agent and accepted a five-dollar bill between her breasts.

Agent Russell sported an embarrassed smile.

40

YOM KIPPUR CONFESSION

SATURDAY, SEPTEMBER 25, 2004

"It never rains on Yom Kippur!" Rona exclaimed.

A cool drizzle fell across Great Neck. Morris and Rona drove to Temple Beth Torah to the soft whooshing of his windshield wipers and the angry proclamations of callers to WFAN demanding that the Mets "trade away the whole friggin' team" before next spring.

Morris was anxious.

It was the strangest Day of Atonement of his life. A man who refuses to make waves generally doesn't have a lot of atoning to do. On this day, however, he had specific sins to acknowledge and some major forgiveness for which to beg. Morris was anxious to get things rolling, to wipe the slate clean.

Suddenly traffic on Middle Neck Road stopped, and brake lights glared at Morris through the rain-streaked windshield. In the distance, he saw the ominous swirl of police lights against the gray sky.

"Oh my God!" cried Rona. "Something happened at the temple! On Yom Kippur of all days!"

Traffic nudged forward and the police lights grew more intense, along with Morris's anxiety. He was close enough to see that the Nassau County Police Department was detaining vehicles that were turning into the synagogue parking lot, and waving ahead those that weren't.

Morris eased his car to the checkpoint and lowered his window. He was always intimidated by police officers. For some reason, their presence induced guilt, as if he'd done something wrong. If the officer at the checkpoint had accused Morris of kidnapping the Lindbergh baby, he would have thought, *Well, they must know something I don't,* and extended his wrists for the handcuffing.

But there was no accusation. Just a question: "Are you a congregant?"

Before he could stammer his answer, Rona proclaimed: "Excuuuuuse me! He's second vice president of the Men's Club! Morris Feldstein!" Which made Morris wince.

The officer checked a list. And when he did, his eyes widened. "Go ahead," the officer said warily.

The High Holy Day at Temple Beth Torah always attracted the high rollers: BMWs, Jaguars, Mercedes, and Lexuses. For a people who wandered in the wilderness for forty years, a Range Rover was now essential for a drive of forty yards. But today, the lot was unusually crowded with bland Fords and Chevys, as if the General Services Administration was having a surplus auto auction.

Morris found a spot, and he and Rona rushed toward the entrance. The Al Lieberman Vestibule was packed with the usual Yom Kippur crowd. They came to the synagogue once a year. They sat in God's general admission section to admit their sins. Then they rushed home to begin a new season of sinning.

On this Yom Kippur, however, Morris noticed many strange, new faces.

• • •

Tom Fairbanks stood inside the Leonard Cooperman Auxiliary Catering Hall, set up to accommodate the overflow penitents from the main sanctuary. He scanned the crowded room and scowled. This undercover operation had all the subtlety of the Normandy Invasion. It would take, maybe, a half second to expose the Feds. They were the ones who propped yarmulkes crookedly on their scalps and seemed puzzled by prayer books printed from right to left. In this room, the G in G-Men meant gentile.

As second vice president of the Men's Club, Morris was entitled to two seats near the front of the main sanctuary, about ten rows from where the rabbi and the cantor led the services. Close enough to the action but far enough not to be noticed. But on this Yom Kippur, Morris sensed that as he and Rona worked their way up crowded aisles, several heads turned toward them, following their progress until they sat.

The congregation fell silent as the rabbi began the service:

"In the tribunal of heaven and the tribunal of earth, by the permission of God—blessed be He—and by the permission of this holy congregation, we hold it lawful to pray with the transgressors."

For a moment, Morris thought the rabbi was staring straight at him.

The service continued. The congregation read silently and aloud, in English and Hebrew. They arrived at the core of the worship, the Amidah, a series of blessings recited silently while standing. And since it was a silent prayer, Morris took a liberty and asked God to bless the Mets and help them win the National League eastern division playoffs. But Morris also prayed for Rona and Jeffrey and Caryn.

And for himself.

Then they came to one of the most familiar Yom Kippur prayers, the "Al-Chet" (which Morris always pronounced with guttural exaggeration as "al cccchhhhaaaayt"). It was a literal checklist of sins, to be recited one by one, each punctuated by a clenched fist beaten against the heart. It was the Super Bowl of sin, a collective gathering of Jews reciting transgressions and mistakes, crimes and misdemeanors, vices and violations. Confessions uttered through stammering lips, the words rising to heaven, like bringing out a soiled blanket and flapping it in the air and watching the dirt and dust carried off by the winds, chanted in tiny shuls and glittering synagogues throughout the world.

Morris began reading aloud sins of generality. All-purpose sins. One size fits all sins.

"For the sin which we have committed before You with immorality . . .

"And for the sin which we have committed before You by improper thoughts . . .

"For the sin which we have committed before You by a gathering of lewdness . . .

"For all these, God of pardon, pardon us, forgive us, atone for us."

And he chanted some sins he didn't quite understand:

"For the sin which we have committed before You by casting off the yoke . . .

"And for the sins for which we are obligated to bring a burnt-offering . . .

"And for the sins for which we are obligated to bring a guilt-offering for a certain or doubtful trespass . . .

"For all these, God of pardon, pardon us, forgive us, atone for us."

And then, pounding his fist against his chest a bit harder, Morris confessed some more. Silently. Urgently:

For the sin of putting a personal lunch with Victoria D'Amico at the Sunrise Diner on my Celfex credit card . . .

For the sin of coveting Doctor Kirleski's receptionist and taking her to the Bayview Motor Inn for a total of twenty-two minutes . . .

For the sin of calling in sick that Friday just so I could go to Boca with Rona . . .

For the sin of fighting with Rona and referring to her clients as patients . . .

For all these, God of pardon, pardon me, forgive me, atone for me . . .

He closed his eyes. So tight that his face seemed twisted in pain. Trying to squeeze out the guilt and the sins and the anxiety.

And when he opened them, having confessed his sins, he couldn't help but wonder: *Why is everyone looking at me?*

BABKA & BULLETS

SUNDAY, SEPTEMBER 26, 2004

Morris awoke the next morning and groggily wrapped his flannel robe around his striped pajamas, slipped his feet in his leather slippers, and lumbered outside in search of the morning *Newsday*, which was usually flung at his curb.

The morning was crisp, a sign that autumn was arriving on Long Island, and that maybe Morris's summer of tsuris was over. As if God had sent the fresh winds to cleanse Morris. A Yom Kippur miracle! He pulled his robe tight and shook off a chill.

Soundview Avenue was unusually busy, especially for a Sunday morning, as if an army of landscapers, utility companies, and home-improvement contractors had mounted a coordinated Fall Makeover of the block. For a moment, Morris thought that some kind of movie was being filmed and that he was the star. All the workers nearby seemed to pause for a split second to steal glances at him.

As he leaned to pick up the blue plastic bag that contained his *Newsday*, he noticed something else, something that confirmed that his paranoia might be deserved. His neighbor Col. McCord had left the sanctity of his gleaming driveway and was crossing the street. Toward Morris! Now the Feldstein Anxiety Anticipation Index was triggered. In the past, on that infrequent occasion when the Colonel and Morris made unavoidable eye contact, both would mumble a forced "Hi" while maintaining a thirty-foot barrier of road between them. But now the Colonel was almost sauntering toward Morris.

They stood face-to-face.

"Good morning!" said the Colonel cheerfully.

"Hello" was all that Morris could muster in response. He tried to flatten his sleep-whipped hair with his hand.

"Feels like fall is comin' in, huh?"

"Yes. Chilly."

The Colonel turned his sharp nose into the air and sniffed. "I'd say fifty-six, maybe fifty-seven."

"Yes. Fall" was all Morris could think to say. He began to turn away, clutching the *Newsday* against his chest.

And then the Colonel said, "The wife thought we should get together one night. For coffee."

Oh God, thought Morris. *Not that. Please, pass the cream, Colonel. But put down the AK-47 first.*

"Yes, I'll mention that to my wife. They can organize things."

"How about tonight? Seven o'clock work?"

Morris felt a twinge in his stomach. *Tonight? Well, I have an appointment on cable TV with Cary Grant and Deborah Kerr at eight, and then I'm expecting Spencer Tracy and Katharine Hepburn at ten. So, no, tonight just isn't possible. But thank you anyway.*

"Seven-thirty?" McCord offered.

The discomfort flared from his stomach to his lower chest.

This was not going in the right direction for Morris.

Another moral dilemma.

On one hand, saying no would be making waves. And lately, Morris was barely keeping his head above the darkening waves.

On the other hand, Morris could not fathom how to pass a Sunday evening with the McCords. The only thing they shared was the thirty feet of asphalt that separated them. What would they talk about? What's the dress code? Weekend casual or desert camouflage? *Just say no, Morris. Just look at the Colonel and tell him you cannot accept his invitation and maybe another time but thank you very much.*

He heard the Colonel ask, "Eight okay?"

Morris Feldstein stood straight, gathered his shoulders, looked the Colonel directly in the eyes, and said, "Eight sounds fine."

As they left for the trek across Soundview Avenue, Morris asked, "Are you sure a chocolate babka from Bruce's Bakery is appropriate?"

Rona held the white cardboard box tied with red-and-white string protectively close, as if it were the Hope Diamond. "Oh, Morris, who doesn't love Bruce's babka?"

A guy whose favorite meals are rations in Iraq, thought Morris.

They proceeded across the street. Leaves were beginning to scatter on front lawns across Soundview Avenue, and Morris heard Rona emit a soft *brrrrr* against the cool night air. At night, the McCords' house had all the charm of a state prison. There were small lights directed at the perimeter of the lawn, larger lights aimed at every door and window, and several lights that bathed the entire property in a luminance so powerful that it might be detected by the International Space Station. Squinting, the Feldsteins approached the front door and rang the bell. Morris thought he heard the "Marines' Hymn" inside.

The door opened and Linda McCord appeared. Morris thought he last saw her on a *Leave It to Beaver* rerun. Coiffed blond hair, a face untouched by age, conservative dress, and even pearls around her neck. "Well, hello neighbors," she said with a sparkling smile. "Come in. The Colonel is in the gun room. I'll get him."

They stepped inside and Morris whispered, "It seems like a lovely house."

"Morris, did she say 'gun room' or 'fun room?' "

"I think the gun room is the fun room," he replied.

A door opened, and the evening's master of ceremonies appeared. He wore stiff khaki pants and a starched white shirt. And he greeted his guests by looking at his watch and saying, "Five after eight. Traffic?"

Rona and Morris exchanged nervous glances. And before either could stammer an excuse, the Colonel erupted into staccato bursts of laughter. The kind of laughter that sounds like a machine gun firing. Which seemed appropriate to Morris.

"C'mon in, neighbors. Linda, why don't you and Mrs. Feldstein set out the coffee in the living room? And I'll show Morris around."

Morris wanted to say, "If I'm not back in an hour, call the police and check the fun room." But he didn't.

"Follow me," the Colonel said. As he was a colonel and officially outranked Morris, who was merely a second vice president at the synagogue Men's Club, Morris complied.

They walked through a dim hallway lined with a single row of black-and-white photographs hanging in perfect symmetry and framed in brown-varnished wood. Each photo featured primitive-looking camps of mud huts, guard towers, sand bags, and concertina wire.

Sure, thought Morris. *We have Feldstein Family Fun Photos on display, and you have scenes from the movie* Platoon.

"Some of my favorite places in the world, Morris!" the Colonel said happily. He pointed. "This is a forward operating base in Somalia. That one there is on the Kuwait-Iraq border during Desert Storm, before the shit show. That one, near Hanoi in seventy-two. And this one is—actually I can't tell you where it is without the appropriate security clearances. Do you have any security clearances, Morris?"

The best Morris could come up with was his Nassau County All-Parks annual pass. "Not really," he mumbled.

"That's too bad. I have a slide show that would knock your socks off."

Literally, thought Morris.

"Let's join the wives, eh? Smells like there's a Bruce's chocolate babka calling our names."

Rona and Linda were sitting opposite each other on stiff leather couches, separated by a glass table covered with a coffee service and desserts. Morris noticed heavy brown curtains pulled tightly across a bay window. Near the fireplace, a big dog slept, his back heaving and sinking with every breath. The walls were adorned with the usual knickknacks you might pick up at a home goods store, if the name of the store was Wars "R" Us.

Rona was showing photos of the children, and Linda nodded at each one, her eyes glazed over. Then, with a tone of relief, Linda chirped, "Well, here are our two men! What have you been up to?"

"I've been showing Morris the front!" barked the Colonel.

Morris made a note to tell Rona later that by "front" the Colonel didn't mean his lawn.

Morris sat next to Rona, and as the Colonel positioned himself on the opposite couch, Morris saw something that brought the Feldstein Anxiety Anticipation Index to record-breaking levels.

As the Colonel sat, his khaki pants crept up on his left leg, revealing brown socks, an ankle holster, and a black pistol.

In the "Excuse me, your fly is open" category of social awkwardness, this was entirely new territory to Morris. *Pardon me, your Glock is showing.*

The Colonel, realizing the exposure, tugged his cuff over the gun and said, "I've been all over the world but there's nothing like Bruce's babka!"

That bit of small talk out of the way Colonel McCord began his interrogation.

"Sooo . . . what do you think of the elections?"

Rona hesitated. Morris followed her eyes. She was watching him spilling sugar all over the saucer, missing most of his cup.

"It looks like a close race," she offered.

"Nah," McCord scoffed. "Bush in a landslide. How can any patriotic American vote for Kerry? Bush showed the world: You mess with America, you get a Hellfire missile so precise it'll find you in your tent and slice off your dick."

Morris and Rona slurped their coffee at the same time.

"Language, Chuck," said Linda.

The Colonel grumbled "Sorry," then said, "anyway, Linda and I vote the three Gs: God, guns, and gays."

Gottenyu, thought Morris.

"Where do you stand on those issues?"

Morris popped a healthy chunk of babka into his mouth to avoid answering.

"Well, we're not exactly one of those gun nuts, if you know what I mean," said Rona.

Morris assumed that "gun nut" was not a term appreciated by a man who wore a gun. On his ankle. For coffee and babka.

"And as for gays," Rona continued to Morris's accelerated chewing, "Morris and I have always believed, 'Live and let live.'"

The Colonel smiled. "Yeah, that's a nice attitude. If you're living in a dream world. But I've seen the real world. And it's not too pretty. I mean, take the Muslims. You want to live and let them live in our country? When they're trying to impose their laws on us? How do you feel about that?"

"What time is it?" Morris croaked through a mouthful of babka.

"Well," Rona exhaled, "I certainly don't want to surrender my civil liberties and tear up the Constitution out of fear. That would give the terrorists a victory. And besides, not every Muslim is a terrorist, you know."

The Colonel fixed his eyes on Rona like a radar scanning for signs of imminent threat. He leaned back in his chair, folded his hands and said, "My dear, if nine-eleven wasn't a wake-up call to this country, I don't know what is. And if we don't deal with the radical-ization of Muslims right here in America, you can kiss it all good-bye. We're in a clash of civilizations, Mrs. Feldstein. It's the fourteenth century versus the twenty-first century. And if we don't buck up and do what's necessary, and even messy, the fourteenth century wins. At which point all your civil liberties are replaced with Sharia law. And something tells me that the Islamic States of America won't look too kindly on people like you."

Morris wondered, *By "you" does he mean Jew? Or is he referring to social workers in general?*

"Enough politics," Linda chided her husband with the wave of a hand. "So, what do you do for entertainment? Any hobbies?"

"Yes," the Colonel exclaimed. "Belong to any groups? Member of any organizations or associations?"

"Oh, you know. The usual. Hadassah, ORT, United Jewish Ap-peal. You're welcome to come to a meeting one day. They can be interesting."

"That would be nice," Linda responded in a tone that said, *We prefer to be with our own kind.*

The Colonel leaned forward. "Getting back to the Muslims. Have you ever associated with a Muslim? Or Muslims?"

"Is it getting late?" Morris asked. "It seems late."

"As a matter of fact, yes. And I found them to be very, very nice. But I'm not permitted to talk about that. For professional reasons," Rona said.

"Professional reasons?"

"I'm a therapist to a nice group of young men. From Kuwait."

Morris saw the Colonel's ankle start twitching. He prayed that it was because his foot had fallen asleep.

The clock began chiming eight thirty, and Morris thought he rec-ognized it as the theme song to *Apocalypse Now.*

"A therapist?"

Strike one, thought Morris

"For Muslims?"

Strike two. Maybe, if we leave now and serpentine across the street, we can get out of range before the first shots are fired.

The Colonel chewed on his babka.

McCord leaned forward and said, "Will you excuse me for a moment? I have to go upstairs to make a phone call."

ROAD TRIP

MONDAY, SEPTEMBER 27, 2004

After morning prayers, Hassan sent Pervez to pick up the car that would deliver them to Paradise. They'd found it two weeks earlier in the classified section of the *PennySaver News*—a rather morbid listing of cars, homes, jewelry, apparel, and other earthly possessions of those who permanently departed South Florida's retirement communities. Dead people were one of the fastest-growing demographics in Boca and its environs. The *PennySaver* was a combination obituary page and Craigslist.

Hassan paid cash for a late-model Cadillac, sold by one Sylvia Goldstein, whose husband, Jules, had just passed away. It was perfect: a deep trunk for the explosives, a GPS that advised misdirected terrorists to turn around "at the next legal U-turn," a Bose sound system to play Rona's relaxation CDs, and a still-active subscription to OnStar ("Hello, OnStar? I locked my keys in my car and have to blow myself up. Can you unlock it for me? Thanks!"). It also had room for a tattered copy of the Qur'an, which Hassan had tucked into the glove compartment.

They assembled around Jules's black Caddy in the employee parking lot of the Paradise Hotel and Residences. Pink clouds dotted the early-morning sky, and the lights of distant vessels bobbed on the dark horizon of the Atlantic. Collectively, almost intuitively, they inhaled the sea air, knowing they would never smell it again. They knew Paradise had seventy-two virgins, but there was no theological commentary on whether it had a beach. Or even a pool. They slid into the car, closing the doors gently, Pervez at the wheel, Hassan next to him, and Achmed and Azad in the backseat. Hassan couldn't resist turning his head and taking his own final look at the towel hut standing in the glare of a single spotlight, a light that grew dimmer as they drove out of the lot.

Their orders were to move the cell to an industrial park in Miami, closer to the presidential debate. Fakhir, the Martyrs of Militancy cell manager/waiter, had procured a warehouse where the cell would be sequestered for the next three days. This phase was the most critical of any suicide bombing operation. Most suicide bombings fizzled in the final days, when the "suicide" part became more real to the bomber. A special place was needed where Fakhir could keep his eye on the bombers and they could keep their eyes on one another, ensuring no second thoughts—no dropping out—limiting loose talk that could be overheard by the wrong people. For the next three days they would eat together, sleep together, plan together, and dream about virgins together.

As Pervez steered onto Collins Avenue, Hassan sensed tension in the car.

Achmed said, "Turn on the radio."

Pervez pressed the radio's scan button, and the Caddy was filled with bursts of Latin music, then pop rock, then angry conservatives, and, finally, gospel preaching.

"Switch to another station," said Azad.

"I want to hear this," Pervez insisted.

Why? Hassan wondered.

"Put on some music," Azad insisted. "Put on some Beyoncé."

"I hate Beyoncé!" Pervez said. "Besides, I am the driver and the driver decides what to listen to. And I choose this."

"And I choose to tell you to pull over so I can get out!" blurted Azad.

The car fell silent, except for the staticky voice of the preacher, who had finished with the Jews and was now moving on to the homosexuals. Hassan knew Muslims couldn't be far behind in the pastor's hate parade.

Pervez turned his head toward Hassan, as if to ask for guidance. "Keep driving," Hassan ordered. "Everyone use your breathing exercises. Like Rona instructed us."

Something is wrong, he thought. A sense of doubt was corroding the mission. For that split second when Azad demanded that they pull over, there was an unspoken relief in the car. As if the best course to Paradise was a U-turn. Even Hassan thought, *What's better, to sunburn at a hotel or to burn in hell?*

He felt a sudden urge, and reached into the glove compartment for his Qur'an. He leafed across worn, dog-eared pages and his eyes scanned type-print faded from fingertips that had swept across the words for so many years in search of comfort.

Hassan silently read: "Oh you who believe! What is the matter with you, that, when you are asked to go forth in the cause of Allah, you cling heavily to the earth? Unless you go forth, He will punish you with a grievous penalty . . ."

In other words, go forth, Pervez!

The pastor began reviewing the range of foreign policy options in Baghdad: "Thou shalt surely smite the inhabitants of that city with the edge of the sword, destroying it utterly, and all that is therein, and the cattle thereof, with the edge of the sword!"

Hassan flipped some pages. "And slay them wherever you find them and drive them out of the places whence they drive you out . . ."

The preacher cried: "And Jee-suss said: 'Do not suppose that I have come to bring peace to the earth. I did not come to bring peace, but a sword!' America, it is time for the sword!"

Hassan found this passage: "Smite you above their necks and smite all their fingertips off them."

The preacher countered: "Fear God who is able to destroy both soul and body in hell."

Hassan read: "I will punish them with severe chastisement in this world and in the Hereafter . . ."

And so it went. Passage versus passage, attack and counterattack, violence against violence, now and forever. An eye for an eye and a truth for a truth.

Hassan continued scanning, desperate for a particular passage about the seventy-two virgins that awaited him. But there was nothing. Sure, there were some references to Paradise, mentions of ornate decor and fine wines, and one's choice of fruit and meat. And there was something about dark-eyed, untouched maidens, which had potential. But Hassan couldn't find anything that pointed to seventy-two virgins on the menu. *Maybe it is all-inclusive,* Hassan thought, *like at the resort,* which troubled him. Because the joke at the resort was that all-inclusive meant all-out sucker.

He turned off the radio. The car rolled from one paradise to another in silence, and the words of the pastor and the Qur'an tumbled together in Hassan's mind.

Sitting inside a retrofitted U-Haul van, Alonso Diaz reported into a microphone, "Vehicle proceeding south on Collins Avenue." It was the most popular radio traffic report in America that morning.

In Washington, Bill Sully watched a monitor with a dot moving slowly across a map, transmitted by a Species Management

Surveillance drone purloined from the US Park Police in a trade for three FDA analysts and a recently intercepted shipment of Cuban cigars.

In Melville, Long Island, Tom Fairbanks watched another GPS image. There was Morris Feldstein's car. Starting another week of travel across Long Island's North Shore. With a detour ahead.

GOING-AWAY GIFTS

TUESDAY, SEPTEMBER 28, 2004

They slept fitfully, dreaming of martyrdom and of McDonald's, of jihad and Beyoncé, of lives past and kingdom come. The warehouse was sweltering hot. With cots assembled in one corner. A large floral rug sat in the center of the sprawling gray cement floor. Oversized pillows lined the rug's edges, for sit-downs. An office-style kitchenette had been stocked with a nice selection of martyr munchies: herbal teas and diet sodas, crackers, chips, and hummus. Massive industrial shelves lined the walls, jammed with cartons of lightbulbs, black panels, wires, and electrical components.

"We've opened a solar lighting company," Fakhir had explained. "It's the next big thing."

At ten o'clock, a shrill bell pierced the tension of the warehouse.

"What's happening?" Azad asked.

Fakhir smiled. "Nothing to worry about! We have expected company, with gifts selected especially for you!"

Hassan thought, *What do you get a suicide bomber who soon won't need anything? Do they make two-day pocket calendars?*

Fakhir peered outside through an open door. He stepped back in and pressed a button on the wall. A large steel garage door began lifting, squeaking and groaning. A white Mazda slipped in, the garage door closing behind it.

A thin, wiry man popped out of the driver's seat and said in a nasal voice, "*As-salamu alaykum.*"

"*Wa alaykumu s-salam,*" everyone mumbled back.

"Brothers," Fakhir clapped. "This is Hosni. Come, sit."

They all crouched on the rug. Fakhir sprawled against some pillows. Hosni sat cross-legged. Hassan noticed he had a habit of licking his lips.

"So," said Fakhir. "You brought the gifts?"

"Yes. You have the money?"

Hassan disliked the newcomer.

Fakhir tossed a canvas tote bag across the rug. Inside were stacks of hundred-dollar bills. Hosni riffled through it then cradled the bag at his side.

"Now, show us what gifts you have brought to us," Fakhir said, clapping his huge hands.

Hosni pulled a remote keypad from his pocket and pressed a button. The beeping ricocheted loudly off the walls, causing the cell members to twitch in anticipation of the drone missiles. But all that happened was the harmless pop of the car trunk opening. Hosni reached inside and pulled out two heavy backpacks, then two small white boxes. He placed the backpacks in the center of the rug.

"Wow! North Face!" Azad admired.

"Do not open them. They are packed just right. Just for you. If you disturb what is inside it may not work. Or may work too soon. Keep them in a safe place. Store at room temperature."

Contents may explode under pressure, in other words.

"Two brothers will wear backpacks to the target. Two other brothers will drive them, drop them off, and then leave."

I'll drive, all four brothers thought.

Hosni opened the small boxes and produced two Nokia cell phones.

"Do not use these phones. They will be traced. Each cell phone detonates a different backpack. Fakhir will remain here. When he receives a signal that the time is right, God willing, he will use each phone. The numbers are already programmed into speed dial, Fakhir. Brothers, when Fakhir calls, your mission will be accomplished. And you will be true martyrs."

Hassan, who would be on the receiving end of one of those calls, didn't like the idea of speed-dialing to martyrdom. Fakhir, on the other hand, seemed fine with it.

Hosni stood. "I ask Allah to reward you greatly, brothers, for the work you have done. May He grant you sincerity and acceptance of the deeds."

The four men stared anxiously at the backpacks.

Moments later, Hosni pulled his car out of the warehouse, the cash-filled tote bag at his side. He drove according to the specific directions he had been given, and twenty minutes later pulled into a Starbucks. He dialed a number on his cell phone.

The person who answered said only: "You delivered the package?"

"Yes, sir. As I promised."

"And they paid you the money?"

"Yes, sir. I have it with me."

"If any of it is missing, our agreement is off."

"No, sir! No, no, no. It is all here. I swear."

"Did you give them the instructions on how to use the package?"

"Yes, sir. Just as you told me."

"And did they ask questions? Did they seem to doubt your instructions? In any way?"

"Oh, no, sir. They understood. Do not open the backpacks. You call the numbers on the cell phone and . . . boom."

"Do you trust them?"

"Yes, sir."

"You still have to hope I trust you. Now, look in your rearview mirror."

"Sir?"

"Look in your rearview mirror. There is a black Chevy with two men. They will follow you to your apartment. They will pick up the money. And they will give you what we promised."

"First class, sir? As we discussed?"

"Have I ever broken a promise?"

"Never, sir."

"Then don't ask. Good-bye."

"Thank you, sir."

And thank you, Hosni! Alonso Diaz thought. *Thank you for your meritorious service to the people of the United States of America! Thank you for being the best informant a Fed could have!*

As tokens of our esteem, may we present you with one get-out-of-jail-free card, one visa to return to Egypt, and a one-way ticket from Miami to Cairo, departing tonight. Not first class, unfortunately. Center seat in coach, actually. You may like to flee the country in style, but the OMB (Office of Mismanagement and Bullshit) prohibits the use of federal funds for first-class travel. Look at it this way, Hosni, a center seat for a fourteen-hour flight to Cairo beats years sitting in a federal detention center for overstaying your student visa.

As-salamu alaykum.

Vice President Cheney disliked delivering bad news to the President. But that is what he was doing that morning. Holding a newspaper to his chest, walking across the portico that separated the White House residence from the West Wing, and waiting for the President to finish his morning run so he could deliver bad news. Karl Rove walked next to him, huffing with indignation.

Adding to the mood, gray clouds darkened the White House grounds, threatening rain. Secret Service agents stood at odd angles, staring into the space in front of them like well-dressed garden gnomes as the President raced around the track.

Finally, Cheney saw Bush walking across the Rose Garden. He wore gym shorts and a Texas Rangers T-shirt, rested both hands on his hips, and was panting.

"Some greeting committee!" the President said breathlessly.

"Good morning, Mr. President," Cheney said. "How was your run?"

"Good pace, Big Time. You should try it someday," the President chuckled.

"Sir, we thought you should see this. It's a little disappointing." He extended the newspaper to the President, unfolded to the offending page. Rove sunk his hands into his pockets.

The President scanned the page, then blinked as he cocked back his head. When the President blinked and cocked back his head, it meant he was surprised—and not pleasantly.

It was the morning edition of President Bush's hometown newspaper, *The Lone Star Iconoclast*, one of the very few "lame-stream" newspapers the President didn't dismiss. This newspaper was a real newspaper. Small town. Authentic. American! It read the way the President walked—with a swagger!

And its endorsement headline that day read: KERRY WILL RESTORE AMERICAN DIGNITY.

Bush returned the paper to Cheney and stared hard at Rove. "Well, Boy Genius, that's a whoopin' right there. Now what?"

"Mr. President, it's a big zero!" Rove replied. "This newspaper will be out of business before you know it. And you will still be President."

Bush frowned. "Bad timing. Two days before my first debate with our opponent!"

Cheney nodded. "I know, Mr. President. But we are ready for him! Just remember your debate prep. Keep turning it back to national security. Remember what we rehearsed. 'September eleventh changed everything. We must fight the terrorists around the world . . .'"

"So we do not have to fight them here at home!" the President concluded.

Rove coached: "Steadfast and strong versus . . ."

"Uncertainty and weakness!"

The soft thunder of a plane taking off from Ronald Reagan Washington National Airport, only a few miles away, rolled across the South Lawn. The President turned and watched the plane disappear into the clouds.

"You know, I wake up every morning thinking about how to keep Americans safe."

Rove said, "That's good, Mr. President. Let's use that," and wrote it down.

The Vice President said, "Sir, one more thing. About the debate."

"Go on."

"DHS picked up a significant threat. We intercepted it and are running an active counter-operation on it. The threat is against the University of Miami. They are targeting the debate itself."

A blink and shift of the head. "Al-Qaeda?"

"No sir. A new group. Likely more lethal than al-Qaeda. They've penetrated throughout the homeland, I'm afraid. New York. Florida. All over. They call themselves the Abu al-Zarqawi Army of Jihad Martyrs of Militancy Brigade. Probably entered the country during the previous Administration."

"Well, that goes without saying."

"But we can't say it enough," Rove chirped.

Cheney continued: "There is absolutely no risk to the debate.

We have informants embedded and we are in control. But we suggest letting them operate for as long as possible. Then disrupt. Probably tomorrow night. Or maybe even Thursday morning."

"But that's right before the debate."

"Yes it is, Mr. President," Rove said. "And our success in stopping this attack will dominate the news cycle before the debate."

The President nodded. "Am I supposed to know all this or is this one of your deniable implausibilities?"

Cheney said, "That would be plausible deniability, sir. And yes."

"Yes, that I deny knowing? Or yes that I cannot know. Because I know already so if asked I should just deny."

"Yes, sir," Rove said, but wasn't sure what he had just agreed with.

"Sir, just as a precaution, DHS Science and Tech wants to outfit you with a protective device at the debate," Cheney said.

"What kind of device?"

"A new kind of ultra-thin body armor."

"Dick, America can't see their President in some kind of fancy bulletproof vest at a debate!"

"Nobody will be able to tell, Mr. President. It's the latest technology. And undetectable."

"Okay . . . but I think the word is indetectable."

"Yes, sir."

The President gazed again across the South Lawn and thought of what stretched beyond. The full expanse of the nation, which, he knew, was safer. Al-Qaeda had been brought to justice. The Taliban removed from power. Libya disarmed. A strategy of freedom around the world. He thought of that day, when he climbed that pile of debris at Ground Zero in New York and announced to the world what would be done about it. He looked back at Rove and Cheney and said, "We've climbed the mighty mountain. I see the valley below. And it's a valley of peace."

"Not bad," said Cheney. "But then pivot to strength. Peace through strength, Mr. President."

THEY STARTED IT

WEDNESDAY, SEPTEMBER 29, 2004

Hassan had entered Paradise, and found that it was good. Nubile women carried silver trays heaping with the finest foods. Wine flowed and soothing music played. There were lavish banquets and refreshing pools of water cooled perfectly to the touch.

Plus, an upgraded room for members of the Frequent Guests program. Subject to availability.

Hassan had not achieved martyrdom. But he had attained the title of General Manager at the Paradise Hotel and Residences. Now he dressed in a purple blazer and khaki pants and trademark Paradise yellow tie. He strutted through the lobby, followed by his assistant managers, Fakhir, who scurried after him like the supplicant that he was, Pervez, who supervised the kitchen, Achmed, who handled banquet sales, and Azad, who booked entertainment. And on this particular day, he surveyed his dominion and smiled at his triumphs.

There was a new sign at the towel hut: PLEASE TAKE MANY TOWELS. NO LIMIT.

Hassan had never been happier. Free of the pounding headaches and the aching deep in his groin.

And speaking of that, check out the new lifeguard! The way she stared at Hassan from her perch above the pool. How she dangled her thin ankles and how her tanned thighs flattened against her chair, and—

"Hassan. Wake up, Hassan."

Fakhir shook Hassan in his cot. His words raced. And in his sleepy state, Hassan had difficulty comprehending them.

"Hassan, I have news. From Gaza. About your two sisters. They were martyred, Hassan. At the hands of the Zionists. In the Jabalya refugee camp. May Allah give them an easy and pleasant journey and shower blessings on their graves. Are you awake, Hassan?"

Hassan tried to swat at Fakhir so he could return to dreaming about the lifeguard.

"Did you hear me, Hassan? Your sisters!"

He shook off the sleep. "Fakhir, you do not know what you are talking about. My family lives in Gaza City. I grew up there. Not a refugee camp. It is someone else you speak of."

"No, Hassan. Your home was destroyed many weeks ago. Hamas used it to store weapons to fight the Jews. So the Jews destroyed it with their missiles. Your family moved to Jabalya. To the refugee camp."

Now the words were sharper. *Is that why there was no answer when I used Rona's phone?* he wondered.

"Hassan?"

"My sisters?" he said, and it came out as a whimper. "Adiva. Ameerah! Oh God, my sisters." His shoulders trembled and his body shook. Tears pooled in his eyes "Be brave, Hassan!"

He closed his fists, tighter and tighter. Moments ago he was in Paradise. Now he was in hell. He began pounding his fists against the thin pillow. The harder he hit, the more he gasped.

"Do not cry, Hassan. The Zionists martyred your sisters. But rejoice! They only struck because our Qassam missiles killed two Israeli children. In Sderot. The vengeful arm of our Prophet reached into the land of the Jews and took their children!"

Hassan thought, *To which the vengeful arm of the Jews reached into Gaza and took my sisters. Who avenged first? And when would it end?*

"God willing, you will see your sisters in Paradise, Hassan. How blessed you are!"

Hassan glared through his tears at the fat man who didn't suffer anything except the occasional under-tipper, who got to stuff grape leaves into his mouth and blow-up everyone from a safe distance. All of the hate that Hassan had built up over the years—for the oppressors and the Americans, the infidels and the Zionists, and the demanders of more than two towels—turned toward that one fat man. His lips rolled back and he bared his teeth. And the words spilled out of his mouth, coarse and seething: "Get away from me, Fakhir! Get away before I fucking kill you!"

Fakhir bolted.

Hassan lowered his head to the pillow, which was wet with tears. He thought of his mother wailing at the funeral of her daughters and the Jewish mothers wailing at the funerals of their daughters.

Later, they sat cross-legged on the carpet, staring at the backpacks that Hassan had placed before them, as if they would blow up at any moment. It was stifling hot, and Hassan noticed that Fakhir was sweating heavily. Whenever Hassan made eye contact with him, Fakhir's eyes darted elsewhere.

Hassan began. "Brothers, you have been trained well for our mission. We have been ordered to strike tomorrow. Now I must ask: Are you ready?"

They mumbled their ascent. *Not exactly a ringing endorsement,* thought Hassan. *That is fine.*

"Then today you must make final preparations." He pointed to a video camera mounted on a tripod in a corner of the warehouse. "You must record your final messages. For your families." He felt his throat tighten. "Think of what you will say to them. These will be the last words they ever hear from you."

Silence.

"Will you miss your family, Azad?"

Azad nodded slowly. "I will see them one day in Paradise." Then he looked up and asked, "Won't I?"

Hassan shrugged. "That is what they say. Although no one who has ever been to Paradise has returned to say for certain. Sooooo . . ."

Azad looked uncomfortable.

"How about you, Achmed? What will you miss after you are gone?"

Achmed stared for several moments, then said, "You know, I have given this much thought . . . I am willing to make the sacrifice not to go to Paradise. I can drive you guys to the debate, drop you off, then I will be able to tell your families personally how you became martyrs and pleased God."

The others glared at Achmed, and Hassan thought, *A great sacrifice, indeed. We blow ourselves up and your biggest risk is a speeding ticket on the ride back.* Then he said, "Actually, Tora Bora has commanded that Pervez drive the car."

Pervez smiled.

"Of course, the American CIA will find Pervez, torture him until he begs for death, but keep him alive and imprisoned forever in Guantánamo. May God be with you, Pervez."

Pervez stopped smiling.

"What will you miss, Pervez? What will you think about while they are waterboarding you in Guantánamo?"

Pervez sighed. "I will miss working at the McDonald's. I was told the assistant manager's position puts you on what they call an executive track."

"I was thinking of one day opening up a landscape design company," Azad offered. "I would call it Mujaha-Green." And when no one laughed, Azad said, "That is a joke. I have been watching standup comedy on HBO. At the Feldsteins'. I will miss that too. And *American Idol*."

Hassan let the quiet and doubt sink in. He watched as their eyes moved from the backpacks to the carpet and back, as their legs and fingers twitched.

And then said, "My brothers, you must decide what to do. As for me, the decision is made. I will not be joining you in Paradise. Or at the debate. My mission has been completed."

"What are you saying, Hassan?" asked Fakhir. "We have a duty!"

"Then do your duty, Fakhir! Blow yourself up and kill the people around you tomorrow. A week from now, the Americans will avenge those deaths with more death. Maybe they will kill *your* sisters. A week from then we will kill the ones that killed us. And so on and so forth, as the Americans like to say. Meanwhile, I have a life to live. I am sick of death. I am going into the hospitality business."

Fakhir protested, "You cannot do this! You must be steadfast! You must persevere! What about the seventy-two virgins?"

Pervez growled, then pulled his favorite fruit-cutting knife from a pocket and waved it in the air. "Fakhir is correct!" he snarled.

Hassan's eyes narrowed as Pervez approached him.

"But I require some proof of these virgins." He spun toward Fakhir, who remained seated and cross-legged, now trembling. "So I will now slice off your head and send you to Paradise. When you get there, if you see any virgins, text us. And we will meet you there."

"A head start, without the head!" Azad giggled.

"Yes, Fakhir, save a virgin for me," Achmed said, clapping.

Pervez leaned over Fakhir, waving the knife over his head. The sweat poured from the fat man's face, draining it of all color.

"Peace be with you, Fakhir!" Achmed proclaimed.

"Merry martyrdom!" Azad giggled.

Hassan put his body between Pervez and Fakhir.

"You have the authority to terminate the mission, Fakhir. You can call Tora Bora, end this operation, and disband the cell. And save all our lives. One day, Pervez can return to the McDonald's. Azad to the lawn service, Achmed to cleaning planes—"

"We prefer to call it aircraft comfort services," Achmed said.

"And you, Fakhir, maybe you can go back to Souvlaki City. Collect your tips, eat all the shish kebab you can, and live happily ever after. Because, from the look of things, living in America has not treated you so poorly."

Fakhir lowered his head, grateful it was still attached to his torso, and shook it slowly. "Even if I end this mission, the FBI will find us. We are dead men in America."

"No. We will be American heroes. We will go to a different paradise. With palm trees and mountains. They will pay us a great deal of money and give us beautiful homes and free health care." Hassan thought of the groin pain he once suffered. "We will meet women on Match.com and have unlimited cable television."

He unfolded a slip of paper. Earlier, he had copied a number from a tattered phone directory. He pressed the keypad on his cell phone and waited.

A voice answered: "FBI, Miami."

"My name is Hassan Muzan. Of the Abu al-Zarqawi Martyrs of Militancy. I have information to share. Who may I speak to about your witness protection program?"

Dick Cheney hated when a VPOTUS briefing began with "We have good news and bad news." The good news was never as good as the bad news was bad. So in the White House Situation Room, when the Director of the FBI began with a good news/bad news scenario, the Vice President snapped, "Just tell me what I need to know."

As the Director nodded, Jon Pruitt noticed the other officials around the table reverting to eighth grade—lowering their eyes, squirming in their seats, and trying to be invisible.

The good news was that in exchange for new identities, homes, and part-time salaries tucked into the payroll lines of various federal agencies and offices, the terrorist cell in Florida was now a cooperating witness cell.

The bad news was that the Vice President's plan to expose the cell just before the presidential debate was now terminated. The cell not only called off their attack, they left the harmless backpacks on the curb outside their hideout with a sign that said PLEASE TAKE, like a piece of old furniture discarded for neighborhood scavengers. Then they cut their deal to provide intel to the Feds as long as no one ever knew they existed.

Which meant no dramatic announcement. No three-night CNN special coverage complete with blood-chilling mug shots and specially composed "The Plot to Kill the President" theme music.

No post-debate, pre-election bounce so high that Kerry would strain his scrawny neck watching it.

Cheney sat straight in his chair, shoulders pulled up to his chin, listening to the FBI Director drone.

"Finally, sir, there is the matter of Mr. and Mrs. Morris Feldstein. Of Great Neck, New York."

"Ah, yes," cooed the Vice President. "Let's not forget the Feldsteins."

Pruitt could swear he heard the FBI Director gulp. "Sir, the Zarqawi informants insist that the Feldsteins had nothing to do with their plans to attack the homeland. They claim Morris and Rona Feldstein just happened to meet Hassan at his place of employment. The Paradise Hotel and Residences. They struck up a friendship and—"

"They're lying," Cheney hissed.

"They did pass multiple polygraphs on this point," the Director replied.

"Ohhhh, a polygraph!" Scooter Libby exclaimed. "A five

thousand dollar polygraph! And all we have is NICK, the most sophisticated NSA intelligence software ever written."

"The Feldsteins are definitely up to something," Cheney said. "Otherwise NICK would not be tracking them. The question is, do we have enough to arrest and question them?"

"Not without violating their civil rights," the Attorney General replied meekly, which was appropriate because he was generally meek about civil rights.

Cheney said, "Even if there is no direct tie between the Feldsteins and al-Zarqawi, they did something to merit NICK's suspicion. Where there's smoke, there's fire. Stay on them. Move the resources we had on the al-Zarqawi cell to the Feldsteins. If they so much as make an illegal right turn on red, I want them arrested."

Heads nodded.

"Anything else?" Cheney asked.

The Secret Service director raised his hand. "Sir, we did have a pretty nifty personal protection device engineered for the President to wear at the debate. It wasn't exactly cheap. Now what?"

"Let him wear it. It may come in handy."

DENIM BLUES

WEDNESDAY EVENING, SEPTEMBER 29, 2004

Caryn had to work that night, but didn't mind. She considered her job an observation post, where she could collect material for her planned documentary on the economic plight of retail workers, tentatively entitled "Mall Stall." Plus, the overtime was decent and she had a 401k.

Caryn was certain that one day she would win an Oscar for Best Documentary. Meanwhile, she was vying for employee of the month at the Gap.

As scenes from her documentary unfolded in her mind, Caryn refolded piles of autumn wool turtleneck sweaters on the twenty-percent-off table. She knew that her meticulous aligning of sleeves, collars, and hems would be disrupted by the next gang of shoppers who bulldozed through the display.

For now, the mall was quiet. It was dinner hour. A few teenage girls combed through endless shelves of jeans in all shapes and sizes: original cut, skinny cut, incredibly skinny cut, and cut-off-your-circulation cut. An exhausted-looking mother and her daughter argued quietly near the fitting rooms about how "your father will have a friggin' heart attack if you wear those things." Caryn's manager, who always wore a headset, like one of those Borgs on *Star Trek*, was reorganizing a rack of designer sweatshirts.

And there were those two men. Definitely not holders of the Gap Loyalty card. Dressed in dark suits and shiny loafers. Their hands always clasped in front of their crotches. Pretending to browse but more interested in Caryn. Peering at her over racks and around tables.

They're right out of one of dad's Bogart movies, thought Caryn. *Like those nineteen-fifties black-and-white detectives. All they need are fedoras and cigarettes.*

Ever since her arrest at the Republican Convention, Caryn had the feeling that people were studying her. But she knew that couldn't be true. As the daughter of a therapist, she even created a name for her anxiety: post-arrest stress disorder. The self-diagnosis helped her cope, but lately she felt her condition worsen. Glances became stares. Things were closing in. The aperture was narrowing.

Caryn was taught by Rona to confront trouble. So she swallowed hard, pulled her frizzy hair behind her ears, and marched toward the two men.

"Hey, can I help you guys?"

They glanced at each other uncomfortably.

"Just looking," said one.

"Browsing," said the other.

Caryn nodded. "Okay. Just let me know. And don't forget our September Sock Sale. Two pairs for the price of one. Ends tomorrow."

"We won't forget," said one.

"We never forget," said the other.

Caryn turned away. Troubled.

THE EARLY BIRD &
THE WORM

THURSDAY, SEPTEMBER 30, 2004

During the ride to work the next morning, Tom Fairbanks repeated to himself, through his fixed jaw, "The early bird gets the worm. The early bird gets the worm."

It was so early that there was hardly any traffic on the Long Island Expressway, meaning plenty of road and little road rage. No cars to cut off, no assholes to shout at, no middle fingers to put up. So early that a dimming moon lingered in a purple sky. So early that he found a spot close to the entrance of his building and walked through a lonely atrium to the rapid-fire echo of his steps against the granite floor.

"The early bird gets the worm!" Fairbanks said again, as an elevator whisked him to the fourth floor.

The worm was Morris Feldstein, twisting and turning on his own country. A piece of slime trying to burrow deep into American soil where no one could find him.

Except that Feldstein could not hide. The entire federal bureaucracy was waiting to bring him to justice, writhing and wriggling. Fairbanks had to act fast. To get that worm before anyone else.

A pile of newspapers lay cluttered at the front door of the DHS suite. *Newsday*, the *Daily News*, and the *New York Post*. As he inserted his key and stepped over the papers, Fairbanks smiled. Or thought it was a smile. These were muscles he rarely used.

Tomorrow I will be in the morning papers! Famous for the arrest of Morris Feldstein. That unlikely terrorist. That enemy within. That worm.

He walked through the lobby and saw the portraits of President Bush and Homeland Security Secretary Ridge on the wall. Would either man call to offer the thanks of a grateful nation after the apprehension of Feldstein? Perhaps they would fly him to Washington for an award ceremony.

Probably not. It would be his bust, but everyone else would try to take credit. Elbowing him out of the camera angles, pushing him back to anonymity. Where they thought he belonged.

Not this time. This time, Tom Fairbanks would rescue America from its enemy. And liberate Tom Fairbanks from his own career.

In the years that followed, Morris Feldstein would have plenty of time to reconstruct the most bizarre day of his previously blasé life. And the precise moment, at one twenty in the afternoon, when everything crashed.

It began after he showered and shaved and put on his beige Van Heusen wool trousers and the navy blue blazer from Macy's, and approached Rona in the kitchen for their perfunctory have-a-good-day-Rona-yes-you-too-Morris peck on the cheek. Only this one tasted of the coffee she had been nursing over an unfolded *Newsday* on the kitchen table and maybe a trace of guilt for all the problems he had caused since that night at the Bayview Motor Inn. And just as he started down the long dark hall to the front door, he heard Rona ask "Morris, are you watching the Mets game tonight?"

He turned back toward the kitchen, swallowed hard, and thought, *Tsuris ahead.*

Actually, not just tsuris. This day would bring a tsuris tsunami.

"Is there something you want to watch, Rona?" He studied her. But this time, there was only this matter-of-fact pronouncement: "I'm watching the presidential debate." Settled with a clasp of both hands on the table.

Since the Mets were off that night, and since Turner Classic Movies was showing a colorized film (which defeated the whole purpose of showing classic movies, Morris thought), and since he was in no position to assert his television-program preferences Morris nodded and said, "Yes, the presidential debate should be very interesting," in a tone of voice that masked Morris's belief that nothing—nothing—could be less interesting, except, maybe, the vice-presidential debate.

There was that slow shuffle to his car and the standard peek inside the trunk to make sure all his Celfex samples were there. He had that sensation of being watched, just like the other morning. There was the drone of a helicopter that seemed to hover over only his house, the curious glances of the utility workers and gardeners, the home improvement contractors and road crews who mobilized on Soundview Avenue. Morris was reminded of that episode of the *Twilight Zone,* the one when Earl Holliman finds himself secluded in a small town, yet can't "shake that crazy feeling of being watched." Only now, instead of viewing Earl Holliman in black and white from the safety of his RoyaLounger 8000, Morris felt that he was the star of this show, live and in color.

Across the street, Agent Russell peered through the McCords' living room blinds, a cell phone attached to his ear, and Colonel McCord almost attached to his hip. Crouching next to him, as if they were in a foxhole rather than on a faux suede couch, both men surveilled Morris and watched those who watched him as well.

"How much company do we have?" Fairbanks asked from the phone in his Melville office.

"Sir, it's quite a crowd," Russell replied. "Plainclothes county police, NYPD, New York State, a guy I recognize from the FDA. Hold on . . . There's a guy standing by a landscape truck with a weedwhacker. I think that might be Miller. From DHS!"

"We are DHS, Agent Russell!"

"Yes, sir. But Miller is DHS Counterintel. Not Intel and Analysis."

Fairbanks hissed: "Spy versus spy and we're the same goddamn spies. Jesus H!"

All these federal assets watching Feldstein while watching one another.

Morris pulled out of his driveway and crept down Soundview Avenue, listening to WFAN lament the Mets' 6–3 loss to the Braves the night before. He noticed a helicopter that seemed to ride just above him and the cars that seemed to follow his every turn.

Something is happening, he thought. But he kept driving.

As the morning and the miles passed, Morris grew more nervous. Dark vehicles pulled close behind him. Additional helicopters seemed to accompany him everywhere. The doctors' offices he visited were unusually crowded, as if there were a sudden virus that only attacked well-groomed men in sunglasses, who tapped impatiently at their knees and peered suspiciously over magazines.

And as Morris continued to ply his sales territory, with each tick of the odometer in his car, the Feldstein Anxiety Anticipation Index nudged up. His fingers were moist around the steering wheel and Morris noticed his knuckles were pale. But even when he sensed that some uncontrollable wave was building against him, about to knock him off his feet and sweep him into the unknown, he did nothing. Even against a big wave Morris would not make waves. Not until it was too late.

And so he pushed on.

Promptly at noon, Morris led a caravan of sedans into the parking lot of Antonio's Pizzeria of Glen Cove. It seemed as if the entire federal government had a craving for a chicken Parm. And as Morris sat at a wobbly table, nibbling at his meal, he sensed that everyone around him was assessing every queasy nibble. Which made him particularly self-conscious about leaving crumbs on his face.

Morris stood, brought his tray to an array of trash bins, and, as the signs instructed, deposited his plastics in the recycling bin and his unfinished meal in the food waste bin.

Outside, as he entered his car, he heard a dozen echoes of doors closing and engines starting.

Gottenyu, he thought.

It's a case of mistaken identity. Like Cary Grant in North by Northwest. *I'm Roger Thornhill! Being chased by spies across the country and not knowing why! Only, instead of running away from planes and hanging on the edge of Mount Rushmore, like Cary Grant, I'm being surrounded at Antonio's Pizzeria in Glen Cove! Gottenyu! Glen Cove! That's where* North by Northwest *begins! Maybe this isn't a nightmare! Maybe it's a sequel! But why me? I didn't do anything!*

Morris reached for his cell phone. His fingers fumbled across the keypad. The sound of Rona's voicemail message comforted him—the sound of normalcy in this horrifically abnormal day. After the beep, he said, "Rona, this is Morris. I'm just . . . I'm checking to make sure everything is okay over there . . . It's the strangest thing, Rona . . . I'm sure it's just my imagination . . . But . . . You know what? I think I may call in sick and come home. Just a little rest . . . Okay. So I'll see you soon, Rona. We'll watch the debate tonight. Good-bye."

He called his district manager, and got her voice mail. "Hello, Laurie," he said, his voice dry and scratchy. "This is Morris Feldstein. I'm not really feeling very well. It's nothing serious. Just—" he looked at all the cars in the lot, engines humming, stiff figures behind windshields. "Just some kind of bug, I think. So I'm going to go home, if that's okay. To rest up. And I'll be back at work tomorrow. Tomorrow will be better. Thank you. Good-bye."

In his many years at Celfex Pharmaceuticals, Morris had called in sick only twice. The first was to make that fateful trip to the Paradise Hotel and Residences at Boca. This was the second.

There would be no more.

After Morris's phone messages had become one of the highest-rated broadcasts in the metropolitan area that morning, Tom Fairbanks proclaimed: "Jesus H! Feldstein's coming home early!" He sat in the McCords' dining room, which he commandeered earlier, sipping his fifth cup of coffee. It was cold and bitter and made him scowl, which was just the way he liked it. Coffee mugs, cell phones, and a tattered Hagstrom's map of Nassau County, marked with Morris's route that morning, cluttered the table. A set of car keys was within arm's reach of Fairbanks.

McCord and Russell were still at their post, peering through the large bay window.

"Oh-oh," McCord warned from behind a pair of binoculars. "Lots of sudden movement at Feldstein's house. Numerous vehicles repositioning."

Everyone's waiting for the worm to slither home, Fairbanks thought. Jockeying for position in what was now a game of inches. Ready to grab Feldstein. And take all the credit.

He scooped up the car keys and leaned toward the map.

"Soundview Avenue is the only route Feldstein can take home?"

"Affirmative," McCord responded. "The LIE to Lakeville. Lakeville to Middle Neck. Middle Neck to Soundview."

And Soundview to Guantánamo! thought Fairbanks as he hurried from the room.

In the FDA control room, Bill Sully stared into a screen at the grainy image of a man racing toward a car in the McCords' driveway. "Who the hell is that?" he asked.

A metallic voice transmitted from Soundview Avenue:

"Uhhhhh . . . Name's Fairbanks. DHS agent on Long Island. He's been trolling on this case for weeks."

Sully nodded his head unhappily. "Well he's fishing in my waters! This is an active FDA case! And where's he rushing to, by the way?"

"Maybe to beat us to the punch?"

"Morris Feldstein is a counterfeit drug criminal. We get him first! Follow Fairbanks!"

"Yes, sir."

And so it went. The FDA following Fairbanks who was intercepting Feldstein. Other Feds following the FDA following Fairbanks to meet Feldstein, being followed by still other Feds.

The race was on.

The sign arched across the Long Island Expressway, reflective white letters that glittered against a green background:

GREAT NECK
NEXT EXIT

Morris tightened his grip on the steering wheel. One more exit to the comfort of his RoyaLounger 8000 and Turner Classic Movies, where he followed the Mets and no one followed him. One more exit to the safe intersection of anonymity and conformity. He pressed on the gas.

For a man who spent his entire life safely at fifty-five miles an hour, Morris didn't even notice that his speedometer was nudging above seventy. He did, however, notice that he was about to race right past his exit, into Queens. He tugged hard at the steering wheel. So hard that his car swerved out of the center lane, almost clipping the vehicle that had been pacing him in the right lane. The driver of that car, a special investigator from the Bureau of Alcohol, Tobacco, Firearms and Explosives reflexively pounded on his horn and slammed hard on his brakes, triggering a twelve unmarked-car pileup. A literal bureaucratic clash.

As he careened onto the exit ramp, bouncing in his seat and clutching the steering wheel, Morris didn't hear what he had left behind on the Long Island Expressway. The screeching brakes, the blaring horns, the sound of metal against metal. He didn't smell the odor of burnt rubber on the pavement. That was all behind him now. He was alone on the expressway's service road. For the moment.

"Subject's driving erratically!" someone transmitted breathlessly. "All units proceed with caution."

Morris made a hard right onto Lakeville Road. The urgent wail of police sirens grew closer. He cut across a major intersection to a chorus of horns and obscenities. Now his heart pounded against his chest and his stomach twisted in excruciating knots. His eyes darted from side to side.

He looked in the rearview mirror, hoping he would see Hillel. Or Assistant Rabbi Kaplan. But all he could see was the frantic swirl of police lights growing closer.

Morris made this ride countless times, but never at seventy miles an hour in a chase scene right out of *The French Connection*. Storefront facades whizzed by: white-brick yogurt shops and bakeries, clothing stores and restaurants. All a blur through the car's windows. Morris Feldstein's past life in Great Neck, passing by at breakneck speed.

Then, he saw it. The weathered street sign that said SOUNDVIEW AVENUE.

"I'm coming, Rona!" he yelled, and aimed the car straight for the corner of his street. His foot pressed on the brake pedal as he began turning right. But, being unpracticed at such maneuvers, he felt the car veer out of control, tires on the left side seeming to lift off the pavement. Morris felt the steering wheel slip from his perspiring fingers. His body strained against the seat belt.

"*Gottenyu!*" he cried. And just as the steering wheel turned naturally back and the car balanced itself, just at the moment where Morris could see his house down the block and the RONA FELDSTEIN CSW sign on the lawn, Morris realized something.

In addition to the many traffic laws he had just broken between the Long Island Expressway and here, he had just violated a precious section of the Great Neck Village motor vehicle code.

He had just made a right on red. Just under the sign that said NO RIGHT ON RED.

He stopped. Sedans and panel trucks converged on him from all directions. Helicopters hovered so low that Morris's car shook and autumn leaves spun around him. Car doors swung open and Morris saw a wave of people rushing toward him, wearing windbreakers stenciled with acronyms. The windbreakers flapped like capes around the runners as they charged. Racing to be the first to reach Morris.

Thrusting elbows and arms and feet and legs. A forty-yard dash for the gold medal in the global War on Terror.

The wave of windbreakers broke around Morris's car. He sat still, almost paralyzed, hands resting on the steering wheel.

A face appeared at Morris's window.

"Get out of the car with your hands up!" Tom Fairbanks commanded.

Morris knew what to do. He had seen it in countless movies. He pushed open the door, raised his hands, and stepped out gingerly. Dozens of guns appeared, trained on him.

"It's all a case of mistaken identity. Like Cary Grant, in *North By Northwe*—"

Fairbanks grabbed Morris's arm, spun him around, and shoved him against the hood so hard that Morris grunted. Then there was a blow to his upper back. His face landed with a thud against the hood. He felt a foot kicking between both of his own, forcing them apart. Hands worked over Morris's body. Yanking his arms so far behind him that pain streaked across his shoulders.

"I can explain. I met a woman. We went to lunch . . . ." But Morris's words were lost under the drone of the helicopters, the screams of sirens. And the shouting of police—at one another. Something about whether he was entitled to be read his Miranda rights or whether, as an "NEN—native enemy noncombatant," he had involuntarily waived those rights.

Native enemy noncombatant! Morris thought. *That's a far cry from second vice president at the Temple Beth Torah Men's Club!*

As the constitutional debate raged, Morris's neighbors gathered on their lawns, pointing in disbelief at the quiet man who never bothered anyone, now surrounded at gunpoint by twenty-seven separate law enforcement agencies.

When the officials finally agreed that Morris had forfeited his Miranda rights, Tom Fairbanks grabbed him by the elbows and spun him around so they were face-to-face.

"You're under arrest, Mr. Feldstein! What do you have to say for yourself?"

Morris thought. But all he could come up with was this: "I'm sorry I cheated on my expense account."

"Hey, Dark Side, does this look funny to you?"

In a green room behind the stage at the University of Miami, President Bush gazed in a mirror, tugged the bottom of his jacket, and noticed the slight bulge in his shoulders. It was bad enough he had to go on stage in minutes to debate John Kerry. But the high-tech body armor the Secret Service asked him to wear looked like a prop from *Star Trek*; it scratched uncomfortably against his torso and bunched up under his suit.

Karl Rove rubbed his thumb under his chin. "It's for your own protection, Mr. President," he answered.

"People are going to think it's some kind of device to cheat. Like you're transmitting answers to me during the debate or something." The President chuckled.

I wish, thought Rove. But he said, "No one will even notice, sir."

Rove's cell phone rang. He walked to a corner of the room and cupped his hand over the phone.

"It's Scooter," he heard. "I have an update on that, uhhhh, traffic infraction in New York."

Rove thought, *Is that what we're calling it? Traffic infraction? Morris Feldstein committed treason against his country and it's considered a traffic infraction? Driving under the influence of terrorists?*

Scooter Libby continued. "I just spoke to VPOTUS. He does not want the President mentioning today's arrest."

In the background, Rove heard Bush rehearsing his lines: "September the eleventh changed how America must look at the world. . . . If you harbor a terrorist, you're equally as guilty as the terrorist. September the eleventh changed how America must look at the world. . . . If you harbor a terrorist, you're equally as guilty as the terrorist. . . ."

"Why not?" Rove snapped.

"Two reasons. Number one, the Bureau of Bleeding Hearts at DOJ is still concerned there's no case against our guy. Other than speeding, reckless endangerment, and making an illegal right on red, his record is ridiculously clean."

"Which is exactly why the terrorists recruited him!" Rove replied, annoyed.

"I agree. But if somehow our bad guy turns out not so bad, VPOTUS doesn't want the President's fingerprints on it."

He heard Bush repeat: "We've climbed the mighty mountain. I see the valley below, and it's a valley of peace. . . . We've climbed the mighty mountain. I see the valley below, and it's a valley of peace."

"Okay," Rove sighed. "What's the second reason?"

"The FBI thinks making this a high-visibility case is not in the best interests of national security at this time."

"Why not?"

"Well, if we are right, if our friend is one of the bad guys, we need to . . . uuuhhh, encourage him to cooperate. You know . . . uuuhhh, incentivize him to give us information. We need time and space for that. Without nosey lawyers, talk show producers, or ACLU rallies. So far the media has been cooperating and we've contained the story. For at least a few weeks, we need to keep our friend the best kept secret in town."

So there it was. Morris Feldstein, whose lifelong goal was to be the best kept secret in town, now had a new and powerful ally in the pursuit of his goal. The United States government.

Who knew?

PART FIVE

FROM ▮▮▮▮▮ WITH LOVE

SEPTEMBER 2004–SEPTEMBER 2008

In his first year of imprisonment, with little else to do with his time, Morris made a mental list of all the interesting places he had visited in his life.

There was the United Jewish Appeal mission to Israel; the family trips to Disneyworld, Lake George, and the Poconos; the two Caribbean cruises, the condo in Boca, of course; and that camping trip to the Catskills. "Look," Rona had said of the latter, "you take the kids and I'll stay home. Sitting in the middle of nowhere covered in bug spray and eating *schmutz* from a campfire is not my idea of a vacation."

And now Guantánamo. Does that count?

Morris spent the first year of imprisonment in a general state of confusion. Between the shock of what had happened to him and the surety that it would be corrected, by the government or by God.

He occupied a four-by-six cell with a metal cot, a tiny writing desk, a toilet, and a video camera that peered at him from the ceiling. The only thing they let him hang on the whitewashed cinderblock walls was his Jewish calendar, with COMPLIMENTS OF GUTTERMAN'S FUNERAL HOME printed at the bottom of every month. At the end of each day, he scrawled a large red X.

Once a day, they would let him out for a walk around the grounds. It was scalding hot, although he enjoyed catching occasional glimpses of his fellow "guests": all Middle Eastern looking, wearing the same white jumpsuit that he wore. But he kept his distance. How does the second vice president of the Temple Beth Torah Men's Club strike up a conversation with someone plucked from the battlefields of the global War on Terror?

He was losing weight. He didn't enjoy the food slid under his cell door on a tray. Pita, rice, curried eggs, spinach, lamb, more pita and more rice. You couldn't get a decent bagel and the fruit seemed ladled out of a can, thick and syrupy. He wasn't comfortable sitting in the communal television room with the other inmates because Arabic-language movies on the DVD player didn't particularly interest him. So he mostly sat in his cell, staring at the COMPLIMENTS OF GUTTERMAN'S FUNERAL HOME calendar, wondering how long before he could stop marking his days with a big red X.

They gave him some reading materials, and an occasional letter from home:

Dear Dad:

I miss you. They told me you are somewhere in ████████ *I'm doing okay. I've enrolled in a filmmaking course at* ████████ *and maybe one day will do a documentary about what happened to* ████████*. The working title is* ████████ ████████*.*

xoxoxox
Caryn.

And this letter from Rona:

Dear Morris:

I don't think it was your expense account. Anyway, I am doing ▓▓▓▓▓▓▓▓▓▓▓▓ although my ▓▓▓▓ has hurt bad since they ▓▓▓▓▓▓▓▓▓▓ it. I am living in a ▓▓▓▓▓▓▓▓▓▓▓▓ in ▓▓▓▓▓▓▓▓▓▓▓▓▓▓▓. Who knew ▓▓▓▓▓▓▓▓▓ could be so ▓▓▓▓▓? My lawyer says that if I cooperate, I can probably go back home in ▓▓▓▓▓▓▓▓▓▓▓▓▓ ▓▓▓▓▓▓▓▓▓▓▓▓▓▓, but I don't know how I could show my face again in ▓▓▓▓▓▓▓▓▓▓▓ or ▓▓▓▓▓▓▓▓!!! Talk about shondas! I told them what I knew about ▓▓▓▓▓▓▓▓, ▓▓▓▓▓▓, and even ▓▓▓▓▓▓▓▓▓▓▓. But they seem to think there's more to it. Is there anything you haven't told me? Now would be a good time to mention it. I hope they're feeding you well. Are there any Chinese restaurants where you are? Where are you?

Miss you!
Love, Rona.

In his second year, there were no more pages to mark in the Gutterman's Calendar, and no one had thought to send him a new edition for 2005/2006 (or 5765 depending on one's orientation). Still, he felt optimistic, because it had been a year, and he figured his incarceration couldn't possibly go on much longer. He'd developed a kind of rapport with his two regular guards—one from Minnesota and one from Texas—and didn't feel so alone. They debated important issues like baseball's designated hitter rule and the various strengths and weaknesses of the National versus the American League. For approximately twenty minutes each afternoon, if he craned his neck at just the right angle, he could see out of his cell to the end of the hallway to where a wan sliver of sunlight shone onto the wall. This light was a great relief for reasons that Morris didn't question. *This same sun is on Great Neck*, he thought. Warming Rona and the kids. *They don't seem so far away and it can't be much longer before we are together*. Plus, he found himself developing a taste for pita and rice.

In year three, his spirits sank again, smothered by an isolation that now seemed infinite. His guards had been replaced several times, and the new detachment seemed to enjoy sneering at him. When they led him outside they held his skeletal arms tight, strategically digging their fingers into pressure points that triggered sharp pains but left no marks. They giggled when Morris stumbled, which happened more as he ate less. The Gutterman's calendar from his first year was still on the wall, every day marked in red, the scenes from Jewish history fading. But Morris's eyes now focused on what was printed on the bottom of each curling page: COMPLIMENTS OF GUTTERMAN'S FUNERAL HOME. A reminder to Morris that he might as well be dead.

And, now, in year four, Morris's emotional state was best described as numb.

One day, a military officer entered Morris's cell and sat with him. He had a blond crew cut and a tanned face and his uniform was so stiff it crackled when he sat. He wore aftershave strong enough to saturate the small cell. BRUT, Morris guessed.

"I'm Lieutenant Colonel Myers," he said. "I'm here to be your advocate."

"You're my lawyer?" asked Morris.

"Well, not exactly. You're not entitled to a lawyer. You do, however, get me. A United States Army officer with the appropriate security clearances, appointed by the military to make sure your rights are protected. Even though you don't have any rights. As a native enemy noncombatant, I mean."

Morris blinked. He was going to ask what the point was of having someone protect his rights if he didn't have any, but he didn't want to make waves with his advocate. And he felt now more than ever before that he really needed an advocate.

"So here's the drill," Myers announced. "At some point—I'm not permitted to say when, or even if—you may go before a Special Native Enemy Noncombatant Military Tribunal. It consists of three military judges chosen by the President. Of course, you won't know who they are nor will you ever see them. They sit in another room. Or another country. I'm not supposed to say. For national security reasons. You will have an opportunity to present your defense. However, you will not be able to see any evidence against you. I will see it. Or whatever my level of security clearance allows me to see. The whole thing should take about a day. Then the sentencing. Or the acquittal. Though an acquittal, well, that would be a first!" He snorted through a laugh.

Morris didn't laugh. "I should be acquitted. I mean all I did was cheat on my expense account, take one unauthorized sick day, and have attempted extra-marital relations while married. That's all."

"Mr. Feldsmith, may I give you some advice?"

"Feldstein. My name is Feldstein."

"Feldstein! You sure? Guess it doesn't matter. Look, take some advice from your advocate. The judges spend all day listening to 'all I did': 'All I did was make a wrong turn on my way to the in-laws in Kabul, and the next thing I know I'm on a mountain near the Pakistani border firing an AK-47.' 'All I did was deliver a package of brownies to the Ministry of whatever, and the next thing I know, there was a crater where the Ministry used to be.' Get my drift?"

"But all I did—"

"I don't think you're listening here. I'm trying to help you. As your advocate."

"Sorry," Morris mumbled.

"Look, here's what I know. There is some scuttlebutt about your case; that maybe the government's evidence is . . . on the thin side, that maybe the higher-ups in Washington wouldn't mind this case going away at some point. So you have a choice, Feldstein."

"What is it?" Prior to now, Morris would've cringed at the thought of choices, of having to decide on one thing over another, for fear of offending someone, anyone.

"You can insist on your innocence. Fight the government. Go into your hearing and make a scene. You know what that'll do?"

"Prove my case."

Myers laughed. He laughed so hard his crisp uniform shook. "It will prove you're an idiot. You'll piss off the government even more than you've already managed to and get yourself sentenced to life in prison in some foreign country with more syllables than vowels. Or rot here for the rest of your life. Not that we do such things to American citizens," he said. "Or don't do them. I'm neither confirming nor denying. I am just saying."

Morris's throat tightened. "What's my other choice?"

"I might be able to work out an . . . arrangement. Maybe you go to a federal penitentiary somewhere, at some point in the near or far future. It's not a bad place if you can stand the politicians. Then, when things calm down, they let you go home."

"Home, to Rona? How is she?"

"I'm not permitted to say."

"What would I have to do?"

"You tell the tribunal everything. How you were recruited by terrorists. How they got to you during a moment of weakness. How remorseful you are. Give 'em what they want. Juicy stuff that validates their existence. Proves the government right about the threats we face. Tell 'em how the Abu al-Zarqawi Martyrs of Militancy Brigade operated in Great Neck. How it's creeping across the nation, from suburb to suburb, infiltrating our schools and our country clubs, taking over our malls and our bowling allies, destroying our town halls and village greens."

"But none of that is true. I'd be lying."

"Would you?"

"Yes."

Myers blew an exasperated "Okay" and stood up. "Look. It's up to you. Give them what they want, and I think you get some of your life back. Stick with the 'all I did' stuff, and you'll be living in solitary confinement for, let's see . . . forever. Totally your decision. It's your life. Decide what you want to do with it."

The door closed with a thud.

Morris fell onto a paper-thin mattress that stank of urine. He curled both hands at his sides and slumped his head into his chest. He was alone again, except for a video camera poking from a corner ceiling, watching his every move.

Gottenyu.

He thought about the Colonel's proposition. "Such a deal!" Rona would say. All he had to do was admit to terrorist conspiracy against the government of the United States of America and he could go home, to his Mets and his movies, to Rona and his RoyaLounger. He could almost taste the Kung Pao chicken.

And then it turned sour. The reality of the life he bargained for, leaving a bad taste in his mouth.

What a homecoming it would be! Maybe a large banner stretched over Soundview Avenue: WELCOME HOME, TRAITOR! Probable impeachment as second vice president of the Men's Club. Not to mention a lifetime ban from the Beth Torah fantasy football league. Plus, Celfex would take away his sales awards. Along with his sales territory. And his sales job.

And the neighbors! Standing in sanctimonious judgment in front of his house or when he passed on the street. Clucking their tongues and proclaiming: "Such a *shonda!*"

He thought about the shame his presence would bring his family. For them, worse than guilt—guilt by association. Rona's expulsion from the mahjong club. Revocation of credit at Bloomingdale's. The gossip and the snickering; the glares contorted by fear and anger, by pity and paranoia.

They're better off without me. They should sit shiva, as if I were dead. They should live happily ever after like one of my classic movies.

Meanwhile, I'll go to one of those foreign prisons, maybe Siberia.

He shook his head and his body trembled. His jaw throbbed angrily, forcing his teeth to grind. He stared angrily at the camera and felt an overwhelming urge to scream at it. To say, "Fuck you" to the President or whatever government official sat on the other side, staring at a monitor. Watching.

Do it! he thought. *Stand up and demand your freedom. Shake your fists and scream out loud until they open the damn doors and set you free.*

Why not? They've taken everything.

He lifted himself from the bed, attempting to assume the defiant posture he'd used so haplessly during that argument with Rona so long ago. Reflexively his hands searched for some loose change to jiggle in his pockets, but he was in a white prison jumpsuit. There were no coins or even pockets.

So he returned to the mattress and glared at the camera.

OPERATION FAST & FURIOUS

THURSDAY, OCTOBER 9, 2008

It was Yom Kippur. And since Morris was suspected of violating multiple provisions of local, state, and federal law, as well as several international treaties and at least three of the Ten Commandments, he thought it might be a good idea to fast. So when a dinner tray was slid through a small opening in his door the night before, he refused it. He wondered, fleetingly, when he'd last refused anything. When a breakfast tray of pita bread, boiled eggs, milk, and fruit was slid through this morning, Morris slid it back.

Later, as Jews around the world searched their souls, two Marines searched Morris's cell. They shoved Morris out of the way while doing so, and then shoved him again a moment later because, after all, the cell was tiny and Morris could never get out of the way. When they were satisfied that it was safe, they escorted in a Rabbi who had been flown to Gitmo from the US military's Central Command in

Tampa (because there wasn't exactly a huge call for a house rabbi to conduct Yom Kippur worship in a place that housed hundreds of suspected Muslim jihadists).

The Rabbi wore an army dress uniform with the Jewish chaplain insignia on his chest. He had puffy cheeks and wet lips that barely moved when he introduced himself. His sad eyes dwelled uncomfortably on the video camera. A yarmulke was clipped to a thick tangle of gray hair on his scalp.

He clutched a beaten leather briefcase and mumbled something about how hard it was to gather a *minyan* in Guantánamo, but that he would lead Morris in private prayer. Then he slid a metal chair toward Morris's bed, groaned as he sat, and passed him a High Holy Day prayer book. It had been screened by the prison authorities.

He began the official Yom Kippur request to God for permission to pray with Morris Feldstein. Transgressor. Traitor. Terrorist. He didn't use those words, but Morris assumed that God got the idea.

They prayed. Most of the prayers involved the concept of God forgiving man for wrongdoing, but Morris took the opportunity to request that God answer certain questions of his own on the subject.

Why are You doing this to me? Morris asked, feeling desperation seep into his inner voice.

What did I ever do to You, to deserve such a punishment?

There was no answer from God, but Morris didn't expect one.

After the last prayer, the Rabbi packed up his books and shook Morris's hand again and looked at the video camera as if to say, "May I please go back to Tampa now?"

He approached the door, scratched his head, turned back to Morris, and said, as if he had read Morris's mind: "God has forgiven you. And soon the answers will come."

Morris asked, "How soon?"

"Only God knows," the Rabbi replied with a shrug.

Which angered Morris even more.

Later, the guards attempted to serve Morris lunch, which he declined.

Why would a broken man break a fast? His sins may have been forgiven by God but not by the government. Yom Kippur was all about starting with a clean slate and moving on, but unknown forces had stomped on Morris's life, leaving broken shards of slate, irreparably destroyed and scattered from Great Neck to Gitmo. He didn't feel like he was anywhere close to moving on, and so he continued his fast, with nothing to digest but his anger.

That night, twenty-four hours after his fast began, hunger pains arced across Morris's belly. His head throbbed. On that thin and rancid mattress, he drifted into a strange and troubled sleep.

Morris dreamed in black and white, of Caryn, crouching at the foot of the RoyaLounger, watching classic movies with happy endings, of Alec Guinness in *The Bridge on the River Kwai* and how realistically he portrayed starving in solitary confinement. Morris dreamed of Rona, and Feldstein family fun, of the sleek condo in Boca with the Emeril Signature kitchen and Arab towel attendants, of the prophet Hillel, and Victoria seducing him on the floral comforter in that room at the Bayview.

But mostly he dreamed of food: of Chinese takeout and chicken Parmesan and the golden square knishes from The Noshery with those crisp brown ridges, just the way he liked them; of his daily toasted bagel with Swiss, and the smell of fresh coffee in the kitchen. He reached out for that coffee in his empty, dank cell in Guantánamo, his arms weak and trembling, but he felt only the cold cinderblock wall that had defined his world for the past four years.

He fell back asleep with a groan.

In and out of sleep.

Between dreams and nightmares.

Between resignation and rage.

49

BREAKING THE FAST

FRIDAY, OCTOBER 10, 2008

The Colonel plopped a red folder marked SECRET on the Brigadier General's desk with a brisk "Good morning, sir."

It was not a good morning for the General, and it would get worse.

The sun had already brought Gitmo to a slow boil. The General cursed the low-bid air conditioner that wheezed and rattled from a window. He ran his enormous hands over his bald scalp and shook the sweat from his fingers.

On a nearby television, *Good Morning America* was agitating America, breaking the news that the federal government was eavesdropping on the phone calls of American citizens.

"Big fuckin' deal," the General mumbled. He thought that if you had nothing to hide, you shouldn't mind Uncle Sam cupping his ear to your gossip about the office, or your plans for tomorrow's carpool, or your argument with "Brad" or "Megan" in India about a discrepancy on your credit card bill.

And now this! The report that the Colonel had dropped on him like a bunker buster bomb, destroying the General's day and maybe even blowing up his career.

"Hunger strike," the General read aloud. His stomach gurgled.

Hunger and *strike* were the only two words that rattled the medals on the General's tree stump chest. Hunger strikes attracted celebrities, candlelight vigils, speeches at the United Nations, and questions from the President. Hunger strikes meant lawyers from the Pentagon and the Justice Department breathing down the General's thick, stiff neck. Worse, the Department of Defense's Public Affairs Office would dispatch those annoying little gnats called "public information specialists." The General could tolerate jihadists at Gitmo, but not the public information specialists.

Altogether, a hunger strike meant the one star on the General's collar might never get company. He'd be pushed into retirement, landing as a consultant to some defense-lobbying firm on Capitol Hill. Worse than getting shot at by terrorists was getting shaken down by congressmen.

All because of an enemy of the state who decided to go on a no-calorie diet.

This fast had to be stopped, and fast.

"Who is this . . . Feldstein?" he asked.

"High-value detainee, sir. Hasn't accepted a meal. Refuses to cooperate."

The General rolled back his squeaky chair and stood, towering over his desk. "Let's get Mr. Feldstein something to eat," he said.

In what he thought was a dream, Morris heard, from the depths of his nutrient-starved oblivion, an explosion followed by angry voices barking his name. His eyes opened onto a small army bursting into his cell. They surrounded his bed and shook it. They barked commands and spat sharp pellets of saliva. Then, dozens of rough hands locked under his arms and pinned him against the wall.

A face approached. Oversized, red, and snorting like a bull. With thick lips and hot breath that stank of chewing tobacco.

By way of introduction, the General screamed at Morris: "You wanna starve yourself, Feldstein?"

Morris groaned weakly.

"I'm giving you two options. Option A: I drag the scrawny remnant of your ass to the clinic. I strap you in a chair. I stick a feeding tube so far up your nose it hurts your brain. I pump fucking blueberry Pop-Tarts up that tube. And I keep you strapped there so you can't try to puke anything back out. Not exactly a picnic, Feldstein."

Morris's mind locked only on the word *picnic*.

"Here's option B, Feldstein. You cooperate and I'll give you a more pleasant dining experience. How about a nice pastrami on rye? We can fly it in from Miami. With sides."

This tempted Morris.

"What do you say, Feldstein? You gonna cooperate or you gonna give me trouble?"

Morris struggled to straighten his back, which involved stiffening a spine rarely used.

He lifted a limp, bony hand. He wriggled a finger, inviting the General to come closer. The General put his ear to Morris's dry lips, so close that Morris could see the soft nicks and stubble on his scalp.

Morris searched for whatever strength was left in his malnourished body. He felt something swelling in his otherwise empty belly.

Morris croaked into the ear of the Brigadier General:

"Fuck the pastrami."

There was a time in his life when Morris couldn't muster the courage to send back a lukewarm cup of coffee at the diner, much less tell a Brigadier General to perform a sexual act with his favorite cold cut.

But, as Hillel might have said, if not now, when?

LIGHTS, CAMERA, ACTION

JANUARY–MAY 2009

The world premiere of Caryn's feature documentary film took place in the Feldsteins' den on Soundview Avenue. The audience was Caryn and Rona. Jeffrey was in Chicago, and Morris was—well, no one really knew where Morris was.

Caryn fed a disc into the DVD player and joined Rona on the couch.

The RoyaLounger was empty, like a riderless horse at a funeral.

"I hope you like my film," Caryn said. "I wish Daddy could see it."

The film was Caryn's final exam at a New York University adult education course called Documentary Filmmaking. Her professor was best known for the not-so-blockbuster exposé: *Chase Lounge: Inside the Patio Furniture Industry*. It took third place at the Lackawana Independent Low-Budget Film Festival.

The professor had coached his students to use their lenses to search for justice.

Caryn, of course, had the perfect subject: her missing father. So she pointed her digital video camera at the strange life and the alleged crimes of Morris Feldstein. A documentary in black and white but mostly gray, with occasional splashes of faded color: the Betamax footage of long-ago trips to Disney, and the station wagon rides upstate. She interviewed the people who had major and bit roles in Morris's life. Here on the screen was Rona, whose shoulders now slumped and who sighed constantly, not to convey guilt but because she was miserable without "My Morris," as she said on camera. Here were the Soundview Avenue neighbors and the people behind the take-out counters that lined Middle Neck Road. The members of the Men's Club. All nodding their heads and saying, "It couldn't be" and "He couldn't have," except for Colonel McCord who said, "I knew it!"

She interviewed Victoria, who said, "I've dated some real sleaze balls in my life, and was married to Jerry, the king of all sleaze balls, but never have I dated a terrorist."

Caryn even managed to get an interview with a Senator from New York, a man physiologically incapable of declining any request that involved a camera. He had a ravenous appetite for publicity; and even when he consumed massive amounts, he still felt malnourished.

Publicity made his heart beat. And a documentary about a constituent from Great Neck—an area he had won with a less than overwhelming margin—made it beat even faster.

Caryn set up her camera in the Senator's Manhattan office. He entered with outstretched arms, bear-hugging her as if they were friends for life. Caryn noticed a thin veneer of makeup on his cheeks, either from a prior interview or for this one. The Senator was perpetually pancaked.

She trained the camera on him.

"Senator, some say that my father, Morris Feldstein, is an

innocent victim in the War on Terror. That he was falsely accused and unjustly imprisoned."

The Senator nodded empathetically. He had mastered empathy on demand.

He responded with a brief but salient history of the tension between civil liberties and national security. And concluded with: "I take no backseat to keeping us safe from terrorists who would do us harm. At the same time, we must be vigilant in protecting our own precious freedoms. And I vow to do both."

Caryn continued. "But, specifically regarding Morris Feldstein, is he to spend the rest of his life in detention without even a trial? Isn't that a massive injustice, Senator?"

The Senator proclaimed, "Justice must be done. And I pledge to look into this issue and get back to you. Forthwith!"

"When?"

"Forthwith!"

"There are reports that this may extend beyond Morris Feldstein. That the government may be secretly spying on innocent Americans. Are you aware of such a program? Are you willing to call for oversight hearings?"

The Senator loved the sound of "oversight hearings." The clack of the gavel, the glare of the television lights, the condemnatory questions fired at witnesses who cocked their heads toward lawyers who whispered responses. An oversight hearing meant elevating this story from the *Great Neck Record* to the *Washington Post*; from an obscure film hardly anyone would watch to gavel-to-gavel coverage on CNN!

"You read my mind," said the Senator, imagining the headlines as he spoke.

When the film was over, Rona wiped tears from her eyes and sighed. She said, "Morris loved watching his television. Now he's on it! If only more people could see this beautiful movie."

"They will," Caryn promised.

Her NYU professor was well connected in the documentary film industry. He knew someone who knew someone else who once worked at HBO and still had a connection with an executive there who might be able to arrange for Caryn to pitch her film to another executive.

Her hopes were high.

They were quickly dashed.

In filmmaking terms, things didn't pan out.

HBO passed on the film before Caryn could get past the door to their Manhattan office. The Independent Film Channel also declined, along with the Sundance Channel, Current TV, Al Jazeera, the Jewish Television Network, and so on, up and down the cable channel lineup, from basic to the premium package and back.

But finally, after weeks of effort, Caryn landed a deal.

A one-week airing on the Public Access channel of Great Neck, wedged between *High School Sports Review* and *Great Neck Restaurant Recap*.

And a commitment for a one-night screening at the Great Neck Cinema.

It was a very limited engagement.

The White House Counsel in the newly installed Obama Administration disliked two particular words: *oversight* and *hearing*. Put together, the words made him tremble. When an unhappy aide reported that the Senator from New York was preparing to investigate the case of Morris Feldstein, the counsel acted quickly.

First he planned a strategy to prevent the hearing.

Second, he asked: "Who is Morris Feldstein?"

He called the new Attorney General, who checked with the Secretary of Defense, who referred the inquiry to the new Secretary of Homeland Security. Her staff identified an official who survived the transition from the Bush Administration by burying himself deep in something called the Office of Intergovernmental Relations, Division of Intermunicipal Affairs, Bureau on State, Local Cooperation, Region Three (which the new Administration didn't even know existed, much less in multiple regions).

His name was Jon Pruitt.

Pruitt wrote a report to the Secretary of DHS, who shared it with the Department of Justice, which referred the matter of Morris Feldstein back to the White House Counsel, who called the White House Chief of Staff.

Said Chief of Staff, enraged that he had been pulled out of a strategy meeting on something called Obamacare, ordered that "this fucking problem be fucking taken care of right fucking now!"

In so many "fucking" words.

One night soon thereafter, the Brigadier General at Guantánamo received a phone call. It was from one of the Defense Department lawyers he loathed. After listening to a quick question he asked, "Feldstein? The guy with a tube up his nose?"

The White House Counsel called the Senator to talk him out of the hearing. He knew exactly what to do.

"Senator," he purred into a phone. "I have good news. We have reviewed the case of Morris Feldstein. And we believe it's time for him to be reunited with his family."

"That is good news," said the Senator, emphasizing the word *news*. "But I still have some concerns about how my constituent ended up imprisoned in . . . wherever he's imprisoned. And about whether there's a secret surveillance program that's spying on innocent Americans."

"Well, first, I can assure you that there is no such program. But of course, it's your prerogative to convene hearings. No need for subpoenas. We'll cooperate."

"Good."

"Or—"

"Or?"

"Perhaps, rather than the Administration announcing your constituent's release, you could do it. You know, reunite him with his loved ones. At some kind of press event."

"Let's talk," said the Senator.

51

*REEING *ELDSTEIN

SATURDAY, MAY 30, 2009

The black sedan, arranged courtesy of the Department of Defense, slipped through a gate at the Stewart Air National Guard Base.

It turned south on the New York State Thruway, leaving behind the distant ridges of the Catskill Mountains. Sitting alone in the rear, Morris smiled. It seemed a lifetime ago when he brought Jeffrey and Caryn camping in the Catskills (as well as Rona, who succumbed to the kids' entreaties but not without leaving them with a full weekend's worth of guilt scars about being "eaten alive" by mosquitoes). The car drove across the Tappan Zee Bridge, then through low hills that skirted the Hudson River. Before long Morris was winding through the suburbs of Westchester. Then the car crept across the Bronx, brakes squealing in stop-and-go traffic. Morris felt asphyxiated by the boxy apartment buildings that loomed everywhere, by the subway cars that rattled back and forth, by the dull yellow lights that peeked at him from the grimy walls of bridges and overpasses plastered with graffiti. *Still, it could be worse,* he thought.

It could be Guantánamo.

Finally, Morris saw it. He was almost free.

It welcomed him to Long Island with both of its massive steel arms stretched across Little Neck Bay, green lights twinkling their familiar greeting from end to end, all the way to the top of its graceful towers, so high they seemed able to touch planes as they approached LaGuardia Airport. The Throgs Neck Bridge. Joining Long Island and the Bronx geographically, but no more than that. Because one end had nothing to do with the other. It wasn't simply a bridge.

It separated two worlds for Morris.

Halfway across, Morris smiled as the car veered right, under the green-and-white sign that said EASTERN LONG ISLAND. The car curved onto the Cross Island Parkway, where Morris gazed at the tiny lights of a few boats in the cool water, hovering near the protective embrace of the bridge.

Close. They were getting close.

They exited onto Northern Boulevard, in urbanized Queens. But with every block eastward, it became more gentrified, until Morris saw the glittering familiar storefronts, the clothing stores and bakeries, and the little Italian restaurants. The places that fed Morris his dinner almost every night, ladled from white cartons, aluminum tins, and Styrofoam containers.

Morris thought, *Five more minutes and I'll be home. Maybe Rona and I will have a little bite to eat. Because almost five years without a pastrami on rye had to set some kind of record. And after dinner, maybe I'll relax a little. In the RoyaLounger 8000. Maybe watch a movie. And I'll worry about tomorrow, tomorrow.*

But Great Neck had something else in mind for Morris.

"Gottenyu!"

Middle Neck Road looked like Times Square on New Year's Eve.

Thousands of people blocked the street, whooping and chanting and laughing in the crisp night air. They waved signs that said FREE FELDSTEIN!, WELCOME HOME, MORRIS!, and WE MISSED MO! The Nassau County Police, New York State Troopers, and Village of Great Neck Police were out in force, the lights of their vehicles flashing constantly, so that the whole thing looked like disco night to Morris.

The police parted the crowd away from Morris's car as it eased forward.

"Mor-ris! Mor-ris!" He heard them chant.

The car pulled to the front of a red carpet unfurled from the curb to the entrance of the Great Neck Cinema. Morris had to shield his eyes from the glare of the giant marquee:

*REEING *ELDSTEIN. A *ILM BY CARYN *ELDSTEIN
WELCOME HOME MORIS!!!

The theater had run out of Fs and was low on Rs. Times were tough in the movie theater business.

A figure appeared at the car window. It was vaguely familiar to Morris. A wide grin spread across fleshy cheeks. Giving Morris a thumbs-up with both hands.

The Senator from New York.

The Senator opened the door. Dozens of cameras jostled for position behind him. Morris squinted at the lights. He felt the Senator's hands lock around his wrists and pull him from the car. He remembered for a moment the last time he had stepped out of a vehicle in Great Neck.

The Senator wrapped Morris in a bear hug (making sure that the Senator's face was to the front of the cameras). Then he pivoted Morris toward the press and shouted, "Let me be the first to say, Welcome home, Morris Feldstein!" He locked hands with Morris and thrust them into the air. As if they had just been nominated to a presidential ticket.

The crowd roared. Morris smiled meekly, and waved as if it were only Colonel McCord standing across the street instead of half of Great Neck.

Morris had never had a receiving line. So many *machers*! The Senator stood shoulder to shoulder with Morris, refusing to cede any ground in the war for camera angles. The Mayor of Great Neck Village and his entire Village Council was there, presenting him with a parchment proclamation affixed with a gold seal and red ribbon, saying whereas this and whereas that until resolving that the day was officially "Morris Feldstein Day." It was nearly nine PM, and there wasn't much left of Morris Feldstein day for Morris to enjoy. The Great Neck Village Merchants Association pressed some discount coupons into his hand, just in case he felt the urgent need to stop off on the way to freedom to procure a home audio system from Great Neck Audio or a leaf blower from Village Hardware. There were hearty congratulations from the Rotarians, the Kiwanians, and the green-jacketed, silver-haired members of the BPO Elks. The Rabbi and the entire board of the Temple presented him with a golden shofar and a nice plaque referencing the call for freedom. And all of this activity unfolded to the accompaniment of the Great Neck High School band's rendition of the theme song to *Rocky*.

He stepped into the theater lobby, where Rona was waiting, across the room, looking no different from when he had last seen her. A lifetime ago.

"Hi Morris," she said. She bit her lip to squelch a sob, but that just made her shoulders shudder. Once that happened, the tears flowed. And instead of heaving her shoulders, she thrust them forward, rushing toward him, and this time he knew how to hug. His arms stretched wide.

Just before they made contact, the Senator slipped between them. Grabbing both their hands, then joining them. As if orchestrating the official handshake between two foreign leaders at the signing of a peace treaty.

Morris and Rona hugged to an explosion of flashbulbs. Hugged so tightly that Morris felt as if he were losing his breath. But it was okay. Because at that point, he didn't mind suffocating—not that way, with Rona's arms wrapped around him and her wet cheeks pressing into his neck.

She pulled away and stared at him, stroking his face to make sure he was really there. "Look, I could never get you out of the house to go to a movie. Now you're in one! Could you *plotz?*"

They sat in the front row. Morris and Rona and Jeffrey and Caryn. And the Senator. Morris turned his head behind him. He saw Dr. Kirleski. Victoria blew him a kiss and giggled. The front desk clerk from the Bayview Motor Inn sat next to the waitress from the Sunrise Diner. Winking.

The lights dimmed and the theater fell silent. The screen glowed and a granular image came into focus: the medical office building where Morris showed up that day and found the courage to talk to Dr. Kirleski's receptionist. Which is how, and when, all his tsuris began.

When the final credit rolled—the one flashing Caryn's name— Morris and Rona went up the aisle and out the doors to a brand-new car donated by the Greater New York Automobile Dealers Association. A Cadillac with a trunk large enough to hold a full year's supply of Celfex Pharmaceutical samples. And when the doors closed with a cushioned thud, they were alone.

Finally alone.

Morris stared ahead.

Rona sighed. Not a sigh of guilt or sadness. Just a content sigh.

Morris turned to her. "So *nu?* I'm not sure what I'm supposed to do now."

"Look," said Rona, "the last time you were home, we were supposed to have Chinese takeout."

"You mean—"

"God fahbid we have a bite to eat. You're skin and bones, Morris.

Let's go home. I brought in dinner. And taped some Mets games for you to watch. From all the seasons you missed."

They drove to Soundview Avenue, where a brown bag filled with white cartons from the Great Neck Mandarin Gourmet awaited. And Morris's RoyaLounger 8000. And over four hundred Mets games, faithfully recorded by Rona.

Morris wasn't in the mood to watch the Mets. And he wasn't really in the mood for Chinese.

So he looked straight at Rona and said, "No thanks. I'd rather eat kosher deli."

Which made Rona smile.

That night, Rona ate Chinese food. And Morris devoured a pastrami on rye.

And there was no tsuris.

THE NSA

MONDAY, SEPTEMBER 3, 2012

William Sully, who had moved from agency to agency in the federal bureaucracy, sat in his spacious new office at Fort Meade, Maryland, enjoying the distant view, across his giant mahogany desk, of plush couches, an antique coffee table, and landscape oil paintings. All had arrived in a recent trade with the Smithsonian Institution (now the proud recipient of vintage chemistry laboratory equipment from Sully's former employer, the FDA). There was also a fine Wedgwood coffee set, ready to serve distinguished visitors, or undistinguished visitors, or any visitors at all. Which seemed unlikely since hardly anyone was aware of William Sully's transfer.

He had himself put on "temporary detail" with the title Acting Deputy Assistant Director of the Division of Intelligence, Office of Foreign Intelligence, Bureau of Analysis and Surveillance, Special Programs Section. He had a desk the size of an aircraft carrier and a nice view, through parted yellow drapes, of the rolling hills of Maryland.

Sully had almost forgotten Ricardo Montoyez and his counterfeit drug operation. He was onto new threats. Countless threats.

He glanced at a wall-mounted television. Vice President Joe Biden was revving up a crowd at a Labor Day rally in Detroit. Biden thundered: "You want to know whether we're better off? I've got a little bumper sticker for you: OSAMA BIN LADEN IS DEAD AND GENERAL MOTORS IS ALIVE!"

The crowd roared.

True, Sully thought. There had been many changes in recent years. George Bush was in Texas; Barack Obama was in the White House. In Afghanistan, where the 9-11 War on Terror began, al-Qaeda was on the run. In Iraq, where the War on Terror was diverted, American troops had exited. At home, the Great Recession was starting to mend.

And yet, some things in Washington didn't change at all. They just grew bigger. Much bigger.

Which is exactly why Sully transferred himself to the National Security Agency.

He ran a hand over his short cropped hair, leaned toward his computer, and released a satisfied sigh. Thousands of NSA-intercepted telephone records scrolled across the screen. A torrent of calls, foreign and domestic. Records of phone calls made and phone calls received. Suspicious calls. Curious calls. Hard to explain calls. Connections that sparked the interest of a sophisticated NSA computer program, an NSA intel analyst, an attorney at the Department of Justice, and an anonymous judge at something called the Foreign Intelligence Surveillance Court.

Sure there were a few times when the Feds may have inadvertently spied on the harmless phone conversations of innocent Americans. Few, as in thousands. Or hundreds of thousands. Maybe millions. No one knew. The whole matter was classified.

But that was a small price to pay for freedom, wasn't it?

Sully stared at the screen as a smile spread across his face. A proud smile.

NICK was all grown up.

And growing all the time.

EPILOGUE

Tom Fairbanks remains in Melville, staring angrily at colored pins on his sprawling map of Long Island. Convinced of conspiracies behind every pizza place, Chinese takeout, nail salon, and Starbucks from one end of Long Island to the other.

William Sully, formerly of the Food and Drug Administration and the National Security Agency, transferred himself to a new federal post. He now heads the Special Investigations Unit in the Department of Commerce/Office of the Undersecretary for Waterways Management/Bureau of Clean Drinking Water/Division of Sewage Infrastructure/Office of Compliance/Department of Monitoring & Evaluation. Over six hundred agents work for Sully. They aren't quite sure what they do exactly.

Ricardo Montoyez is still at large. He was last seen slipping out of a Red Lobster in Toledo, leaving his fiancée behind. She worked as a part-time cashier in the local Walmart. In the pharmacy department.

Azad and Pervez relocated together to upstate New York. Pervez co-owns and cooks at a highly popular hibachi restaurant, Tokyo Joe's Steak 'n Sushi. Azad works there as a comic deejay during weeknight happy hours. They are developing a cooking show for a local Public Access channel.

Achmed owns Virgin Office Cleaning. He received a huge contract from the General Services Administration, tidying offices in the Pentagon.

Hassan's cooperation with federal authorities led to the breakup of the Abu al-Zarqawi Martyrs of Militancy Brigade. Today he is Assistant Director of Security at the corporate headquarters of Paradise Global Ventures, LLC. He is married with one daughter. She is the only student at Scottsdale Road Preschool named Rona.

Victoria D'Amico is happily remarried. She fell in love with one of the federal agents who interrogated her for three days after Morris's capture. He "is-everything-Jerry-wasn't-but-I-still-wish-nothing-but-the-best-for-that-miserable-SOB-and-the-pizza-slut-he-left–me-for."

As for Caryn, the eventual success of *Freeing Feldstein* launched her career in film and social commentary. Following the release of her sequel, *Feldstein: Finally Free*, she negotiated a six-picture deal with HBO Films. Next month she begins shooting *Male Strippers: Not So Undercover*.

Today, Morris and Rona Feldstein live in their condo in Boca Raton. They moved out of Great Neck so that Rona could escape the "yentas" and "get some peace and quiet." There, she opened up a social work practice focusing on Great Neck residents who live part-time in Florida and have developed what she calls SAD, "Snowbird Anxiety Disorder." Morris won election to The Residences at Paradise Homeowners Association Board of Directors. He is trying to avoid being swept into a battle between the clubhouse mint-green paint versus lime-green paint factions.

Among other waves.